ONCE AGAIN
BRACKENROYD HALL
HAD A VICTIM

Fern stared at the handsome face and powerful,
rigidly erect figure of the man who was now
legally her husband. His arrogant lips were
smiling—at her uncertainty, her fears.

Fern forced herself to ask her question:

"Did you come to my room in the night?"

"Do you need to ask?" he replied.

"You knew that I was unaware of what was
happening."

"Really?" His thick eyebrows shot up
questioningly. "Then your response was
remarkably warm in the circumstances."

"You treated me like . . . like a woman of the
streets."

"And you reacted like one." Then, still
smiling, Bruno held up two gold sovereigns.
"Would you consider these adequate
payment?"

*Even as Fern ran from his room with tears
burning her eyes, she realized there was no
escape. She was prisoner of the same curse
that claimed the other women who now shared
her body—unless she found the hidden
key to release. . . .*

D1324871

SIGNET Books You'll Enjoy Reading

THE BRACKENROYD INHERITANCE

by
Erica Lindley

A SIGNET BOOK
NEW AMERICAN LIBRARY
TIMES MIRROR

SIGNET TRADEMARK REG. U.S. PAT. OFF. AND FOREIGN COUNTRIES
REGISTERED TRADEMARK—MARCA REGISTRADA
HECHO EN CHICAGO, U.S.A.

SIGNET, SIGNET CLASSICS, MENTOR, PLUME AND MERIDIAN BOOKS are published by The New American Library, Inc., 1301 Avenue of the Americas, New York, New York 10019

FIRST PRINTING, DECEMBER, 1975

3 4 5 6 7 8 9

PRINTED IN THE UNITED STATES OF AMERICA

For my kinsfolk, the Armitages,
whose history reaches back through
the mists of Colne Valley antiquity.

I tell the things I know, the things I knew
Before I knew them, immemorially.

—VICTORIA SACKVILLE-WEST, *The Land*

Chapter 1

The master was coming downstairs. Fern Saxby, like all the other occupants of this imposing London villa in Elton Square, held her breath and hoped that the master's Monday morning humor, usually indicative of his mood for the whole week, would be sunny, for the weather decidedly was not. She ushered the two Hastings children hurriedly before her into the parlor to be ready to greet their papa and mamma.

"Now, remember, children, greet your papa first, and then your mamma. As soon as they enter, mind, don't wait until I have to nudge you," Fern advised them gently. A quick glance around the room reassured her that all was as it should be; though the grandfather clock in the vestibule was only now chiming eight, the parlor had hours ago been swept and dusted and the fire lit. No trace of skimped effort or sloth could be detected in the gleaming fire brasses by the fender to arouse Mr. Hastings' swiftly awakened disapproval.

Heavy footsteps approached the door. Fern ran her hands quickly over her smoothly coiled fair hair, then clasped them dutifully before her as the door swung open and Mr.

Hastings, his pallid wife on his arm, entered slowly and majestically. Lydia Hastings smiled timorously at her children and then glanced nervously at her husband. He, tall, graying, and imposing, stood glaring at his offspring expectantly.

"Good morning, Papa. Good morning, Mamma," two stifled voices breathed in unison.

Mr. Hastings nodded. "Good morning, children. Good morning, Miss Saxby."

He expected no reply from her, Fern knew, and from habit bred of the last two years' experience she walked across to the bell, anticipating the master's next command. Never on any one morning, except the week he had once been confined to bed with influenza, had the ritual of morning prayers in the Hastings household varied.

"Summon the staff to prayers," came the order as Mr. Hastings took his seat at the head of the chenille-covered table. Opening the great family Bible, he began to select the text for the day. Almost as soon as Fern released the bell rope the door opened and the servants shuffled in at the far end of the parlor. Under the vigilant eye of Bunting, the butler, they had all been awaiting the summons just beyond the green-baize door that marked the boundary between house and servants' domain.

Heads bowed now, they all stood respectfully before the master and mistress, the one inspecting their caps and uniforms critically before beginning to pray, the other surreptitiously smiling at her offspring while her husband's attention was diverted. Fern stood behind her little charges, midway between the seated Hastingses and the standing servants, as befitted her anomalous position as governess. A strange creature is a governess, she thought for the thousandth time, neither gentry nor common folk, but a curious hybrid, left to fend alone, vulnerable and friendless, in the no-man's-land that yawned between them. Mrs. Hastings, despite her undoubted warmth, dared not befriend a governess, however lonely she herself might feel. Nor dared Hetty and Rosa and Clara, the kitchen and parlor maids, for venturing to presume friendship with one above their own station would undoubtedly bring a sharp reproof from the butler. Bunting knew well the boundaries of class, and firmly instilled the knowledge of these unalterable limits into the minds of his staff.

So I'm trapped, thought Fern as she stared directly ahead at the William Morris wallpaper and dimly heard Mr. Hastings' ponderous voice droning in prayer. Like the pimpernel entwined in the inexorable intricacy of the fronds on that wallpaper, I am trapped in this mesh of class boundary. If only Papa and Mamma were alive; if only we were all still comfortably wealthy and free.

Sighing, she turned her attention to Mr. Hastings' words. He was reading from Ecclesiastes, giving full emphasis to every word, conscious of his captive audience and of the resonance of his voice. From the corner of her eye Fern saw Hetty fidgeting restlessly.

"Vanity of vanities, saith the Preacher, all is vanity," intoned Mr. Hastings, pausing to lower his pince-nez a half-inch down his nose, the better to survey the effect of his words on his hearers. "What profit hath a man of all his labor which he taketh under the sun? One generation passeth away and another generation cometh."

Fern permitted herself a covert glimpse of the maids. Hetty, up before six to clear and relay the grates, was already trying to hide a yawn. Was she too speculating as to the uselessness of her labor? Fern wondered, for the grate would be dirty again tomorrow morning, and the next, and the next, and still even when the next generation came.

"All things are full of labor," Mr. Hastings pontificated. "Man cannot utter it; the eye is not satisfied with seeing nor the ear filled with hearing. The thing that hath been, it is that which shall be, and that which is done is that which shall be done; and there is no new thing under the sun."

The staff shuffled to their knees for the Lord's Prayer while Mr. Hastings assisted his wife to kneel as gracefully as her rheumatically stricken joints would permit. This London fog and damp, thought Fern. No doubt, as Mr. Hastings' business grew more lucrative day by day, he would eventually consider sending his wife abroad to a spa or to a sunnier climate. It was possible, even though he seemed to spare little thought for the comfort of others, even for his patient, uncomplaining wife. Matthew Hastings' vision seemed to be bounded by his own comfort and seeing to the continuing prosperity of his business. Little else existed in his world, save the fluctuations of national and international affairs, and only then insofar as they might affect trade.

Fern's musings were interrupted by the rustle of skirts and shuffling of feet as the company rose from its knees. Mr. Hastings closed the Bible and put down his pince-nez.

"And now, to your duties," he commanded his flock. Mrs. Paddock, the cook-housekeeper, led the servants out, all save Bunting, who stood at attention awaiting the customary order. "Order breakfast to be served, Bunting, and bring me the morning post."

"Very good, sir." Fern stood hesitantly, a hand on the shoulder of each child, awaiting Mr. Hastings' decision as to whether he would allow his son and daughter to remain in the parlor for breakfast or dismiss them to the day nursery to eat with their governess.

Mrs. Hastings, noticing his air of abstraction, ventured to resolve the dilemma. "Shall the children return upstairs, my dear, or would you prefer them to remain?" she asked timidly.

"They must remain, of course, to hear our decision. Very well, Miss Saxby, you may go."

As Fern made to withdraw, Rosa, the housemaid, entered bearing a large tray laden with a tureen of porridge and a platter of scrambled eggs and kidneys. It was a relief to Fern to quit the pretentious parlor with its gloomy oil paintings and its ponderous, ornately carved furniture. Fern felt sorry for Lydia Hastings, trapped in that claustrophobic room with her domineering husband, unable to escape the pattern which marriage dictated, the undeviating pattern of husband, lord and master of his universe, while his wife was no more than his servant, trained always to listen and obey. Poor Mrs. Hastings, her lot is no better than mine, thought Fern, and possibly even worse. Marriage seems a deadly, stifling affair for a woman, for she gains nothing from it but her children.

Fern breakfasted alone in the nursery, her meal being served, not by Rosa, second in importance only to Mrs. Paddock, the cook, but by Clara, whose humbler position as kitchen maid would not be offended by having to serve a mere governess. Clara grinned as she set down the dishes.

"So you can eat in peace this morning, eh, miss? Miss Sarah and Master Robert been allowed downstairs for once."

Fern smiled. It was true, the children were rarely allowed to disturb Mr. Hastings' morning reading of the *Times* over breakfast. Though they were not permitted to speak at table, Mr. Hastings found their foot shuffling annoying and their manners distasteful, declaring it ruined his digestion. Today there must be something special he wished to impart to them if he was prepared to suffer their presence. Idly Fern wondered what it could be.

When the breakfast dishes were cleared away, Fern took out the schoolbooks from the bottom of the cupboard and laid them on the table. The grandfather clock was chiming nine. If Mr. Hastings had finished with the children, it was time for their lessons. Fern descended the stairs and knocked at the parlor door.

"Enter," Mr. Hastings commanded. He was relaxing in an overstuffed armchair while his wife and children still sat at the dining table, their white faces and tight expressions indicating that Mr. Hastings' news had not been pleasant.

Before Fern could speak, he rose from his chair. "Ah, Miss Saxby, the mistress would like to speak to you. Please be seated," he said, indicating a straight chair by the window. "And, children, return to the nursery. Miss Saxby will join you shortly." The children, rising obediently, shuffled quickly and silently out of the room.

Fern dutifully sat down, smoothing the skirt of her dark merino dress and folding her hands in her lap. Mr. Hastings went to follow his children, but paused in the doorway and glanced at the letters in his hand. "Oh, by the way, Miss Saxby, there is a letter for you among my mail this morning," he commented in tones of surprise. He held the intrusive letter toward her. Fern started in surprise. Who could possibly have written to her? She, with no friends and not a relative in the world. Never before in her life had she received a letter, save those that used to come at regular intervals from her parents in India, but that was long ago, before Afghan bullets had claimed their lives.

Even Mrs. Hastings' puffy face registered alarmed surprise at a governess's letter finding its furtive way into the master's correspondence. Fern took the letter from Mr. Hastings' outstretched fingertips and thanked him quietly. A quick glance at the neat, spidery handwriting on the envelope revealed no clue as to the sender, for it was completely strange to her.

Mr. Hastings cleared his throat noisily. "Now, remember, my dear," he addressed his wife, "tell Miss Saxby what has been decided and make arrangements accordingly. I wish everything to be clear-cut and orderly, as in business. No shilly-shallying or compromise, as is your wont, you understand?"

"Yes, Mr. Hastings, indeed," murmured Lydia unhappily. Fern felt sorry for the woman. Whatever unpleasantness Mr. Hastings had to communicate to his children's governess, he was deputing the task to his weary little wife to perform, and it was evident that Mrs. Hastings did not relish the prospect. A reprimand perhaps, thought Fern, some mistake or oversight on my part which has displeased him. As the master departed, closing the door sharply behind him, Fern forgot the letter on her lap and waited for Mrs. Hastings to begin.

The mistress's eyes shone unnaturally bright, Fern noted, as she sat twisting her fingers nervously in the folds of her skirt. As though she were feverish, or her eyes held unshed tears. As a good servant should, Fern sat in silence and waited to be addressed. At length Mrs. Hastings rose and crossed to the window, looking out at the square outside over Fern's shoulder.

"I . . . I really don't know where to begin, Miss Saxby," she stammered without looking down at her. "I don't, and that's the truth of it."

6

"Perhaps you could tell me what decision the master has taken, madam," Fern prompted.

The other woman's voice quivered yet more as she answered. "He ... he has decided to send Sarah and Robert away to school."

It was a bald statement, terse and to the point, yet Fern's sympathy rose at once for Mrs. Hastings, for the fact she had just revealed meant far more to the wretched woman. Her children, the only joy of her life, were to be wrenched from her. Fern's dislike for Mr. Hastings grew more intense as she realized his unfeeling callousness toward his wife.

"Both of them?" she queried, aghast. "But Miss Sarah is only seven."

"I know. But Mr. Hastings feels that since Robert is now old enough to go to boarding school, it might be wise to send Sarah away as well. He feels they are not developing as they should. ... Oh, not on your account, Miss Saxby, please don't misunderstand me. Mr. Hastings has said no word against you."

Her tear-filled eyes turned full on Fern now, anxious not to hurt. "It is not your fault at all, but mine, I fear. My husband feels that I indulge them overmuch and that they would be better removed from my influence."

Her voice caught on a sob as she spoke. Fern had to resist the urge to rise and comfort the woman, which would have betokened criticism of her master. Instead she tried to divert Mrs. Hastings from her misery.

"So I understand you will soon have no further need of my services, madam. Is that what the master wished you to inform me? Do not worry unduly on that account, for I am sure I shall be able to find another position soon."

Mrs. Hastings gripped Fern's hands between her own. "Oh, my dear, I would not lose you for the world if I could keep you here, but there is nothing I can do. I shall give you an excellent reference, of course, but ..." Her voice trailed away in anguish. Making a firm effort to regain her self-control, she turned sharply away. "I shall do what I can, of course. No doubt Mr. Hastings will permit me to recommend your ser-

7

vices to others of our acquaintance who may be in need of a governess. We do entertain on occasion, as you know, and if the opportunity arises, I shall speak of you. . . ."

On occasion, thought Fern sadly. Mr. Hastings had long ago despaired of his wife as a hostess, and although Mrs. Paddock could be relied upon to provide a substantially appetizing if not inspired meal for his guests, his wife's social inadequacies left much to be desired. He could impress his business acquaintances far better over a meal in town.

"Well, now"—Mrs. Hastings wiped her eyes hastily—"I must begin the arrangements. The master wants me to order new clothes for the children, so if you would see that they are dressed in their street clothes, Miss Saxby, I shall take them to the dressmaker this morning."

"Very well, Mrs. Hastings. Shall they have their lessons this afternoon instead?"

"Oh . . . er . . . no, I think not. Mr. Hastings has not said what he wishes done then. Best leave lessons today. You may have the day off."

"Thank you, madam." Taking Mrs. Hastings' words as a dismissal, Fern rose and left the room, thrusting the letter into her pocket. Mounting the steep, balustraded staircase to the nursery, she found two disconsolate children sitting at the nursery table, their books unopened and their faces vacant. Poor little things, thought Fern, never the brightest or most rewarding of pupils, but amiable and anxious to please nonetheless, like their mother.

"Come, children, no lessons today," she said brightly, sweeping the books away from in front of them. "Your mamma is to take you to the dressmaker's instead, to buy you new clothes. Aren't you lucky?"

Robert looked up mournfully. "New clothes for school," he commented in a lackluster voice. "I don't want to go away to school, nor does Sarah."

Sarah's little white face stared beseechingly at Fern. "No, we'd rather stay here with Mamma . . . and Papa," she added quickly. "Please ask Papa if we can stay, Miss Saxby." The little voice was so plaintive that Fern could have hugged the child, but instead she spoke cheerfully.

"But you haven't really thought about it, Sarah. Just think, lots of playmates every day and all day. You haven't anyone to play with here, save Robert. Now you'll have lots of little girls your own age, and Robert will have boys of his age. You should be glad your father is so concerned for you. Come now, let me help you button on your boots while Robert fetches his coat."

She watched the two dispirited figures leave the house with their mother before returning to her room. A cheerless, sparsely furnished room, in strong contrast to the heavily overfurnished parlor, it was nevertheless a more congenial lodging than those the servants shared in the attic. On the second floor, far removed from the main bedrooms, it was yet close to the children's rooms and heated by a small coal fire in the hearth.

Fern seated herself on the edge of the bed and reflected. So, events would seem to decree yet another upheaval in her life. Soon she would be forced to leave this secure if monotonous existence, and what then? Two years ago had seen the first upheaval, when her father and mother had died suddenly and she had been obliged to leave her pleasant life at Miss Danby's Academy for Young Ladies in order to earn a living. She had coped then, so why not now? After all, at twenty-two she was no longer the immature miss she had been once, cosseted and indulged. Now she was both abler and wiser in the ways of the world. She would manage. Something would turn up. An advertisement in the columns of the *Times,* perhaps. That might produce a suitable position.

Suddenly Fern remembered the unexpected letter that remained still unopened in her pocket. She withdrew it curiously.

The letterhead indicated it was from Nathaniel Lennox, a solicitor in London. That was clear enough, but the text of the letter was puzzling: "If you would be so kind as to call at my office as soon as it is convenient to your good self, you will

9

hear of a matter which may be greatly to your advantage."
What matter? How could it be of advantage? puzzled Fern.

It was not far from Elton Square to the solicitor's office,
and as Fern threaded her way through the streets, among
fashionably dressed ladies and their frock-coated escorts
mingling with the shabby poor who scraped a living selling
matches or flowers and blacking boots, she wondered about
the letter. Could it be a legacy of some kind? Fifty pounds
would be extremely welcome just now, but who could possibly
have named her in a will, since she had no living relative in
the world? But if it were not a legacy, why should a solicitor
speak of a matter "to her advantage"? It really was most per-
plexing.

Mr. Nathaniel Lennox sat smiling benignly behind his wide
oak desk, his chins dimpling above his constricting high stock
and his fingertips arched together as he surveyed his young
visitor. The ordered regularity of his chambers with their
bookshelves lined with huge legal tomes lurched suddenly into
confusion to Fern's disordered mind, for his words were
senseless, crazy, and fantastic beyond all imagination.

"What is that you are telling me, Mr. Lennox?" she ventured at last, her breath seeming to catch helplessly in her
throat. "I cannot fully follow . . ."

"Yes, I admit it is a trifle overwhelming, but it is the truth,
Miss Saxby. There is no mistake. Mr. Thomas de Lacy, deceased, has bequeathed to you his estate in Yorkshire—subject to certain conditions, as I mentioned."

"But . . . but I have never heard of this Mr. de Lacy! There
must be some mistake!"

"None whatever, I assure you. I have checked most carefully. Though no blood relation of yours, Mr. de Lacy was
nonetheless distantly related to you, and anxious to redeem
what he considered to be an oversight in the past."

"An estate," murmured Fern, still too dazed to comprehend. "A sum of money, do you mean?"

"Money, as well as a mansion, a mill and several farms that
have quite a sizable acreage." He drew a sheaf of papers

toward him. "Would you like to know the precise figures at valuation of the mansion, the mill and the farmlands?"

"No, no. Let me think a little, Mr. Lennox. First, are you *certain* I am the person Mr. de Lacy intended to inherit? It seems so unlikely, as I have no relatives."

"I am certain, be sure of that, young lady. But the matter is a little more complicated. There is also another legatee to share the estate—a Mr. Bruno de Lacy, who again is distantly related to you."

A relative! A living relative—it seemed too good to be true. Fern's hitherto blank face broke into a smile. "Do explain to me, Mr. Lennox, I beg of you. How do these gentlemen come to be related to me?"

"It is a long story, dating from some seventy years ago, but I'll do my best," the old gentleman replied, drawing a blank sheet of paper toward him and dipping his pen in the inkstand. "At the turn of the century, or soon after, there was a Dorian de Lacy at Brackenroyd Hall, the only son and heir. He was to have married a young lady named Annot Radley."

"Radley? That was my mother's name!" Fern interrupted unthinkingly. "But I always understood her to say she had no kin. She did say her family had come from Yorkshire, but she rarely spoke of them."

"Well, Annot Radley bore Dorian de Lacy a son—your maternal grandfather. But she never married Dorian. She died suddenly," Mr. Lennox continued. "He later married a Sarah Ramsden, and it was his son and Sarah's, Thomas de Lacy, who bequeathed Brackenroyd Hall jointly to you and his grandson, Bruno."

"But why?" questioned Fern. "I do not understand."

Mr. Lennox shrugged. "I know it seems odd, for your claim through an illegitimate line would seem thin, but you did not know old Thomas. He was a very Christian gentleman, extremely conscientious and scrupulous, and it troubled him that had his father married Annot, then his elder half-brother would have inherited, and not he. Having lost sight of his half-brother, he resolved to reinstate his descendants if he could trace them. It took time, but I traced you. Thomas' own son, George, being dead, his grandson, Bruno, inherits, along with you."

Mr. Lennox pushed across to Fern the sheet of paper on which he had been writing. She saw that he had written two neat columns, each one representing the line of descent from Dorian de Lacy.

Annot Radley	= Dorian =	Sarah Ramsden
William Radley		Thomas de Lacy
Fern Saxby		George de Lacy
Sophie Radley		Bruno de Lacy

"I see," murmured Fern; then, pointing to the last name on the list, "And this Mr. de Lacy—Mr. Bruno de Lacy—we share a common great-grandfather in Dorian de Lacy. Does he know of me and of the terms of the bequest?"

"Oh, yes, and is quite content with the arrangement, for the inheritance is a substantial one." He beamed encouragingly at Fern. "Well, now, young lady, does the prospect appeal to you, of becoming an heiress and living high on the Yorkshire moors?"

Fern bit her lip dubiously. "To be quite honest, Mr. Lennox, I find it difficult to believe it is true. But if it is, it could hardly have occurred at a happier moment." On seeing Mr. Lennox's bushy eyebrows arch in question, Fern went on to explain. "It's a blessing, and that's a fact. You see, I find I am obliged to leave my present post and had no idea where to turn next to find work. Because money with which to live is vital."

"Indeed it is, my dear. Well, now, your problems would seem to be solved."

"It would be such a relief to leave the . . . restrictions of the household where I live. Oh, just to think of it! Breathing pure fresh air on the moors! Does the house have gardens, Mr. Lennox? Orchards, a lake perhaps?" Fern's eyes grew bright and enthusiastic as she reviewed the potentialities of this un-looked-for future.

"I have never actually seen Brackenroyd Hall, I'm afraid.

Mr. Thomas used always to come to London to transact his affairs with me. But I believe it is a fine house with all you mention in its grounds. On the edge of Brackenroyd village, I believe, not far from the river, with the moors above."

It sounded wonderful. But what of the other legatee, the grandson Bruno? Would he too wish to live in the Hall, or dispose of it and share the proceeds? she wondered. Pointing to his name on the list again, she inquired of Mr. Lennox if he knew the gentleman.

"Not personally, I regret, though no doubt the omission will be rectified in time. A fine, upstanding young man by all accounts, some ten years older than you, at a guess. He's a doctor, you know, and already earning himself quite a reputation in his field."

Mr. Lennox paused, toying with the pen between his fingertips. "But there is more to be discussed, Miss Saxby," he said tentatively, and Fern sensed that he found it difficult to pick his words with care. "As I mentioned before, there are certain conditions attached to the legacy, and these must be met before you can complete your claim."

Ah, yes, the conditions. Having held out a promise of heaven to her, what stumbling block was he now going to produce to make the vision fade? She felt a prick of anger and dismay at the thought of losing Brackenroyd Hall. She would not be cheated of it lightly.

"What are the conditions, Mr. Lennox?" she asked levelly.

"First, that on obtaining the Hall you do not sell it again, at least for five years after your marriage."

"Marriage? That is highly unlikely, Mr. Lennox. I have seen marriage at close quarters, and do not like what I see. It destroys the soul."

"Really?" The lawyer's bushy eyebrows arched again. "You surprise me, my dear young lady. Such a cynical view for one so young. I cannot say *I* have found marriage to be so destructive."

No, possibly not, she reflected, you have such a warm and kindly face. You, perhaps, would not sap a woman's happiness. You would not tear her beloved children from her.

Mrs. Lennox is a far more fortunate creature than Mrs. Hastings.

Mr. Lennox was studying her closely. "Are you quite determined against marriage, Miss Saxby?"

Fern looked up, puzzled. "Why do you ask?"

"Because I come to the other condition of Mr. Thomas de Lacy's will. In order to inherit and share Brackenroyd Hall equally with Dr. Bruno de Lacy, it is conditional that you and he must marry each other."

Fern sat aghast. Marry—and a man she had never even met? It was unthinkable! Ridiculous! The old man must have been crazed when he dictated his will. Mr. Lennox, watching the reactions on her face, seemed to follow the drift of her thoughts.

"It was a sensible enough solution on Mr. Thomas' part, my dear, if he wished to ensure that both legitimate and illegitimate lines of the family were secure. This way, your claim is valid and no one could ever contest it. I know the idea appalls you, as it would any sensitive young lady, but if you would like to go home and think about it for a few days, I believe the logic of the arrangement will become clear to you. Think it over, my dear, and let me know when you have decided."

Too numb to answer, Fern sat stiffly, clutching her gloves nervously.

Mr. Lennox murmured more persuasive words. "Just think of it, a fine young man, of very presentable appearance, with excellent manners and taste, I am told, and a respected doctor besides. A marriage partner many young society ladies would no doubt find highly desirable, I'll be bound."

A good catch for a governess, thought Fern, a chance I shouldn't sneer at—that's what he means. But the inheritance meant more than that. It meant escape from frustration and claustrophobia, escape from London's filth and poverty and drudgery, freedom to breathe and be one's own mistress. Was marriage to a stranger too high a price to pay for such bliss?

Impulsively Fern rose, stretching out her hand to the lawyer. "I thank you for your courtesy and interest, Mr. Lennox. I would not wish to take up yet more of your valuable time, so I will give you my answer now. I agree to the terms. If Dr. Bruno de Lacy is in agreement, I shall marry him as you request."

And Brackenroyd Hall will be mine, she thought ecstatically to herself as she retraced her footsteps to Elton Square. Whatever this Bruno de Lacy is like, handsome or ugly, human or demonic, I will not let my husband rob me of my inheritance!

Chapter 2

Matthew Hastings' change of attitude toward his children's governess was quite astounding when he learned of her sudden rise in fortune. Now he no longer banished her from his presence as quickly as possible, as an indeterminate thing neither quite gentle nor baseborn, but instead he became openly affable.

"Perhaps you would care to dine with us, Miss Saxby—this evening, if you would, when the Blandings come? We have never really conversed, have we? Let me see, now, your family are the Saxbys of Lincolnshire, are they not?"

But Fern declined his magnanimous offer, having no wish to be paraded with pride as Mr. Hastings' friend, the heiress of Brackenroyd. Lydia Hastings, however, was genuinely pleased at her governess's good fortune, relieved that the problem of her future was thus happily resolved and no longer presenting a problem to her conscience.

"You must let me help you choose new clothes, befitting your new station," she murmured anxiously. "Come with me to the dressmaker's when I take the children."

Fern, armed with the prodigious sum of twenty pounds that Mr. Lennox had pressed upon her once all the necessary papers had been signed, was glad to accept Mrs. Hastings' offer. The solicitor had said that Dr. Bruno de Lacy had given orders that Fern was to be furnished at once with all necessary funds for preparing for the journey, and a first-class railway ticket to Bradford.

"Dr. de Lacy will be writing to you himself shortly to make the final preparations," Mr. Lennox had said in his kindly, avuncular manner. "In the meantime, buy whatever fripperies a young lady needs, and do not hesitate to call on me if you require more."

Fripperies indeed. Fern smiled. Twenty pounds represented a half-year's salary as a governess, wealth indeed to one accustomed to budgeting carefully. It would more than pay for her few needs.

Lydia Hastings was touchingly helpful. "The violet wool gown enhances your fair coloring beautifully, and I think the gentian blue becomes you very well too," she would say in the privacy of the dressmaker's parlor, and the quick surreptitious dabs at her reddened eyes betrayed her misery. The children, Robert and Sarah, stood impassively, lifeless little waxwork figures, while the dressmaker's deft fingers measured and pinned.

What a sad duty for Mrs. Hastings, Fern thought, to be preparing her beloved children to leave her, while her governess prepared for a new life as a bride. These gowns were her wedding trousseau, Fern reflected, though Lydia Hastings did not know it. Fern had not disclosed to her employers that her inheritance entailed an unlooked-for marriage, only that she and a very distant relative, a doctor, were to share the bequest.

As the days slipped by, little Sarah and Robert seemed too bemused to register what was happening to them. Life had somehow slithered out of its familiar routine, for Father had decreed that lessons in the schoolroom were no longer necessary, and the household was in a state of upheaval, trunks everywhere and drawers and cupboards ransacked and emptied.

The departure of both children and governess was imminent. The atmosphere in the house was heavy with unspoken misery. It could have felt no more oppressive if they were funeral arrangements being planned, thought Fern, and she could feel no pang of nostalgia at leaving Elton Square. Mr. Hastings, however, seemed quite oblivious of the air of mournful silence in his household.

Then the letter came, crisp and practical. Fern stared at its strong, masculine handwriting, boldly self-confident yet with a trace of something remote, withdrawn, and intense in the firmly closed-in tails of the letters. Bruno de Lacy would seem, from his handwriting at least, to be more complex than his simple letter indicated. It told her the easiest way to reach Bradford by train, the most convenient train times, and assured her that he would meet her at the Bradford railway station.

"A Pullman coach, of course," Mr. Hastings dictated. "Second class would be most unseemly for a lady of your means. Yes, a Pullman will ensure comfort and privacy. I shall see you to the station myself."

Her trunk and smaller hand case loaded aboard the hansom cab, Fern turned on the step to bid farewell to Mrs. Hastings and the children. A momentary stab of pity compelled her to lean forward impulsively and kiss the older woman's cheek before climbing hastily inside. The poor woman looked so frail, so vulnerable in her misery, and Fern was obliged to force her mind to other matters.

Mr. Hastings seated himself cheerfully beside her and bade the cabman drive on. The dismal February afternoon dulled quickly into evening as they rode, and as the lamplighters touched the gas lamps into life, Fern could see in their flickering light the forgotten citizens of London still desperately seeking the means for supper. A forlorn flower seller sitting on an upturned box, her basket of limp violets on her lap and her threadbare shawl clutched about thin shoulders; a wizened man bent over his barrel organ, his equally wizened monkey holding out a pathetic tin cup to passersby as the thin, tinny music wailed on the evening air; the bootblack; and the rickets-twisted little boy trying vainly to sell his matches—all their cries vied with those of the street vendors selling baked potatoes or muffins. London's night air rang shrilly with the sounds of the poor.

It seemed odd to be setting out on a lengthy journey at so late an hour, thought Fern, but according to Dr. de Lacy's letter, the evening train was the most convenient of the day, necessitating no delay in making connections. It was odd, too, that the prospect of the journey and the unknown life ahead seemed to stir no expectancy within her, glad as she was to leave London and its claustrophobic atmosphere.

Luggage safely stowed in the guard's van and Mr. Hastings' final exhortations made as to securing a porter at the journey's end, Fern settled down in the Pullman coach.

The guard's whistle shrilled along the vast platform, and the train slid ponderously out from under the great dome of King's Cross station, out into the night and the unknown. As it chugged more and more rapidly and the clatter steadied into a regular rhythm, Fern began to drowse. Unbothered by other travelers, the nearest being two gentlemen at the further end of the coach, and soothed by the comfortable seats and upholstered head cushion, she remembered earlier days as a child when she had last traveled on a train, on a dearly longed-for day excursion to Brighton. It was on one of Mother and Father's infrequent home visits to England; tanned and handsome and laughing, they had appeared such benevolent gods to her child's eye. Gaily all three had gone down to the seaside for the day, and the indulgent parents had permitted her to ride on a donkey along the beach, to watch a Punch and Judy show on the sands, and to dabble her feet in the sparkling water. It had been such a glorious day of sun and buoyant laughter and freedom, one of the rare golden days of childhood she would always treasure, for she barely knew her parents after that. Her father, tall and resplendent in his captain's uniform, had borne Mother away again to India, and life had become a routine of lessons at the academy once more, until the day the terrible news had arrived. An Afghan raid, they had said. A marauding band in search of food or ammunition had crossed the northern frontier in the night. Papa had been very brave, they said, in defense of his bungalow and wife, but he and his few men and Mamma had all fallen victim to the Afghanis' bullets.

"Doncaster!" The guard's strident voice aroused Fern. Doncaster already? She must have been dozing, for it was now past eight o'clock. Fern sat upright and stared out into the darkness. Within an hour she would be meeting her future husband, and for the first time she felt a twinge of apprehension.

At Wakefield, Fern alighted, beckoned a porter, and followed his measured tread as he carried her luggage to the awaiting train that was to take her to Bradford. He helped her to mount the step into the coach and held out a grubby hand for his tip. As Fern gave him a coin, she became aware of a gentleman's eyes surveying her curiously, and as she seated herself opposite him, she saw he was looking from her to the label on her suitcase and back to her again.

He wore a clerical collar, she noted. Quite young, sandy hair showing beneath his top hat, a well-cut coat which had seen better days, and a now studiously averted thin face indicated that he was a harmless enough traveling companion. She sat back and watched the little station signposts as they flickered under their gas lamps—Ossett, Dewsbury, Batley—not far now. At Laister Dyke the young clergyman leaned forward.

"Forgive my impertinence, madam, but I see from your case you are traveling to Brackenroyd Hall. Allow me to introduce myself. I am Edgar Amos, vicar of Brackenroyd. I should be honored to see you safely to the Hall if you would allow me."

Fern looked up, pleasure irradiating her face. How pleasant to meet a future neighbor who seemed so friendly and welcoming! He was smiling a little diffidently, as though uncertain of the propriety of his action. Fern leaned forward with a smile, extending her gloved hand.

"How very kind of you, Mr. Amos. My name is Fern Saxby, and I am delighted to make your acquaintance, as no doubt we shall be near neighbors. Thank you for your kind offer, but there is no need to incommode yourself, for I believe Dr. de Lacy is to meet me at Bradford himself."

The young clergyman's sandy eyebrows had risen fractionally as Fern spoke, and she wondered why he should register surprise. His next words explained.

"Miss Saxby? Then you must be the new heiress of Brackenroyd, along with Dr. de Lacy? I am delighted to meet so charming a young mistress for the Hall, and sincerely hope your new life in the village will be a most happy and rewarding one."

"I have no reason to doubt it, sir." As she watched the comfortable smile settle over his bland features, she wondered what Mr. Amos was thinking. That she was not what he expected, that she must be a strange creature indeed to agree to marry a complete stranger? At least he knew something of Brackenroyd Hall and its present tenant. She resolved to try to glean something of his knowledge.

"The Hall?" he replied seriously in answer to her question. "Ah, yes, a fine building, constructed at the beginning of the century on the site of the old Hall, built in the sixteenth century. In fact, one wing of the old Hall still remains, and the new Hall was added to it, though I believe the old wing is now unused. Too cold and drafty, you know."

"And the De Lacys—have they always lived there?"

"Since the late sixteenth century, yes. They are a wealthy family of Norman descent, and the lifeblood of Brackenroyd village. Lords of the manor, as you might say, building cottages and later a mill for their tenants. Most Brackenroyd villagers even now still work in the woolen mill."

"And Dr. de Lacy—has he always lived at the Hall?"

"As a child he came frequently, but he lived mostly in Germany. His mother was German, you know, and as his father died young, she kept Bruno in her native country to be educated. He has only recently returned to Brackenroyd, on his grandfather's death."

The train rumbled to a halt at a small station. "St. Dunstan's," commented Mr. Amos brightly. "Nearly there, Miss Saxby. We shall be in Bradford in a few minutes."

Fern gazed out of the train window, anxious for her first glimpse of the great Yorkshire city, but in the darkness there was little to be seen save the occasional gas lamp. The train rumbled noisily into the great station, and Mr. Amos rose to hand down her suitcase before dismounting.

Few people other than those leaving the train loitered about the vast platform, for the February night air was chill and damp, but a greatcoated man, tall and impressive despite his gauntness, strode purposefully toward them. He doffed his hat, exposing his thick dark hair clinging damply about his temples, as he addressed Fern.

"Miss Saxby? I am Bruno de Lacy." His handshake was firm despite his few words, and he granted the young clergyman at her side only the curtest of nods.

Fern could not resist staring at him. He was uncommonly handsome in a dour sort of way, with no hint of a smile about his compressed lips, though the fullness of the lower lip indicated a generous nature. His dark eyes were surveying her intently.

Amos fidgeted slightly and excused himself. "Well, since the young lady is now safely delivered into your hands, I shall leave you, Dr. de Lacy. No doubt we shall meet again soon," he said, and disappeared quickly.

De Lacy's hand cupped Fern's elbow firmly. "The carriage is waiting, and the porter has seen to your trunk," he commented laconically. "Allow me to carry your hand luggage."

With a quiet, proprietary air he took the suitcase and led her to the waiting carriage and helped her inside. As the coachman whipped up and set off into the darkness, De Lacy sat silent at Fern's side.

"Is it far to Brackenroyd Hall?" Fern inquired timidly at last, fearful that he might resent her breaking his air of absorption.

"A half-hour's ride, no more."

He made no further effort to speak. Fern sat equally silent, wondering if he was assessing her appearance and bearing as his prospective bride. She could not beat down the confusion which caused her cheeks to flush in embarrassment. For a long time no sound broke the tense silence save hoofbeats and the clatter of wheels.

At length he leaned forward and gazed out of the window. "Brackenroyd village," he said curtly. Fern could discern in the darkness only the glimmer of oil lamps in uncurtained cottage windows and the hulking outline of a great building, the mill perhaps. Then she spotted the spire of a small church, the one where Mr. Amos was vicar, no doubt, and she wondered why Dr. de Lacy had not offered a seat in the carriage to him.

"This is the way to the Hall," said De Lacy as the carriage turned off the cobbled street and began to climb a steeply graveled drive. The drive wound on and on, uphill all the way, until at last Fern could see the outline of the house starkly silhouetted against the skyline, right on the crest of the hill. She drew in her breath sharply. It was not only the strangely weird appearance of the vast building with its battlemented turrets which disturbed her, but also the uncanny feeling that she had seen the place before. And the half-recollection brought with it an unaccountable sense of sadness.

"Oh!" The sigh escaped her lips almost inaudibly, but De Lacy was quick to note it.

"What is it, Miss Saxby? Does the Hall disappoint you?" he asked with a wry smile.

"Oh, no, not at all. It was just an odd sensation that I have been here before, though I know I cannot possibly have done so. I seem to recognize it—that there will be a flight of steps and stone balustrades, a wide vestibule, and ..." She could remember no more, for the fleeting vision had dissolved. De Lacy was frowning slightly, as though he considered he had burdened himself with a half-witted girl.

Fern smiled as the carriage halted. "Silly, isn't it? Perhaps I am overtired after the journey."

"It is not an uncommon sensation, Miss Saxby. The French have a name for it—they call it *déjà vu*."

Found only in flighty, irresponsible females, thought Fern.

She wished she had never mentioned it to him. But as he helped her alight and mount the stone steps to the balustraded terrace, and a woman opened the huge front door revealing the wide, warmly lit vestibule within, Fern trembled again. It was exactly as she had visualized it. The woman smiled in welcome.

"Miss Saxby, may I present Mrs. Thorpe, the housekeeper," De Lacy said tersely, indicating the generously built, matronly figure. "Is there supper ready for Miss Saxby?" he inquired.

Before Mrs. Thorpe could reply, Fern intervened. "Indeed, I am not hungry, Dr. de Lacy, and should much prefer to go straight to bed if you do not mind. The hour is already very late."

He glanced at the oak grandfather clock in the corner, whose hands pointed to just after eleven. He nodded in agreement. "Very well. Good night."

At once he turned and entered a room off the vestibule. Mrs. Thorpe smiled and crossed to the staircase. "I'll show you to your room, then, miss. This way."

Fern mounted the wide, shallow steps behind her and followed her along the gallery, guided by the lamp in the housekeeper's hand. When at last Mrs. Thorpe opened a door and ushered Fern into a large, well-furnished bedchamber with a huge four-poster dominating the center of the room, Fern could feel only grateful relief. Sleep and rest at last. Her curiosity about the vast old house and its occupants could wait until morning.

"There's hot water in the jug, and a hot bottle in the bed," said the housekeeper as she fussed about, turning back the bedcovers and opening the doors of a huge press. "Leave your unpacking until the morning, and I'll send Cassie up to help you. If there's anything else you want, there's the bell rope by the fireplace."

Satisfied that Fern was comfortable, Mrs. Thorpe withdrew, leaving Fern to undress and wash. There was a low fire in the hearth, but the room was still chilly, and Fern was glad to pull her woolen nightdress over her head and climb into the downy depths of the great bed. How comfortable it was, a feather mattress and blanket-covered stone bottle full of hot water on which to warm her feet. How luxurious, how vastly different from the plain narrow bed in the Hastings household, to be in this enormous four-poster with its brocaded hangings. As sleep crept over her, Fern mused idly as to the history of this bed. How many De Lacys had slept here, and what were their stories? Had there ever been a De Lacy bride before who had had no knowledge of her bridegroom before setting foot in the Hall?

Sleep came quickly, but with it came oddly tangled dreams of a tall, taciturn man with a thin, sneering lip and of a silently miserable woman who wept as her child was pulled from her arms. She was shabby and thin, gaunt misery in her eyes, but the vision seemed to have no substance, to hover vacantly in space. No house or landscape formed a frame to the picture. The only distinct impression was of the dark-eyed man's mockery and total lack of feeling as the woman, bowed and silent, finally yielded her child and turned away. Fern awoke before dawn, thin shafts of light entering the high window where she had left the curtains undrawn. She felt uneasy and not at all rested. Strange she had slept so fitfully when she had been so tired.

As the light grew stronger and sleep did not return, she rose, and pulling on her dressing gown, crossed to the window. Far below, down the hill, beyond the gravel drive which curled out of sight behind ancient oak trees, she could see the cluster of cottages that was Brackenroyd village. To the side of the house and sweeping up and away behind it rose a vast stretch of gray moorland where occasional sheep grazed in the hollows, out of reach of the sharp wind. She opened the window and breathed in the cold air. How clean and fresh it smelled! For the first time Fern felt glad. It was indeed pleasant to leave behind the fog and stench of London and be able to breathe clean, wholesome country air. As she closed the window again, a knock came at the door, and a housemaid entered. She bobbed a curtsy.

"Morning, miss. I'm Cassie. Mrs. Thorpe says I'm to help you unpack, once you've breakfasted." She laid a tray on the night table and began pouring a cup of tea. A bright-cheeked girl of about twenty, she looked happy enough in her work, thought Fern as she picked up the bowl of porridge on the tray and began to spoon up its steaming contents. She pulled a face. In North Country fashion, the porridge had been sprinkled with salt instead of the customary sugar. Hunger, however, overcame her distaste.

"I'll come back when you've finished," promised Cassie, and with a smile she was gone.

Fern sipped her tea thoughtfully. The strange, wistful feeling of the dreams came back to her, and she pondered again as to their meaning. The tall uncommunicative man—not Mr. Hastings—was probably Bruno de Lacy, about whom she evidently still felt a little apprehensive—and with reason, since she was soon to pledge her life to his. And the woman who wept—that must be Mrs. Hastings, for Fern did indeed feel great sympathy for the poor woman whose beloved children were being wrenched from her. Or was it she? For the woman in the dream was young and ethereally fragile, her face plaintive and vividly clear in Fern's waking memory. No, it must be Mrs. Hastings. Purposefully Fern brushed the dream aside, put down her empty cup, and set about unpacking her luggage. Cassie soon returned to help.

It was only when Fern had completed the task and stood by the latticed window surveying the Hall grounds below that she thought again about Bruno de Lacy. Even as she thought, his tall, gaunt figure appeared below, striding absently away from the Hall, upward toward the moor. Straining at the leash curled about his hand was a huge wolfhound.

Bruno's head was bare, despite the damp mists, and his appearance was decidedly disheveled. Cassie, bustling behind Fern, caught sight of her master through the window and sighed.

"There goes the master on his regular morning walk with Pharaoh," she commented as the figure receded rapidly into the mist.

"Where does he go?" Fern inquired.

Cassie shrugged. "Who knows? To the moor, happen to

think. He's a deep one, Dr. de Lacy, a very clever man, they say."

The mist played tricks with the figure fading into the distance, enlarging and distorting the shape till he seemed a giant with Cerberus at his heels. Fern shivered involuntarily. There was decidedly something very strange about Bruno de Lacy.

Chapter 3

Mrs. Thorpe's warm smiles as she conducted Fern on a tour of Fern, throwing open doors and cupboards proudly, confi- housekeeper at least welcomed her arrival. She bustled ahead of Fern, throwing open doors and cupboards proudly, confi- dent that all was as a fastidious mistress would expect. Fern was overwhelmed by the beauty of the Hall, its vast rooms furnished with taste and heedless of expense.

"Mr. Thomas used to travel abroad as a young man, long before I came here," the plump matron enthused as she led Fern into the parlor. "Much of the furniture here he brought back with him."

From the Far East undoubtedly, for the room was filled with chinoiserie, embroidered tapestry screens, ornaments of jade, lacquered cabinets, and deep-red-enameled side tables. On the hearth, before an embroidered fire screen, stood huge vases filled with pampas grass and dried honesty, cheek by jowl with the gleaming brass fire irons. Fern sank into the depths of the sofa and sighed with pleasure. What a comfort- able room, with its oak-paneled walls and gleaming chandelier, far more welcoming and cozy than the overstuffed pretentiousness of Elton Square. Mrs. Thorpe was hovering expectantly by the door.

"Would you like to inspect the kitchens now, madam? Or if you prefer to remain here, I'll send Cassie up to light the fire for you. Usually it is lit only in the afternoons when Mr. Bruno returns, but if it is your wish—"

"No, no, don't trouble yourself, Mrs. Thorpe. I think I too shall go out for a walk shortly," Fern interrupted as she rose. "Perhaps you would be so kind as to show me the rest of the house later?"

Mrs. Thorpe's plump cheeks dimpled. "But, of course, madam. You are the mistress now."

"I shall be—soon," Fern corrected.

"Mr. Bruno said I was to hand over the keys to you and treat you as mistress as soon as you came. The wedding was but a formality, he said."

Reluctant fingers slid to the bunch of keys dangling from a chain at her waist, or rather, where Mrs. Thorpe's waist would be if she had not been so amply built. Fern laid a hand on hers.

"Please—be so kind as to keep the keys, Mrs. Thorpe. Pray carry on exactly as you did before I came. From you I am certain that I shall learn much of the ways of skillful housewifery, for I confess I am totally ignorant and would be glad of your counsel. When my wedding is over, perhaps then I shall be ready."

As they talked, the women retraced their footsteps toward the vestibule. Turning a corner into a long, paneled corridor, Fern noticed a wide, arched doorway set into the corner, and a studded door. A quiver ran up her spine.

"What is that door? Where does it lead?" she asked the housekeeper.

Mrs. Thorpe spread her hands. "To the east wing, that part of the old Hall we never use now. Mr. Bruno keeps it locked. He goes there occasionally, but he tells me not to waste time cleaning it, for it is so damp with all those flagstone floors, and some of it is crumbling. As I say, it's never used at all, save for Mr. Bruno's cellar."

"Cellar? For wine?"

"Bless you, no. Something to do with his work as a doctor, experiments or something; I never did quite catch on what it was, but he's a very quiet man is Mr. Bruno, and very clever."

In the vestibule Mrs. Thorpe left her, and Fern returned to her room to prepare to go out and inspect the Hall by daylight from the outside. Donning a small, veiled hat and ulster and pulling on her gloves, she walked down the steps, crunching the gravel drive underfoot and turning off the main drive along a flagged path before reaching the gate. The path wound between now barren flowerbeds and rockeries, rising gradually as it circled the house widely, and ending suddenly at an iron gate set in a high stone wall.

The lock creaked rustily at Fern's touch but opened easily. Beyond lay steeply rising rough turf and a pathway worn by countless feet. Clanging the gate shut behind her, Fern set off up the moor.

The path swept steeply across tough, wiry grass, between outcrops of black rock scoured into smooth gigantic monoliths by the searching Atlantic winds. Fern was entranced by the wild Pennine countryside, stark and majestic in its somber wintry mood, not on account of its beauty, for not even a poet could see beauty in the tough brown heather and wild, exposed wastes. But there was power, a kind of repressed strength and primitive appeal in these rugged gaunt mountains protecting the little village in the hollow far below, and in the fierce little brook gushing vigorously down its narrow rocky bed to join the river.

Not a figure broke the solitude of the landscape save an occasional browsing sheep that, startled at her approach, looked up with a distrustful, inimical stare. Fern, out of breath from her climb, and the wind catching in her throat, seated herself on an outcrop of rock to survey the scene. What an impressive countryside this was! Deep within her, something responded, low and vibrant, to the untamed majesty of the Pennines. It was as though their power evoked in her something she had once known and then lost, something she was over-joyed to rediscover. Coming to Brackenroyd was somehow akin to coming home.

Turning, Fern sought out the shape of Brackenroyd Hall. It was not difficult to discern, huge and brooding darkly against the skyline on the clifftop. From here it seemed to dominate and overwhelm the cluster of cottages and the church and mill in the valley below it, standing sentinel as the De Lacy family had done over its vassals for centuries. A shiver caused Fern to rise and resume her walk. The Hall was somehow an object of menace. Turning her back on it, Fern surveyed the view and made out at length the shape of a long, rambling building half-burying itself in the hillside. A strange edifice, neither church nor mill, but rather like a huge barn it stood, neglected and dilapidated, a no-longer-frequented house, per-haps. From a curl of smoke rising above a chimney, quickly whipped up and swept away by the wind, Fern concluded that the house was still inhabited after all.

It was cold up here on the heights, and Fern reflected that her London attire was hardly suitable for braving the gusty Pennine winds, which were laced with frost. Here and there a patch of snow still lay on the heather, and from the wind's icy, probing fingers it would seem that further snow was still to fall. Fern began to retrace her steps to the Hall.

Perhaps it was the wind's shrill rise and fall, or the crackle of her own footsteps on desiccated heather that drowned all other sound, but a sudden voice at her side caused Fern to leap in alarm.

"I see our moorland air has brought fresh color to your cheeks, Miss Saxby." Fern's startled gaze found Bruno de Lacy walking moodily at her side, his dark eyes regarding her penetratingly. She recovered herself swiftly.

"Indeed, it is fine, bracing air. I think I shall come to love Brackenroyd, sir, for it stirs deep feelings in me, a kind of familiarity almost."

He was looking at her oddly, and Fern remembered her re-mark on arriving at the Hall last night. He had looked at her equally oddly, almost mockingly then, when he had spoken of her sense of recognition as a common sensation.

"Do you think it is possible, Dr. de Lacy, that one can feel a sense of belonging where one knows one has never been before?" Fern inquired. "I could almost believe I know this valley and these moors—perhaps a kind of inherited memory through my ancestors?"

He stopped suddenly and faced her squarely, his gaze fierce and compelling. "No, I do not believe such things possible, Miss Saxby. Yorkshire folk are too full of common sense and practicality to have faith in any such nonsense." His voice was sharply emphatic.

"Yorkshire folk? But you . . ."

"I know what you would say. I am partly of German parentage and educated in Germany, but nevertheless one side of me is pure Yorkshire—and of you, too." He began to walk again, adjusting his long stride to suit Fern's shorter one. The dog, Pharaoh, unleashed, bounded among the lichen-spattered boulders.

For a time they walked in silence, Fern feeling she had been reprimanded for her foolishness and at the same time resentful of his superior ways. As they descended the pathway to the gate in the Hall's walls, Bruno spoke again carelessly.

"I presume Mrs. Thorpe has shown you over the Hall. If there is anything else you require in the way of amusement—a piano or embroidery materials or whatever a young lady desires—you have but to order it."

Fern was stung. Amusements indeed! "Thank you, sir, but I do not require diversions of the kind you mention. A library such as the Hall possesses suits me admirably, and a mare to ride would please me well."

He nodded curtly. "Malachi will see to a suitable mount for you. The library is, of course, at your disposal."

At the gateway he paused before opening the gate. "If I might presume, Miss Saxby, to call you by your Christian name, would you be offended? It seems a little . . . odd for a betrothed couple to be as formal as we are. May I call you Fern?"

Fern thrilled to the sound of her name spoken in such resonant tones, a sound as wild and untamed as the wind on the moors. "By all means," she said softly.

If only he were not so stiffly aloof and cold, she could quite like this man she was to marry. His tall frame and subdued manner bespoke strength, a power as repressed and formidable as that of the Pennine moors. Here was a man to lean on in time of adversity, a man in whom to place one's trust—if one could only penetrate his reserve. He had spoken of their betrothal; Fern resolved to press further.

"I think I can see the church spire there below," she said, indicating the gray tower amid the village trees. "Is that where we shall be married?"

"If you wish." How laconic he was!

"When?"

"When you are ready. At once, if you wish the banns to be published."

Fern felt a little mollified. He was not, then, anxious to delay the match lest he did not come to like her or because he resented her intrusion. In that case, she would not rush him. She too would be glad of a little delay while she came to know both Bruno and her new surroundings a little better. She glanced up at the leaden sky.

"It would seem that there is snow to come soon. Let us be married in the spring, when the winter is ended."

"Very well. I shall wait till you ask again."

They turned up the gravel path leading to the door of the Hall, the dog loping ahead of them. Bruno opened the front door for her and smiled, a fleeting curve at the corner of his lips which gave his saturnine expression a brief moment of humor.

"One would have expected your first excursion to be to the village, my dear, and not up on the barren moors. After lunch I must go down to see to matters at the mill. I shall take you down to the village and introduce you to some of our local worthies."

"Thank you. I shall be delighted."

That afternoon Malachi led out from the stables a beautiful

little gray mare named Whisper for Fern to ride, and a lively black stallion for his master. Bruno caressed its nose affectionately before mounting, though Fern could not catch the words he murmured in the horse's ear.

"Phantom and I are old friends," he commented as he swung a long leg over the saddle. "He was with me in the old days, in Vienna."

Strange to think of Bruno de Lacy in Vienna, that romantic city of music and gaiety. Somehow, in his taciturn, brooding manner he seemed to be more at one with this arid, bleak mountain country than with the waltzing beats of that far-off city. Together Fern and he cantered down the gravel drive, swinging sharply down into the cobbled lane leading into the village. Light precipitation began to cling to Fern's riding habit in the shape of miniature, coruscating snowflakes.

"Would you like to return?" Bruno demanded curtly. Fern shook her head. He was considerate despite his abrupt manner. As they rode past the inn, a cheery and red-faced young man at the door waved and smiled. Bruno reined in and turned toward him.

"Allow me to present to you Tom Rawcliffe, landlord of the Woolpack," Bruno said. Fern inclined her head, smiling. "This is Miss Saxby, Tom, new mistress of Brackenroyd Hall and my future wife."

Rawcliffe made a welcoming gesture, half-salute, half-wave, and grinned apologetically at his own gauche manner. "Glad to meet thee, miss. The Hall's been lacking a mistress this many a year, and it'll be grand to see a De Lacy wedding again."

"Thank you." Fern smiled over her shoulder as Bruno led her on down the cobbled street. Almost imperceptible twitches at the curtains of the cottages betrayed that other inhabitants were curious about the newcomer to the village, but no doors opened. Bruno had noticed. He grunted quietly. "Pennine folk are a cautious lot, as you'll find. They'll watch and size you up before they commit themselves, but their friendship is worth the having once you've earned it."

A suspicious race, then, he made them sound, but reliable

and solid once one had penetrated their reserve. Fern resolved to win their confidence, for they were her own folk, were they not, bred of the moors and the millstone grit which was her own heritage?

The gray-stone church was discernible to their left, surrounded by old oak trees. "We shall call on Amos after we have met the schoolmaster," Bruno remarked as he drew up before a low gray building, evidently the school, with the schoolmaster's house alongside it, for Fern could hear childish voices chanting, "Once seven is seven, twice seven is fourteen . . ."

In answer to Bruno's knock, a pleasant-faced young woman with smoothly coiled fair hair came to the door. From behind her skirts peeped a child, a girl with huge violet eyes and the same gilt hair.

"Bruno! How nice to see you," the young woman cried as she stepped aside to allow him to enter. Bruno smiled distantly. "Fabia, this is my betrothed, Fern Saxby. Fern, this is Fabia Armitage, the schoolmaster's wife."

Fern noted the young woman's appraising gaze as they nodded mutually and Fabia led the way into the shabbily furnished parlor. The child clung timorously to Fabia's skirt, and Fern was amazed to see Bruno bend to her, stroking her hair with one gentle finger.

"And how is my little Phoebe today?" he asked softly. "Still as timid as a little sparrow? But you grow more beautiful, like your mother, every time I see you."

Fabia laughed softly, a contented, happy sound. "She is well, I am glad to say, despite the influenza that struck so many of the village children recently."

Fern noted the quick, interrogative gaze that passed between Bruno and the young woman. She too held out her hand to the child gravely.

"How do you do, Miss Phoebe."

The child shrank away, alarm glistening in her huge eyes. Bruno rested his hand on her shoulder reassuringly and spoke across the fair head to Fern.

"I regret she does not understand you. Phoebe is deaf, and

35

consequently dumb. She is afraid of anyone who is not familiar to her."

Fabia's quick smile alleviated the sudden tension in the little parlor. "But she will come to know you soon, Miss Saxby, and no doubt she will care for you then as she does now for Bruno." She turned quickly to Bruno, and Fern could see the light of pure pleasure in her eyes. "You will stay to tea, won't you? I know Luke will be so disappointed if he doesn't see you, Bruno, and your charming bride. Lessons will be over soon."

Bruno shook his head. "I fear there is snow on the way, Fabia, and I must take Fern home soon. Moreover, there is business at the mill I must attend to. Tell Luke I shall come again soon."

"Very soon, Bruno. It does Luke a world of good to talk with you, for I fear I am no match for him. He needs the companionship of another clever man like you. And do bring Miss Saxby to visit us again soon." Her fingers rested fleetingly on Fern's arm as she bade farewell, and Fern felt glad. Here at least she felt she had found a friend. There was something so warm and hospitable, so unassuming and kindly about Fabia Armitage that one could not help but like her immensely. And Bruno's dark face, relaxed now into a warm smile, indicated that he too thought the same. For a brief moment Fern felt envious of the silent intimacy between him and the schoolmaster's wife.

But there was no sign of any such closeness between Bruno and Edgar Amos once they reached the vicarage, Bruno leading the two horses across the village green and tethering them near the lych-gate outside the church. Amos received them warmly enough and led them into his book-lined study, where paper and pens scattered on the desk indicated he had been working, perhaps on Sunday's sermon, thought Fern.

"You have, of course, already met my fiancée," Bruno said coldly, once they were all seated.

"A great pleasure," replied Amos, "and I hope you have settled in comfortably at the Hall. What do you think of your new home, Miss Saxby?"

"A most impressive house," said Fern uncertainly. It was difficult to convey how one felt, confronted by such an overwhelming edifice, and one whose atmosphere was incalculably strange and forbidding yet curiously familiar.

"Impressive indeed—and with a most impressive history, too," replied Amos. "I was working on some old records of the Hall still extant, going back to the mid-seventeenth century." He indicated the papers strewn before him on the mahogany desk. "A private piece of research, you know, a hobby I indulge when time permits. Perhaps you would come to peruse them if you are interested."

"Oh, indeed I am," Fern cried impulsively.

Bruno looked up sharply. "Perhaps it would be as well not to," he commented quietly. Amos' sandy eyebrows rose in question, and Bruno rose to leave, gathering up his coat. "Miss Saxby is perhaps of an ... imaginative turn of mind. She already believes she has some kind of inherited memory of the Hall, acquired no doubt in an earlier incarnation."

Fern was angered by the scornful tone in his voice but controlled her voice smoothly as she spoke. "You are very kind, Reverend Amos, and I should be most obliged if you would permit me to read your records at some time."

His blue eyes sought hers inquiringly. "Do you truly believe in reincarnation, Miss Saxby?"

Fern hesitated. She had never really considered the matter, but Bruno's sneer had roused her. "Who knows the truth of the matter? An intelligent mind remains open to inquiry and does not condemn out of hand. I should be glad to discuss the matter with you."

"You are most welcome here whenever you wish to call," Amos replied warmly, as he led his guests to the door.

"And you also at Brackenroyd Hall," Fern added, glancing sideways at Bruno's set face. Damn the man, how impertinent he was. She would invite whom she pleased to her home if she found their manner more to her liking than her fiancé's.

It was not a very auspicious way for their association to begin, she thought sadly as they cantered homeward in silence. Already Bruno and she were at loggerheads on her first day in

Brackenroyd. As they turned into the great stone gateway that marked the drive, she jutted her chin defiantly.

"I shall invite whom I choose to the Hall. I have a right to select my friends," she stated firmly.

He smiled wanly. "Indeed you have, and as mistress of Brackenroyd I shall not deny you the right. I could only wish your judgment better, that you chose more rational, logical companions than a superstitious creature like Amos, that is all."

Fern felt her cheeks burning with anger, and during afternoon tea in the lavish warmth and comfort of the dining room she could not bring herself to talk to him again. Mrs. Thorpe's hot buttered muffins and thinly sliced fruit cake, accompanied by strong Indian tea, helped to restore Fern's equanimity, but Bruno seemed abstracted, deep in his own thoughts as he sipped from the fine willow-patterned cup. After tea he disappeared, to the mill Mrs. Thorpe said, to conclude the business the afternoon's visiting had delayed.

The afternoon's freezing rain had now coalesced into delicate drifting snowflakes. Mrs. Thorpe offered to show her new mistress around the rest of the Hall.

"Though most of the bedrooms are now unused, of course, and the furniture draped until such time as we have guests again," she remarked. "It's many a year since the Hall had guests, Mr. Thomas being a very retiring and Christianlike gentleman who spent most of his time working or reading. He lost his wife when his son, Mr. George, was born, and when Mr. George went away to school, Mr. Thomas seemed to prefer being alone. Very shy he was, but as kind and considerate a master as anyone could wish. It's a pity Mr. Bruno didn't come home from Germany to keep the master company, for the old gentleman doted on him. Still, Mr. Bruno's home now at last, and to stay."

She looked at Fern appraisingly, and a sigh of contentment escaped her. "Aye, the Hall is a fine mansion, and I'm glad it's to have a young master and mistress to bring happiness back to it at last. It's seen far too much unhappiness in the past. But now is different. Reverend Amos will no doubt be calling often, and Mr. Armitage and all. Before long the house'll be full of company again."

Her warm face brightened at the prospect, and she ushered Fern happily into many bedrooms ornate with four-posters and Chinese rugs on parquet floors, all with marble-topped washstands and flowered ewers and basins, and all white-draped like spectral rooms awaiting ghostly occupants. Fern, while congratulating Mrs. Thorpe on their orderliness and cleanliness, nevertheless shivered again. There was undoubt-edly an odd, forbidding air about the stately old Hall, but she forebore to question the housekeeper about the past's unhap-piness. Instead she inquired idly about the dilapidated old barnlike house high and solitary on the moor.

"Oh, that's Fox Brow," Mrs. Thorpe replied as she relocked the last bedroom door. "Lovely old house in its time, but it's gone to rack and ruin since Mr. Stansfield died. Mrs. Stans-field still lives there alone, but she never receives company nor goes out, though it's several years since she was widowed. Pity. She was a very lovely woman, and no doubt could still have her pick of many a second husband, being still young, but she'd have none of it. They say she's gone a bit queer with grief, but I'm not one to gossip. It's for her to decide how she'll live, and nobody else's business."

It was clear from her firm tone that Mrs. Thorpe had done with Mrs. Stansfield, her duty done in putting the new young mistress into the picture so far as her neighbors were con-cerned. Though curious about the young widow recluse, Fern pressed no more.

They were passing the old iron-studded door to the east wing again. On an impulse Fern stopped.

"Have you the key to this wing, Mrs. Thorpe? I should like to see it."

The housekeeper's genial face became doubtful. "I have a key, though none but Mr. Bruno goes in there." On reflection, she seemed to decide it was the mistress's right to do as she pleased. Selecting a key from the bunch at her waist, she un-locked the door.

"There is no need to accompany me if you wish to attend

to other duties," Fern said, seeing the woman's perplexed expression. "I shall relock the door when I have done."

"Very well, madam." Mrs. Thorpe surrendered the key and pattered away. Fern pushed open the door, wondering what she could expect to find. A long flagstoned corridor led into a vast hall around which a high gallery ran. Windows set high allowed little light to enter, and since dusk was falling fast, the hall was steeped in gloom. Was it the cold air in here that caused that involuntary shiver along her spine?

Dust carpeted the expanse of stone floor, but footmarks back and forth indicated frequent use. Bruno on the way to the laboratory Mrs. Thorpe had mentioned, no doubt. Fern followed the track to a door in the corner, under the shadow of the minstrels' gallery, but the handle would not yield. Locked. No matter; perhaps it was as well if Bruno used this room as a dispensary. Doctors frequently had dangerous drugs and potions that it was safest to keep locked away.

As Fern turned to go, she caught sight of something in the shadows under the gallery, and peering closer, she could just discern a portrait on the wall, apparently of a woman. At that moment firm footsteps rang along the corridor leading back to the newer Hall, and a figure carrying an oil lamp approached. It was Bruno.

"Mrs. Thorpe told me you were here," he said curtly. "It is cold and damp. Permit me to accompany you back." His fingers touched her elbow, but Fern drew back.

"I was exploring, that is all. Pray tell me, who is the woman in the portrait, and why is her picture left here alone?"

By the light of the lamp she could see a young woman dressed in the style of some half-century earlier, her braided hair glinting golden and her pointed, wistful face expressing desolate unhappiness. Fern's sympathy was arrested at once by the girl's huge, saddened eyes. Bruno was staring at the portrait thoughtfully.

"She looks so sad, Bruno, and in some strange way oddly familiar. Who is she?"

"She is Annot Radley, your great-grandmother. The portrait was painted in readiness to hang in the gallery as soon as she became a De Lacy wife, which, as you know, she never did."

"Then why is her picture still here?"

"Grandfather Thomas would not dispose of it. I think it pricked his conscience, and he wished above all things to atone to Annot's son, though he never knew him, of course. Come, let us return." Again Bruno took her elbow, and this time Fern did not resist, for it was a reassuringly firm touch that helped to allay the shivering this hall induced in her.

"I wonder why she looked so familiar to me?" Fern queried idly as Bruno relocked the studded door to the old wing.

His tired features creased briefly into a hint of a smile. "No doubt because it was like looking in a mirror, my dear. You are remarkably like your great-grandmother."

Of course, that was it. Dismissing the thought, Fern inquired how matters stood at the mill.

Bruno sighed and answered absently. "Well enough, but there are many things I should like to change. I'll go again tomorrow and talk it over with Fearnley, the manager."

"Would you like me to come too?" Fern offered. "After all, the mill's affairs will be partly my responsibility too."

Bruno's eyes narrowed, and he looked at her directly, surprise in the dark, intent look. "Business management is hardly woman's work. I would have considered cooking or tending the plants in the hothouse were more to your taste, and I would not wish to trouble you unduly with matters you do not comprehend."

Fern's cheeks flamed. Again he was insulting her, belittling her as a woman of superficial thought; how like that unbearable Mr. Hastings he was! How insufferable he would be as a husband!

She spoke stiffly, but with control. "It is no trouble, I assure you. I should far prefer to occupy my mind with matters of business than my hands with mindless tasks." She was now outside her own door. Fern disengaged her elbow from his fingertips. "I shall see you at dinner. At what time?"

"At eight." He was gone. He too, it would seem, had no wish to prolong the conversation with her.

Half an hour before dinner, Cassie came up bringing hot water and fresh towels, complaining that she had extra work to do in the kitchen today. "Fanny's off ill—the kitchen maid. Got flu, Mrs. Thorpe says, so I've all her work to do as well as me own," she said as she laid the towels over the jug of hot water on the washstand.

"Poor Fanny," commented Fern. "Does Dr. de Lacy tend the influenza victims in the village?"

"Lor' bless you, no, miss. He's not that kind of doctor, isn't Mr. Bruno. Not one that cures illness, I mean. Mrs. Thorpe says he's a doctor of philosophy, whatever that may mean, and does very clever scientific work, but it's all Dutch to me. It's Dr. Briggs from up the far side of the valley who comes to sick folk. Will that be all, Miss Saxby?"

Over dinner in the dimly lit dining room, its oak-paneled walls receding into the gloom beyond the reach of the oil lamps and the candles on the table, Fern surveyed Bruno's dark, handsome features in silence. He seemed reluctant to talk, eating the brown Windsor soup and the superbly roasted sirloin of beef with an air of absorption. She wondered curiously what thought filled the mind of this strangely reticent man who seemed loath to allow anyone to invade the privacy of his mind. Problems of the business in the mill perhaps, or scientific problems currently occupying him in his laboratory, or was he mentally debating the wisdom of taking her to wife? It was already evident to both of them that they had little in common. Once the dessert plates were cleared away, he rose suddenly from the table.

"Allow me to pour you a glass of Madeira," he said, and Fern could hear the clink of glasses at the sideboard before he returned to offer her the glass. "Now I am going to work in my study. Good night, my dear." Abruptly he left her. Fern sighed and rose slowly, replacing the wineglass and her linen napkin on the table and crossing to the window. Outside, snow was still drifting down, silently and relentlessly. By morning the stark landscape would be softened and blurred under the heavy blanket that was swiftly enveloping the house and hillside. Brackenroyd Hall seemed even more isolated and forbidding than ever. Fern let the braided velvet curtains fall into place again, deciding that though it was still only nine o'clock she might just as well go to bed, for it was evident Bruno would not seek her company again tonight.

Perhaps it was the chill of the bedroom, or possibly the strange air of unreality about the loneliness of the house after the hectic atmosphere of London, but whatever the reason, Fern slept badly, tossing fitfully until the small hours. The chill in the bedroom seemed to grow, the cold penetrating her bones despite the blankets and woolen nightgown. And strange dreams flickered in her mind.

Suddenly she sat upright, fear choking her. A gray mist seemed to be trying to force its way into her nostrils, and with it an alien, terrifying sensation. With returning wakefulness the menacing mist receded and Fern clung, gasping, to the bedpost. It was as though something had been trying to invade her body, to take possession of her. She shook her head firmly. What a terrifying nightmare!

But from the dream something still lingered—a wailing, piteous thing that held out its arms and sobbed plaintively. And with a sudden gasp Fern remembered. The woman in the dream the previous night who had wept for her child—it had not been Mrs. Hastings, after all. She had come again tonight—and there was no mistaking the face in the portrait in the east wing. The woman was Annot Radley.

Chapter 4

With a satisfied sigh Edgar Amos pushed back the chair from his mahogany desk and laid down his pen. There, Sunday's sermon was complete. With the contented feeling of a job well done, he rose and crossed to the study window. Snow still lay thick on the village green, graying and slushed by the hurrying feet of his flock as they busied themselves about their work, clogged feet tramping down the lane, at dawn mostly, to De Lacy's mill, and homeward again at dusk. From the window he could just see, beyond the church tower, the tip of the mill chimney belching its eternal cloud of black smoke. Only on Sundays was the Brackenroyd air clean and still; only on Sundays did clogged feet veer toward the church instead of the mill.

Amos' pale-blue gaze shifted westward, up from the village to the jutting crags of millstone grit rocks edging the moor and the stark outline of Brackenroyd Hall, silhouetted against the gray skyline. The De Lacy family had stood there, guardian of the vulnerable village at their feet, for countless generations, their decisions always affecting the lives of the stolid village folk below. It was a De Lacy who had always owned the land the tenant farmers worked; it was a De Lacy who, in this century, had built the mill farther downstream that had robbed the handloom weavers for miles around of their independence, forcing them out of business with his gigantic frames that could weave good Yorkshire woolens far faster than any human hand. They had given in at last, this proud, silent race, and in time they had come to realize that their standard of living had improved as a result; their admission that it was due to a De Lacy's acumen had remained tacit. Pride and independence were a heavy price to pay.

Amos admired the spirit of this dour race who had accepted him a few years back with warmth, if not with overwhelming welcome. Perhaps they had regarded a new young curate, unmarried at that, with a certain degree of native suspicion, but when the old vicar eventually died and Thomas de Lacy's patronage had been extended to young Amos as the new vicar, the villagers had continued the habit of depositing gifts of eggs and freshly baked bread in the rectory kitchen just as they had always done for his elderly predecessor. They asked no thanks nor wanted it. The silent gesture, unacknowledged by either side, was a mark of his being accepted and respected, as old Thomas de Lacy had pointed out to him, and Amos was glad.

He had missed old Thomas, a gentle, scholarly soul who had carried on conscientiously the family business he had inherited, leaving most of the daily running to the mill manager, Fearnley, while he busied himself among his books and papers in the Hall library. It had been Thomas' ambition one day to publish a history of the Hall, and Amos was proud of the old man's faith in him, that he had entrusted all his research to Amos as he lay dying.

"Carry it on for me, Edgar my boy, I beg you. If there is to be any monument to me. I wish it were this, that my papers were published. If you can find the time among your many parochial duties, I shall be eternally grateful to you."

Dear old Thomas, so loved and respected by all the villagers in their begrudging, taciturn way. Edgar had promised willingly to fulfill his obligation. He wondered idly whether the new master of Brackenroyd would ever win the admiration of Brackenroyd folk as Thomas had done. He was a strange fish, this Bruno de Lacy, with his penetrating dark eyes and stern Teutonic manner. One felt he was watching and calculating, unwilling to reveal himself until he had learned what one was thinking. That was due to his streak of Continental blood, no doubt, for Yorkshire folk were blunt to the point of rudeness, and they welcomed honesty in others. But this new master remained comparatively unknown to them, for in the two months he had been at the Hall he had communicated with the locals only so far as it had been necessary. He visited the mill and talked with Fearnley often, he nodded and passed the time of day with the villagers in passing, but with none had he appeared to form any kind of relationship. Amos felt a little slighted. Young De Lacy was reputedly academic and gifted, yet so far he had made no overture to the young vicar, who was, apart from Luke Armitage, the schoolmaster, probably the only other highly educated person in the district. One would have expected the new master to have sought Amos' company, yet he had not. It was Amos who made the first approach, paying a visit to the Hall after a deferential lapse of some days after De Lacy's return from Germany. His words of welcome and condolence left little apparent mark on De Lacy.

"You know, of course," the young man had said brusquely, "that my uncle wishes me to marry my distant cousin, Miss Saxby. When she comes, you will naturally conduct the marriage service."

Of course, Amos had known of old Thomas' wish. All the villagers knew, but since none knew the young woman, all still wondered whether she would agree. No such doubt seemed to enter young De Lacy's mind. Amos at once took a dislike to the dark stranger's self-possession and air of assurance. Such a manner was hardly calculated to win over the cautious villagers. De Lacy would have to strive harder to woo the valley folk than he would to win his bride.

The attractive Miss Saxby. Amos' thoughts dwelt pleasurably on the flaxen-haired young woman he had met by chance on the train, slender and tastefully dressed and with as warm a smile as he had ever seen. Now, she, if she had a mind to, could win the locals over with little effort; of that he was sure. Her gaze was direct and honest, a trait all Yorkshire folk admired, her wide blue eyes indicating intelligent interest. Amos hoped they would renew their acquaintance soon, husband-to-be De Lacy permitting, for there was promise of a worth-while friendship in that warm young face.

"You should be married, Amos." The bishop had said it time and again, implying that the incumbent of this village could hardly carry out his duties effectively unless he were co-zily cared for by a warm and gentle wife. The ministrations of Amos' housekeeper, Mrs. Crowther, did not meet with the bishop's approval. "The sooner you find a young woman of breeding and tact who is fitted for the role of vicar's wife, the better," he had sternly admonished. Miss Saxby's pretty oval face flitted into Amos' mind, and he brushed the impious thought aside. It was easy for the bishop to propound, but how in the restricted round of parochial duties could one find such a wife?

The aroma of freshly buttered muffins preceded Mrs. Crowther's knock at the study door. Amos turned from the window, rubbing his hands in pleasure.

"Shall I set the tray here, Reverend?" the pudding-faced woman asked pleasantly, pausing by his desk. Amos agreed, and as he drew the heavy plush curtains together to shut out the gathering dusk, she poured the amber liquid into a china cup, handing it to him when he crossed to sit by the fire.

"There's rabbit stew and rice pudding in the oven for your dinner, so don't get lost in them books of yours and forget, now, will you, sir? It's time I were off home now."

Her words, though rough and rudely phrased, were kindly meant, he knew. He smiled appreciatively, biting into the buttery depths of a muffin as she withdrew. Her warning was not unfounded, for once he abandoned himself to the pleasure of working on old Thomas' notes, time no longer existed.

There was a ring at the doorbell, muffled voices in the little hallway, and then Mrs. Crowther reappeared, her face suffused in pleasure.

"Dr. de Lacy has come to call on you, Reverend. Shall I fetch another cup when I've shown him in?"

Amos rose suddenly, almost spilling his tea in surprised delight. He brushed the crumbs sharply from his threadbare worsted suit and stood, hands clasped behind his back before the fire, to welcome his exalted guest. Mrs. Crowther entered, bobbed an unaccustomed curtsy before announcing, "Dr. de Lacy, sir," and withdrew.

De Lacy strode into the small study and shook hands with the vicar with a curt, "Afternoon, Amos," and without waiting to be invited, he sank into an armchair, the one Amos had just vacated. Amos pulled forward another chair and sat gingerly on the edge. Mrs. Crowther reappeared with a fresh cup and saucer, which she placed silently on the tray.

"How pleasant to see you again so soon," Amos said a little uncertainly. De Lacy, so taciturn and unpredictable, was a little difficult to handle, but one would not wish to rebuff any advance he made. "Would you care for a cup of tea?"

Amos brandished the teapot invitingly, but De Lacy shook his head. "I did not come to stay, Amos, only to ask you if you would indulge Miss Saxby in a whim she has entertained these last few days."

Amos' sandy eyebrows rose. Miss Saxby did not seem the capricious type, but if he could please her and thereby please the master of Brackenroyd too . . .

"Of course, my dear friend. Anything."

De Lacy was frowning. Amos wondered if it had been a mistake to presume to call this reserved young man a friend. De Lacy fidgeted restlessly.

"The fact is, I think she is bored with having to stay in the Hall. She wanders about and asks if she may come to the mill, but business is hardly a woman's concern. For a week she has asked endlessly about that ancestress of hers, Annot Radley, but since I do not know the story beyond what my grandfather told me, I cannot satisfy her curiosity. To be quite frank, Amos, I consider such curiosity rather morbid, but she insists.

I believe you have my grandfather's notes on Brackenroyd's history. Perhaps you would be so kind as to tell Fern the story or let her read the notes for herself. Then perhaps she will let the matter rest."

Amos smiled broadly, relaxing sufficiently to sit back more comfortably in his chair. De Lacy was not only more loquacious than he had ever known him, but he was taking the young vicar into his confidence too, and asking a favor of him. Matters were indeed taking a turn for the better.

"I should be delighted. Perhaps you would like me to bring the records to the Hall for Miss Saxby to read, since the weather is still so inclement? Tomorrow, if you wish."

"Then that's settled." De Lacy rose abruptly, picked up his riding whip from where he had dropped it on the desk, and strode toward the door. At the doorway he halted and turned. "One thing, Amos. I should not wish you to encourage Miss Saxby too much to talk about Annot Radley once she knows the facts. Already she claims to have dreamed about her, and I think she fancies she has some strange sort of relationship with the girl. Some odd notion about inherited memory, I think she said. Stuff and nonsense, of course, and I would not wish the notion to be encouraged."

He did not wait to ask whether Amos would agree to his request, as though he believed his order would be obeyed without question, thought Amos as he watched De Lacy mount his black stallion and ride off uphill into the gloom. From nowhere the great lumbering shape of De Lacy's wolfhound materalized from the darkness and loped off in the sleet behind the horse. Amos shivered. If he had not been a man of the cloth, he might well have believed that the strange man on a black horse and the devilish hound following them were creatures from a netherworld. Closing the front door against the sleet, he hurried back into the cozy warmth of the study.

By mid-morning the following day an unexpected turn of mildness in the weather had almost melted the snows from the valley. Amos presented himself at the Hall, smiling at Fanny, the parlormaid, as he proffered his visiting card to be borne on a silver tray into the inner regions of the house. Although Miss Saxby had met him and indeed requested this visit, it was nonetheless etiquette to offer his card on his first visit to the new mistress of the Hall. Fanny, having seen service in greater houses in the West Riding, where she had rubbed shoulders with French maids and quickly learned their winsome ways, lowered her lashes demurely as she invited the vicar to step inside, flicking the ribbons on her cap, her heels clicking across the parquet floor before him.

In the drawing room Miss Saxby rose from her chair by the fire to greet Amos, and he noted that her fine features were somewhat drawn, as though she were fatigued or worried.

"A glass of wine after your cold walk, Reverend Amos?" she offered politely. "A glass of Madeira, perhaps?"

As Amos declined courteously, she nodded to Fanny to withdraw, then reseated herself by the fire, signaling Amos to be seated also. He drew a chair closer to hers.

"Mr. de Lacy is not at home this morning, Miss Saxby?"

She smiled wanly. "Indeed no, he is constantly occupied, either at the mill or engaged upon his own work in his study or the laboratory. I could wish he would tell me more of his work or allow me to be involved with business matters, but I think he does not feel it to be a woman's place." Her smile dimpled warmly. "Perhaps you could persuade him otherwise, Reverend, for I should very much like to use my brain a little."

Amos felt sympathy for the girl. She was undoubtedly intelligent as well as attractive. How presumptuous of De Lacy to discount her as useless. Courtesy bade him protect his new patron's actions, for like all the De Lacys since time immemorial, Mr. Bruno had agreed to see to the comfort of the village church incumbent.

"No doubt he considers this wintry weather unfit to take you down to the mill, Miss Saxby. Doubtless when the weather improves . . ."

"But that is not the reason for his silence in other respects, Mr. Amos. He will not talk of his research, nor of any other matter. I think he must by nature be a solitary creature, preferring his own company and thoughts."

By the nervous clenching and relaxing of her fingertips on the arms of the chair he could guess that she spoke against her better judgment. She obviously felt deeply about De Lacy's reticence to be tempted to speak of it with a comparative stranger, and Amos welcomed her confidence in him.

"Perhaps he is a little shy because he does not yet know you. Time will overcome that difficulty."

"Then why does he treat me like an imbecile?" Her pale face flushed angrily, and her eyes glittered with hard fire. Amos shifted uncomfortably. "Since my arrival nearly two weeks ago he has ignored me, offering me only childish pastimes to occupy my time," the girl went on. "He brushes aside my efforts to converse with him, he declines even to eat with me often. I think, to be quite honest, he considers me flighty, or even worse."

She relapsed into silence, knotting her fingers together nervously. Amos eyed her curiously. Worse? What worse could the master of Brackenroyd believe of her? She raised huge, sad eyes as she answered his unspoken question.

"I told him I had a strong affinity with this house, that I could sense an urgent communion with it, and when I told him that I even dreamed of Annot Radley, he stiffened toward me. I think he believes me mad. Do you think it impossible, Mr. Amos, to have a distinct feeling for one's past?"

Clearing his throat nervously, Amos smiled reassuringly. "No indeed, Miss Saxby. Here in the West Riding such feeling goes deep. I'll wager there isn't a man in the valley who doesn't feel as deeply for his heritage as you do. Such sentiments are common, and I think you are not unusual in that respect."

She sat up tautly, her eyes glowing. "But it is more than that, Reverend. My emotions are those of Annot Radley; I know it, though I do not yet know her story. Mr. Amos, tell me truly, do you believe in ghosts?"

Amos hesitated. Here was a tricky situation if he were to retain the respect both of the girl and of the master. "As a man of the cloth, my dear, I believe in the eternal life of the spirit, of course. But here, as you requested, I have Mr. Thomas' notes on Annot Radley. Let me leave these with you to peruse at your leisure." He saw her eyes gleam as her fingers closed about the sheaf of papers. "But do not let your mind dwell on poor Annot's story overmuch. Hers was a pathetic history, and I fear perhaps it would be a trifle ... unhealthy to dwell too long on such a morbid subject."

He rose quickly before she could engage him in further embarrassing discussion, murmuring that he must visit a sick child in the village. She followed him toward the door, the dull glow still gleaming in her eyes.

Amos tried to lighten the tension in the atmosphere. "Perhaps before long you and Mr. de Lacy will be holding a wedding party here. It is time the old house knew gaiety and laughter again," he commented brightly.

Her eyes softened. "Indeed, Mr. Amos. It is time the Hall knew peace and happiness," she agreed quietly.

The door burst open unexpectedly, revealing the tall figure of Bruno de Lacy, the wolfhound at his heels.

Amos, taken aback by the sudden apparition of the gaunt figure, uttered a strangled laugh. "Oh, Mr. de Lacy! I am so pleased to have the opportunity to see you as well as Miss Saxby."

Bruno's gaze flickered over him and beyond, to where Fern stood, motionless, the sheaf of papers in her hand. His eyes narrowed. "Are those the notes on Annot Radley?"

Amos nodded. "As I promised, copied from Mr. Thomas' own notes, verbatim."

"Give them to me."

As in a trance, Amos watched the tableau, the unmoving figures of the master and the girl, the one holding out his hand peremptorily in demand, the other holding tightly to the papers and glaring defiance. For some seconds neither moved.

"You hear me? Give them to me," De Lacy barked.

"Why?" The girl's face sprang into animation, her eyes dancing anger. "Why should I?"

"Because they will only encourage your romantic daydreams. This place has had an unsettling effect on you, it seems, and on reflection, I would prefer you to delay further investigation as to its history until you have regained your self-control."

Black eyes held fiery blue ones in their thrall. Amos could feel the charge that enmeshed their gaze and knew he was forgotten in the battle of wills. Then slowly he sensed the blue gaze weaken, the electric power of the black subjugating the girl. It was like watching a snake mesmerize a rabbit. Slowly she raised her hand and released the papers.

De Lacy took them and turned sharply to Amos. "As I told you, Miss Saxby has some strange notion concerning Annot Radley, which I prefer not to be encouraged for the moment. At some future date, perhaps it will be more opportune."

Chivalry dictated Amos' next words. "But, sir, you do not truly believe Miss Saxby's interest is unnatural? You yourself asked me to bring the notes."

"When I believed her interest normal and natural. Now I have reason to believe she is momentarily . . . unbalanced."

Amos was shocked. Such discourtesy, such uncouth unmannerliness, and such wild words!

The girl was nodding as if in satisfaction. "As I thought," she murmured, "he believes me mad."

"Not mad, my dear." De Lacy swung smoothly to face her. "I think, a little disturbed, perhaps, by the rapidity of recent changes in your life. Let us say I am concerned by the odd vivid dreams you have recounted to me. From my experience, I know such dreams to stem from an imbalance in the mind, which, in time, can be restored. It is only a question of patience."

Irritation prickled Amos at the man's arrogance. De Lacy stood, arms folded, in the center of the room, the high stock surmounting his well-cut frockcoat lifting his chin high and giving his curl-framed head a jaunty, high-handed look. With the massive wolfhound curled obediently at his feet, he looked every inch the dominating master of all he beheld, and Amos' instincts rebelled.

"Who is to say Miss Saxby is not correct?" he said evenly.

"It is not unknown for sensitive people to feel a rapport with their own past. It is not beyond the bounds of human belief that she does indeed recall something, the kind of inherited memory of which she speaks. An intelligent person does not dispute what he cannot disprove."

It was satisfying to see the girl's approving smile, but De Lacy was evidently angered.

"Equally it may be said that an intelligent person would not attempt to maintain that which cannot be proved. Let us discontinue a debate which is pointless."

The girl's voice cut in calmly, though Amos could detect a tremor, whether of anger or dismay. "You spoke of your experience, Bruno. What experience have you, may I inquire, of dreams and their relevance?"

Surprisingly, De Lacy turned a smile upon her. "It is too vast a subject to discuss at length now, my dear. Suffice it for now that my work in Germany with a brilliant young colleague named Sigmund Freud was in precisely that field. Little research has been done into mental conditions, and together we worked upon it for a time. Dreams, and especially in young females, we concluded, were an unconscious seeking for oneself, a search for one's own identity. Once the patient's mental confusion is resolved, the problem is solved and the dreams cease. This was our finding, but I am still researching on it. The rational, scientific mind cannot accept an explanation such as yours for dreams—an imagined rapport with the past. It is a primitive, almost superstitious explanation. To my mind there can be only some psychological reason for it, and once your problem is resolved and the dreams cease, you will have found yourself and be well again."

He called the dog, turning for the door. Amos recognized his movement as indicating that the conversation was now closed. He rose to bid Miss Saxby good-bye, and saw that her gaze rested on him thoughtfully.

"Where is Annot Radley's grave?" she asked quietly. Amos saw De Lacy's thick brows knit irritably. "Is it in the churchyard? I should like to see it."

Amos felt the color rush to his cheeks. "No, Miss Saxby, it

is not. Annot could not be buried there, for she was a suicide."

He turned away too quickly to see her reaction. De Lacy only grunted inaudibly in reply to his farewell, and Amos took his hat and cane gratefully from the waiting parlormaid outside the door. As he rode downhill again toward the village, he wondered whether De Lacy would reveal to the girl that the suicide's grave stood within a stone's throw of the Hall parlor, in a clearing of the copse in the Hall's vast park. If not, she would surely stumble across the little tombstone herself when spring sunlight tempted her out into the grounds. That wouldn't be long now, for already patches of ground were visible through the snow, and in the village's main street was already melting away.

Outside the Woolpack a lone figure leaned desultorily against the stone wall, his head drawn into his upturned coat collar for warmth and a seedy cloth cap topping his graying hair. Amos recognized Joss Iredale, the man whose little girl Amos was now on the way to see. Villagers had told him young Agnes was in a fever. At the sight of the young vicar the man turned and shuffled away toward the steep lane leading to his cottage, just as a buxom woman in a gray woolen shawl came hurrying downhill.

"Joss!"

He stopped and looked at her questioningly, his eyes hollow and bleared. Amos dismounted and approached. The woman caught hold of Iredale's arm, her lined face softened in pity.

"I'm sorry, lad, she's gone."

Visibly Iredale's figure slumped, and Amos felt a stab of apprehension. Not little Agnes, surely? The child was sick yesterday, but not mortally ill, was she?

Iredale turned vacant, misted eyes toward him. "I thowt as much. I knew it, vicar. Not content wi' our Nellie, we have to lose our Agnes as well. There's no justice, God help us, there's nowt."

His voice choked with emotion, Iredale broke loose from the woman's grasp and stumbled uphill toward the cottage. Amos stared disbelievingly.

"I must go after him, Mrs. Shaw, for the family will have need of me. I take it you have been with Mrs. Iredale?"

"Aye, vicar. The poor woman is near demented wi' worry. She loved that little lass, you know, the more so since she lost Nellie last year o' the measles. She never thowt as influenza'd kill Aggie, and she's afeared lest Joss takes it badly."

"Poor man," Amos agreed. "A willing worker and a fine family man, it will undoubtedly grieve him sorely. A terrible blow. Such misfortune. Are you going back to the house?"

Mrs. Shaw shook her head firmly. "There's nowt I can do now. Let 'em grieve in peace. But happen you could help, vicar. Another funeral in a twelvemonth is a great expense for a man on Joss's wage."

Amos looked at her inquiringly. "Ah, the old custom that the master of Brackenroyd should help, as a sign of his kindly patronage, you mean. You would no doubt like me to speak to Mr. de Lacy about it? So I shall. Doubtless he will agree, and Miss Saxby I am sure we can count on for sympathetic cooperation."

Mrs. Shaw's eyes narrowed, her lips tightening as she drew her shawl closer about her. "No point in asking her, vicar. She's a Radley."

Amos' blue gaze widened. "What on earth has Miss Saxby's lineage to do with it? She is a most kindly and agreeable lady and will be a fine mistress. Have you met her yet?"

Shaking her head, Mrs. Shaw pursed her lips tighter. "Nor wish to," she said tersely.

"Why ever not?"

"She's a Radley, like I said."

"And what is wrong with being a Radley? There have been no Radleys in the village for two generations, so you cannot have formed a dislike for any of them. What is all this about the Radleys?"

Mrs. Shaw's tense shoulders eased as she turned a forbearing smile upon the young vicar. "You're a stranger here, Reverend, so you wouldn't know. But for generations, long before I were born, or even my grandparents, the Radleys have always spelled trouble for Brackenroyd folk. That's why the old

Radley cottage is never used now, 'cept as a barn. There's trouble where there's Radleys, and specially when a Radley comes up wi' a De Lacy."

So that's it, thought Amos. The old story of Annot Radley and Dorian de Lacy had left its mark on local legend. Without knowing the details, cautious villagers knew only to avoid a Radley and De Lacy encounter.

"That's an old story, Mrs. Shaw, and one that has no bearing on present-day life. Put it out of your mind and be tolerant, as we should."

"Not where there's a Radley. There's an evil taint in the blood, my grandma told me, and everyone here knows it. No sooner does this Radley girl come to the Hall than trouble starts."

"What trouble, Mrs. Shaw?"

The woman's eyes flickered uphill toward Iredale's cottage. "Well, there's Aggie, for a start."

Amos protested. "You're not blaming the child's death on Miss Saxby, surely? Aggie had influenza."

"Aye. Well, others think differently, vicar. There's none i' this village who'll be happy while she's here, and we all hope as she don't marry Mr. Bruno. If she does, there's terrible grief for us all, mark my words. A Radley always spells evil."

Thunderstruck, Amos watched the woman's ample figure plod purposefully away. She couldn't be voicing the view of all the village folk, surely? If she were, then God help Fern Saxby in her attempt to begin her new life as mistress of Brackenroyd.

Chapter 5

It was nearing time for dinner. Soon the dull throb of the dinner gong would reverberate throughout the Hall's vast space, and for once Bruno had intimated that he would dine with Fern. Mrs. Thorpe's eyes had sparkled in anticipation as she relayed the news to Fern. No doubt, thought Fern bitterly, she thought the master was about to make a belated attempt to behave civilly, if not actually begin to woo his intended bride. At any rate, his company, however diffident, would be some improvement on his hitherto neglect.

Now, what to wear to impress him. The mauve-silk gown with the pretty lace at the throat, she decided, on surveying the wardrobe. And her hair coiled perhaps more softly, draped gently over the ears before being drawn up into pins. Yes. On surveying her reflection in the long pier glass, Fern felt satisfied. Becomingly feminine and yet demurely inoffensive, gold hair gleaming from her efforts with the hairbrush, by candlelight at the dining table Bruno must be just a little impressed. A dab of lavender water behind her ears, and Fern was ready.

As she laid her hand on the brass doorknob of the drawing room, Fern could hear deep voices, animated in conversation, beyond the oak panels of the door. Bruno sat in the great armchair by the firelight, speaking in low, urgent tones to a man seated opposite him, of whom only a fair head was discernible to Fern. She approached the two men with a smile. Bruno, noticing her, rose and laid aside his pipe.

"Ah, Fern, I should like you to meet Luke Armitage," he said warmly, indicating the seated figure, who now rose and turned to her.

By the fire's glow Fern saw a delicate-looking young man in his early thirties, his eyes warm and welcoming and his hand extended. His grasp was firm and his gaze direct, belying the fragile appearance, and Fern felt an instant liking for the man. Fabia's husband, and Phoebe's father. What a pleasant family they seemed. There would be agreeable company for her in Brackenroyd after all.

"Luke, this is Fern." Bruno's voice held such warmth that momentarily Fern wondered. Was it pride or pleasure he evinced? Or simply a residue of warmth that lingered from the conversation with Luke she had just interrupted, and which Bruno was so evidently enjoying?

"I am delighted to meet you, Miss Saxby," the schoolmaster was saying, and as he relinquished Fern's hand, he added, "and may I remark that you are as beautiful as Bruno and Fabia have both told me. Brackenroyd Hall will be graced with a charming mistress once more."

Startled, Fern looked quickly at Bruno. He had called her beautiful? As if embarrassed, he had already turned away and was busy arranging a chair for her. He waited until she was seated before sitting again and resuming his pipe. Luke leaned forward eagerly.

"It was very kind of Bruno to bring me to dinner, Miss Saxby. I do hope you are not inconvenienced by my unexpected arrival."

"Not at all, Mr. Armitage, I am delighted. Have you told Mrs. Thorpe to lay the table for three, Bruno?"

"Yes." He made no explanation of his omission to her as

the mistress, Fern noted. No doubt long bachelorhood had made him accustomed to doing as he pleased, warning only the servants. He had much to learn yet, as a husband. Still, she welcomed Luke's advent, however unexpected.

It was cozy by the fire's warm light, the candles yet unlit and the curtains undrawn. The men sat silent, but the silence was ruminative and companionable, and Fern did not wish to break it. The two men evidently shared a closeness which included intimate silence, and she was glad. Bruno could not be wholly cold and insensitive if he had won such friendship. The peace was shattered by Fanny's clattering entrance.

"Shall I bring more coal, sir?"

"No. Draw the curtains."

Brass rings rattled along bamboo canes as Fanny drew the heavy red-velvet draperies across the tall windows. Lighting a wax taper from the fire, she then lit three tall candles on the table, their glow reflecting on their brass holders.

"Is dinner almost ready, Fanny?"

"Yes, sir. I shall sound the gong immediately."

It was during dinner that Luke first mentioned hypnotism. He had been reading an article on hypnotism and mesmerism in a journal and was curious to know Bruno's opinion, he said. Fern saw the intense look return to Bruno's somber eyes.

"Both are induced states of trance brought about by different means. Most people can be hypnotized if they cooperate, but some are far more easily suggestible than others." Was it her imagination, Fern wondered, that his eyes flickered briefly over her?

"It was Mesmer who first experimented, was it not, in Vienna? I understand hypnotism can be used to good effect, as treatment for a sick patient?" Luke's light-blue eyes were lively with curiosity.

Bruno nodded. "Indeed. I have seen, and on occasion worked with, patients suffering from physical problems such as speech impediments. They have often benefited greatly from hypnotism. But its greatest use, to my mind, is in the treatment of nervous disorders. Someday, when the quacks stop using hypnotism as a music-hall entertainment, I hope it will be more widely used in this field. At the moment it is either distrusted or scorned by many."

Fanny's deft fingers removed the dessert dishes and laid out the decanter of port and glasses for the gentlemen. Reluctantly Fern rose to leave the gentlemen to their port, as was the custom, but as she was closing the door, she heard Luke's question.

"I had a reason for asking, Bruno. I wonder if you could help Phoebe?"

Poor little Phoebe, thought Fern as she returned to the drawing room. Was her muteness a result of deafness or of accident? Evidently Luke considered her plight not entirely hopeless if he was enlisting Bruno's help, but would hypnotism have any effect? Surely not, if the child was deaf and could not hear Bruno's voice.

Evidently Phoebe had remained the subject of the gentlemen's conversation, for they were still discussing her when they came to rejoin Fern. As Luke entered, she could not fail to notice the slight limp, the way he dragged a reluctant left leg after him. Bruno was in a contemplative mood, nodding in reply to Luke's comments and his dark eyes afire with interest.

"I think some effect could perhaps be achieved," he said at length. "We may even arrive at the cause of her disability, but at least no harm would be done. Bring Fabia and the child to tea with us tomorrow."

Luke's eager smile died suddenly. "There is a matter I had overlooked, Bruno. You know my salary as a principal teacher. A hundred and fifty pounds a year does not warrant luxuries such as the services of a specialist for Phoebe. I fear I may not be able to afford your fee."

Bruno's rugged face darkened angrily. "Between friends there is no question of fees," he snapped. "The experiment could well fail, in which case you are not beholden to me. I forbid you to mention money again."

Luke hung his head, a pink tinge coloring his pale face. Fern felt embarrassment for him, for while Bruno's intentions were friendly, his manner was abrupt and reproachful. She felt angry with him for his thoughtless unkindness, but her anger softened when he insisted on sending Luke home in the carriage. Aware of his friend's lameness, he would not consider his walking home, though he made no reference to the limp until Luke was gone.

"A childhood accident, a wagon ran over his leg while he was working at the mill. So he went back to school as a pupil-teacher," he explained laconically. Seeing that he was in no mood for further conversation, his look abstracted and distant, Fern bade him a quiet good night and went to her room.

It was a graceful staircase, wide and shallow, and as Fern mounted the stairs, fingering the carved balustrade affectionately, she reflected with pride on the beauty of her home. Mistress of Brackenroyd. She was a fortunate creature indeed to have inherited such grace and luxury, but still the suggestion of lingering unhappiness in the air troubled her. A ring at the front doorbell interrupted her musings, and Fern could hear Fanny's quick step hastening to answer.

A late hour for a caller. Who could it be? Out of curiosity Fern loitered on the gallery and saw Edgar Amos' sandy head below as he murmured to Fanny, and Bruno's quick exit from the drawing room.

"I regret troubling you so late, Dr. de Lacy, but the matter is urgent," Amos apologized, and Fern could see his nervous fingers clutching at his hat and the glistening droplets on his cape.

"Come in," said Bruno curtly, and the two men disappeared into the drawing room.

Fern hovered for a time on the gallery, filled with curiosity, undecided what to do. Eventually she went down again and crossed to the room, where deep voices could be heard in conversation.

"Do I understand you to say you are requesting me to undertake the funeral expenses?" Bruno's voice was demanding.

"Otherwise it will mean a pauper's grave for the child. Iredale would never live down the shame. And it has always been customary for the master to pay in the past," Amos' timid voice answered.

"Must I, then, for the sake of tradition, be prepared to pay for all my workers and their numerous dependents? It would seem a highly expensive precedent to set."

"For your workers, sir, not their dependents. Aggie herself worked in your mill."

"Aggie? I understand she was a very young girl?"

"Ten, sir. Ten-year-olds are allowed by law to attend school part-time and go to work part-time. Joss and his wife will miss her few shillings a week. And they lost their elder daughter last year from measles, and thus her income too. Joss's wage is barely enough to keep his younger children now, without Aggie's help."

"His wage is adequate, since the weavers' strike in this area last year. He earns a fair rate, the same as the others."

There was a pause, and Fern could visualize Amos' uncertain, blinking gaze while he awaited Bruno's agreement or refusal. If a child had died, a child who worked in *their* mill, Fern could not understand Bruno's hesitation to pay for the poor mite's funeral. With resolution Fern grasped the doorknob and walked into the room.

"Good evening, Reverend Amos. I have heard enough of your conversation with Bruno to understand that our help is needed in burying one of our child workers at the mill."

"That is so," Amos admitted with a quick, nervous glance at Bruno.

"Then have no fear that we shall honor our obligation. If you would be so good as to tell me where the Iredales live, I shall go to them myself tomorrow and assure them that the bill will be met."

As she stopped speaking, Fern turned a direct, challenging stare on Bruno. He stood silent, a thoughtful finger rubbing his chin.

"Will you permit me, Bruno?"

He spread his hands. "You will do as you think fit. I shall not presume to interfere."

Nor could he, she thought angrily. Joint legatees, they could each spend as they wished, but Amos was looking at her oddly.

"I think, Miss Saxby, if you will permit me to comment, that the offer were best coming from the master."

"I am mistress of Brackenroyd, Mr. Amos."

"That is so, but the villagers are queer folk." He was fidgeting with his hat, shifting uncomfortably, and his gaze refused to meet hers.

Fern was curious. "How do you mean? Please be plain, sir."

He hung his sandy head miserably. "They have strange ideas, superstitious almost, and they distrust a Radley. Your offer, though generously meant, could well be misconstrued, simply because you are a Radley. But since the hour is so late, let me leave you and the doctor to discuss the matter."

He made for the door, and Bruno made no comment as he rang the bell for Fanny to show the visitor out.

Fern hastened out after Amos. "I cannot understand your words, but I want to reassure the poor family their child will be decently buried. Surely there is no harm in my visiting them?"

For a moment Amos' bleak expression softened into a smile. "Perhaps your warmth and sincerity will make them forget the old stories," he said, and then turned to follow Fanny to the front door.

Bruno's face was blankly unsympathetic as Fern repeated her intention to go to the Iredales' cottage.

"If you insist, my dear, then I shall accompany you."

"There is no need for you to come."

He looked up sharply. "Indeed there is. You know so little of the villagers, and yet you will insist on interfering. I have warned you once that mill affairs are best left to me, and that includes the welfare of the workers."

"If you apparently care little for their welfare, then it is up to me to act," Fern retorted hotly. "If you—if we—paid our workers a better wage, there would be no need for us to have to appear charitable and bury their dead children for them."

Bruno's expression darkened. "Now you go too far. You know nothing, nothing at all, of weavers' work and conditions or their rates of pay. Nothing of their history, or of their recent strike. Though I admit your equal share in the mill, I will not permit you to make decisions as to its running. That is my province, and I would welcome your assurance that you will trust me and leave it to me."

Fern hesitated. He too was a newcomer to Brackenroyd, but undoubtedly, with Teutonic thoroughness, he had probably already acquainted himself fully with the state of the mill. But she was unwilling to relinquish her right to voice her opinion; it would be setting a dangerous precedent to let this dictatorial man tell her where she could or could not intervene.

"I should like to console the Iredales, nonetheless," she muttered fiercely at last. "And reassure them about Aggie."

"So you shall, if you wish. And I shall come too."

And he did. It was a gray, misty day that hung over Brackenroyd village as the carriage drove along the cobbled street and mounted the hilly lane to the Iredale cottage. Bruno helped Fern out of the carriage in silence. A woman, apparently a neighbor, answered his knock at the door of the tiny stone cottage with its slate roof. She turned at once and addressed the unseen occupants of the living room immediately inside the front door.

"It's t' master, Joss, t' master o' Brackenroyd, and his lady," she added dubiously.

Fern entered the low door, noting the cold stone-slabbed floor of the little room with its handmade rag rugs and deal table. A shawled woman, presumably Mrs. Iredale, glanced curiously at Fern, then crossed to a spindle-backed chair by the fire, arranged a calfskin over its rush bottom, and seated herself in silence. Joss Iredale, seated opposite her, laid aside a clay pipe he had been filling and rose to grunt a curt good day. His wife, ignoring her guests, riffled through a collection of balls of colored wool on the cupboard beside her and selected one to continue a half-done scriptural picture she had stretched over a coarse wooden frame. Fern, daunted by the cottagers' obvious uninterest, stood silent. Bruno cleared his throat while the neighbor stood curious, arms akimbo, by the door.

"Miss Saxby was most concerned about you, Joss Iredale," Bruno said, almost coldly, Fern thought.

"She's no need," Iredale answered gruffly.

"No, she's not," agreed Mrs. Iredale in a mutter.

Fern felt the time had come to speak for herself. Bruno's manner was far too peremptory.

"Do not take offense, Mrs. Iredale. I come only out of sympathy for you in your loss, and I would not wish you to worry unduly over the cost of the funeral. Dr. de Lacy and I would be honored if you would permit us to bear the cost."

Mrs. Iredale scowled but did not speak. Joss Iredale looked hesitantly from his wife to his master. A light footstep on the stone steps leading down directly into the little room from the upper floor interrupted the silent scene. Fabia Armitage, her blue eyes wide in surprise, stood on the lowest step.

"Bruno! I'm so glad you've come."

There was no doubting the genuine pleasure that irradiated her gentle face, and Fern saw the answering smile in Bruno's dark eyes as Fabia crossed the room, hands outstretched. Bruno gripped them silently. Fabia turned to the Iredales.

"There, now, I told you the master of Brackenroyd would honor the old tradition. Now you've no cause to worry."

Joss Iredale shifted uncomfortably, but his wife rose resolutely, clutching her shawl about her.

"So long as it's t' master who's offering, we'll accept. But we want nowt from *her*." And glaring fiercely at Fern, she turned and went into the little scullery. Fern saw her grasp the posser which stood next to a zinc dolly-tub and start pounding the clothes she was washing, suds spattering the stone floor angrily. She evidently had no more to say to her guests.

Fabia drew Fern aside, and while she talked, Fern saw Bruno talking quietly with Joss. It was difficult to hide the hurt she felt at the Iredales' rejection of her offer of help, but Fabia's words were soft and soothing. As they left the cottage together, Bruno suggested that Fabia fetch Phoebe now and drive up with them to the Hall.

"A pretty name, 'Phoebe,'" Bruno commented as they drove to the schoolhouse. "What does it mean?"

"'Shining one,'" replied Fabia with a smile. "It was Ellen Stansfield's suggestion when the baby was born, she was so shining-eyed and interested in everything around her. That was before Ellen was widowed and became so withdrawn."

"Names are so important," Fern said, anxious to share in the closeness that seemed to bind Bruno and Fabia. "Mothers must ponder for hours how to name their children aptly. No doubt Bruno's mother named him so because he was so dark."

Bruno was silent for a moment. "Then why did your mother choose 'Fern' for you, I wonder? A nostalgic reminder of happy hours in the countryside, perhaps?"

"No," retorted Fern swiftly. "She named me for what she hoped I would be. Fern is the Anglo-Saxon word for 'sincerity.'"

For a brief instant his dark gaze darted to meet hers, stared penetratingly, and then withdrew. In total silence they arrived at the schoolhouse.

Phoebe climbed eagerly into the carriage, taking a seat opposite her mother and next to Bruno. Fern noted how the child's hand slid trustingly into Bruno's and how he silently enfolded it, but she was still smarting from the Iredales' treatment and could not resist speaking of it to Fabia.

"They hate me, Fabia. I don't know why they should, but I could feel it."

"No, Fern, they do not know you. The villagers are very parochial in their outlook, and distrust all strangers. It will take them time, but their resistance will be overcome if you are patient."

"They accepted you, and you were a foreigner to them."

"That was many years ago." Fabia smiled. "And I was a curate's daughter, marrying their beloved schoolmaster. It was easy for me."

"And for Bruno." Fern's gaze slid to him, but it was as if he did not hear, buried in his own thoughts.

"Bruno is a De Lacy, hereditary lord of the manor," Fabia countered calmly. "Though a stranger, they will accept him because of his blood. Don't let them hurt you, Fern. Be patient, and you will come to love them."

"But that's just it," Fern burst out. "I *do* care for them. I feel one of them, I feel I belong, but they want to push me out, to dispossess me."

Bruno was listening now, his piercing gaze intent on her. Fern bit her lip and was silent. Now he would consider her hysterical indeed, judging by his thick, knitted brows.

"Well, Bruno, what do you think?" she challenged.

He shrugged. "I was thinking how you sound like a case I once treated, a man who thought everyone was determined to persecute him. The medical name for such a condition is 'paranoia.' Ah, here we are at the Hall."

The business of dismounting, entering the Hall, and ushering their guests into the drawing room absolved Fern from the responsibility of replying, fortunately, for she was too astounded and bereft of words to think coherently. Bruno was by now amused to watch Phoebe's wide-eyed reaction to the grandeur of the Hall, for it was the child's first visit.

"Don't touch, Phoebe," Fabia admonished the little exploratory fingers testing the texture of a china figurine. Fern noticed that Fabia raised her voice, and the child seemed to hear, for she withdrew her hand at once.

"Toasted scones and cream cakes for tea, Mrs. Thorpe has promised," Bruno said in a similarly loud tone. The child watched his lips and smiled. "And your papa will join us later. He has business in Bradford, I understand?" he added to Fabia.

She nodded. "He has to see the School Board in connection with the school's grant this year. He should be back soon."

Luke arrived as they were all seated about the table, apologizing as he limped into the parlor. Bruno indicated a vacant seat at the table. Fern noticed Bruno's genuine interest as he quizzed Luke as to the outcome of his meeting with the School Board.

"We are to have sixty pounds' grant, a slight increase over last year," Luke told him. "That will enable me to replenish a few books and slates." His keen gaze alighted on the newspaper Bruno had tossed on the sideboard.

"I see you have the Huddersfield *Examiner*. How is the war in the Sudan going? Has the Army put down the rebel Mahdi yet?"

Bruno pushed away his plate and sat back. "It seems Admiral Hewitt and General Graham have arrived at Trinkitat and are disembarking the troops. Their spies report that the Sudanese rebels are massing for an attack, so the general is awaiting the authority to advance."

"I see." Luke's lively eyes moved to Phoebe, busily munching Mrs. Thorpe's chocolate cake. "And my little Phoebe? Have you come to any conclusion about her?"

Bruno surveyed the child reflectively. "It would seem she is not totally deaf, so I shall attempt to hypnotize her after tea and see if I can discover the cause of her muteness. Tell me, Fabia, did she ever experience some shock as a small child, as a baby even? Some dreadful experience which could have caused her condition?"

Fabia's eyes took on a faraway look as she endeavored to recollect; then she shook her head slowly. "None that I can remember. She had to suffer a lot of teasing from the other children on account of her silence when she first began school, but the trouble must have stemmed from before that date."

Bruno rubbed his chin thoughtfully. "No sudden death of a beloved relative, or a physical accident?"

"Nothing of that nature. As a baby she would make the normal gurgling and cooing sounds all babies do, but even that ceased."

"Does she weep?"

Fabia nodded. "But they are silent tears, no sobs."

"Have you had her examined by a doctor?"

Luke cut in. "I took her to a specialist in Bradford once, but he was emphatic that there was no physical defect. Her lungs, vocal cords, and mouth are perfectly formed, and there was no reason for her not to speak."

"Which strengthens my view that the cause must be psychological," Bruno commented as he rose from the table. "Come, let us go to my study, and I shall see what hypnosis can reveal."

They all rose to follow him, and as Fern passed through the doorway, she involuntarily placed an affectionate hand on Phoebe's ringleted head. The child stiffened and pulled away, frightened eyes staring up at her, and Fern drew back sharply. It was as sharp a rebuke as the Iredales' abrupt rejection of her. Fabia's keen eye had seen the incident.

"I'm sorry, Fern, she did not mean to be rude. I'm afraid she is always cautious and rather suspicious of those she does not know."

Fern smiled to show her understanding, but the hurt lingered. How could the little one know how genuine was her sympathy and affection?

"Sit here, Phoebe," commanded Bruno, pointing to his own leather chair behind the desk, which he had turned to face the center of the room. An oil lamp on the desk threw a halo of light on the girl's fair head and Bruno's tall figure before her, while Luke and the women seated themselves in the shadows to watch.

Bruno turned to the adults. "Now, I must ask you all to be absolutely silent for the next few minutes. I shall talk to Phoebe, and whatever happens, I must insist that you remain silent. On no account are you to speak, or you will break the concentration. Moreover, it could be dangerous if you disturb Phoebe, for if she sleeps, she must be awakened only by my word. Are you ready?"

Luke and Fabia nodded, Luke sitting back relaxed and confident while Fabia sat nervously on the edge of her chair. Fern could see her fingers gripping deep into the upholstery of the arms.

Bruno dropped on one knee before Phoebe, his dark head now level with hers, and took her hands in his. Phoebe smiled shyly.

"Listen, Phoebe, can you hear me?" Bruno's voice was raised, though still kindly. Phoebe laid a finger on his lips. "Good, then listen, little one."

Bruno rose again and stood before her, his broad back to

Fern, and taking something from his pocket, he held it aloft. Fern could see something small and shiny on a chain.

"Watch this, Phoebe, see how it gleams." The child's eyes fastened on the shining object while Bruno's voice continued to speak. "Think back, Phoebe, think back to summer and warm days in the sun. Think how pleasant it is to be in the sun and watch the birds fluttering in the sky. Isn't the sun bright, Phoebe, doesn't it dazzle your eyes?"

The child's eyes flickered down from the object Bruno held, tried to find it again, and then closed.

"Sleep now, Phoebe, sleep peacefully in the sun's warmth," Bruno's voice urged, becoming quieter and firmer now. "Sleep deeply, little one, and do not wake until I tell you. Sleep, sleep, and dream of when you were a very little girl."

Luke and Fabia were watching and listening as if they too were entranced, soothed by the warm vibrancy of Bruno's voice. Phoebe sighed and stirred but did not open her eyes. From behind Bruno, Fern could see the child clearly, her downy eyelashes curving on her cheek and a peaceful expression on her cherubic face.

"Remember the orchard up behind the schoolhouse where you used to play before you started school," Bruno murmured. "Remember the apple trees and the sunlight flickering through the branches. Remember the sweet smell of the apples and the humming of the bees." Phoebe's expression was dreamily content. "You used to swing on the rope seat Papa made for you. You were very little then."

Fabia was nodding as she too remembered, but evidently Bruno was not satisfied. The child's memory of those years was peaceful; the trouble must stem from earlier.

"Now, think back, Phoebe, to when you were a baby, just learning to totter about the house and watch Mamma at her work." Phoebe's face remained content, a hint of a smile curving her lips. "And back before that, when you were a tiny baby in your cradle, when Papa and Mamma bent over you and made cooing noises to make you smile. Go back, Phoebe, back as far as you can."

Fern watched, fascinated. The child's face was still passive,

71

but Bruno's was growing animated as he willed her to remember. His voice throbbed with determination.

"Go back, child, back. There must be a moment you recall which still offends you. Go back till you find it, Phoebe."

A restless flicker crossed the girl's face, but Bruno would not relent. "Back, Phoebe, back!" A frown rutted the childish forehead, and Phoebe began to roll her head from side to side, her eyes still tightly closed. Fern could feel the tension in the study grow until it became almost tangible. Luke sat upright, staring, and Fabia's knuckles were white with the force of gripping the chair.

"Don't be afraid, Phoebe, go back and face it." Bruno's eyes were staring wildly, his efforts frenetic to discover the fact that eluded him. "You are nearing it now, Phoebe, face it squarely!"

Phoebe's mouth sagged open, and a low moan issued from her lips. Fabia gasped, her fingers flying to her mouth to suppress a cry. It was the first sound the child had uttered since babyhood. Fern watched the scene as though from some remote viewpoint with a strange sense of detachment; Bruno, wild-eyed and farouche, willing the girl back to some far-off incident she obviously preferred to negate and forget, anxious parents sitting tense with worry, and herself, a stranger to this place and these people, witnessing the forcing out of an event in which she had no part. She could feel only pity for Phoebe, having to undergo such relentless harassing, and anger with Bruno for putting her unnecessarily to such torment.

"Back, Phoebe, back!"

Suddenly the child's eyes jerked open, and she sat bolt upright, her gaze roving over the adults in the room and registering only malevolent distrust of them. It was a terrible, baleful stare, and Fern was filled with horror. Phoebe's gaze went past Bruno and came to rest on Fern, and instantly her expression changed. Her eyes rounded and filled with fear, and her lips parted as she began to pant. Then, without warning, she began to speak.

"I didn't mean it to happen. I swear to God I didn't!"

It was not the words which electrified her audience, startling though they were. It was her voice. The voice emanating from the slight figure of the child was the full, throaty voice of a woman.

A strangled moan escaped Fabia, and Luke leaped to his feet, but Bruno stayed him, his gaze never wavering from the child. Phoebe rose slowly, still staring at Fern, and held out her hands. Then she flung herself at Fern's feet.

"Forgive me. I've wanted so long to beg you. Pray forgive me, Catherine, or I am accursed forever."

The enormous eyes, filled with pleading, suddenly closed, and the child fell limp on the floor. Fabia too fell senseless beside her.

Chapter 6

Fern was so preoccupied that night restoring Fabia and then calming the young mother's hysterical weeping until Luke took her and the child home that she did not know what happened to Phoebe. According to Bruno, once he was left alone with the child in the study, she had reverted to her silent, trancelike state, and he had then awakened her from her hypnotized condition normally. Apart from being sleepy, Phoebe showed no sign of distress, he said.

Fern did not discuss the incident of Phoebe's strange behavior with him that night. She was still too bewildered and benumbed with horror by Phoebe's unexpected outburst. It was not just that the child, a lifelong mute, had spoken at last, but the unnatural voice and strange words she had spoken. It was more than unnatural; it was supernatural, Fern was convinced—another sign of the disturbing atmosphere of Brackenroyd Hall.

Or was it some power in Bruno himself? Fern shuddered at the memory of his face contorted with frenzy, and pushed out of her mind the sudden notion that he could have some demonic power. Now she was thinking like a primitive, uneducated savage. He was a strange man, it was true, dark and secretive, and in some odd way restless and turbulent, but evil, no; surely the man she was to marry was capable of no malefic doing.

But it had been uncanny in the silent lamplit study, the way Phoebe, as if pushed back too far in time by Bruno's urging, had overstepped the boundary of her present life and revived an earlier one. Was it possible? Too tired and bewildered to speculate further, Fern began to undress and prepare for bed.

Sleep came reluctantly to Fern that night, doubt and the chill air of the bedroom combining to make her feel restless. Strange shadows, cast by the last dying flares of the fire, flickered beyond the curtains of the bed, leaping and fading by turns. In the gloom of the far corners it was easy to visualize phantom figures from the past who watched and waited, as though to see how the new mistress of Brackenroyd would conduct herself. At last sleep ventured to mist her drifting thoughts, Phoebe's words echoing in her mind. Catherine, she had called Fern. "Catherine, forgive me, or I am accursed." "Accursed"—that was an oddly archaic word, one a child was not likely to know. It was decidedly odd.

Dreams came, as they had done nightly since her arrival at Brackenroyd Hall, enveloping her in a hazy limbo world where pale faces gazed bleakly at her, but they were tangled, confused visions that were meaningless to Fern. The faces came, melted, and changed; cries turned to moans; and hands without substance reached out to her in pleading. Then a terrible, nauseous miasma enveloped her, reaching into her nostrils and threatening to suffocate her, and Fern awoke, trembling and struggling to push the mist away from her.

"No, no, I don't want you," she was crying out as she realized she was sitting up in bed, flailing her arms about her head in the effort still to ward off the menacing mist. The whole house was still and silent. Fern snuggled down again under the blankets, shivering. It was only a nightmare, and no one seemed to have been disturbed by her cry.

This time when she slept, the dream was clear. Annot

Radley, pale and thin and clutching a shawl about her, was walking in a woodland clearing by moonlight. She was glancing nervously about her, as though afraid of being discovered. Suddenly, from among the trees, a young man, elegantly dressed in frock coat and breeches and a silk cravat, strode toward her. Annot's anxious face softened.

"Oh, Dorian, I thought tha'd never come."

He enfolded her in his arms. "Now, Annot, you know me better than that," he said, a teasing smile curving his sensual lips. "I promised, didn't I, and I never break my promises to you."

Her face was buried in his chest, but she lifted her little pointed chin and regarded him seriously.

"Me dad's fair mad wi' me, Dorian. He threatens to send me away to me aunt's i' Nottingham. Says I've disgraced t' family's name."

Dorian's smile was sardonic. *"You've* disgraced the family name? It's surely little to be ashamed of, to be bearing a De Lacy child. My father, however, is probably justifiably furious with me, for fathering a child to a village girl."

"It's just as shameful for me, Dorian," Annot replied sullenly; then she clung closer to him. "What's to happen to me, love? Tha won't let 'em send me away, will tha? I couldn't bear parting from thee now."

Dorian's handsome face darkened. "My father has given me a choice. I may marry you, or return to London without my allowance. So I'll marry you."

The girl's upturned face grew radiant. "Dosta mean it, truly? Me, marry a De Lacy? Me father'll never credit it. Will thy parents truly let thee marry a lass from t' mill? Will they own me for a daughter? Oh, Dorian, could it really happen?"

"It will happen, there's no two ways about it. My father is insistent because he has his pride to uphold, though I must warn you that my mother does not really approve. They are to send for your father tomorrow to tell him."

"He were going up to t' Hall any road, to tell thy father tha should be horse-whipped. 'Appen he'll take a kindlier tone wi' thee when he hears tha's to make an honest woman of me."

"So he should. There's not many village folk who've captured a De Lacy. He should be proud. And being a Radley too, he should be especially proud."

The girl looked perplexed. "Why? What's being a Radley to do wi' it?"

He withdrew himself from her embrace and sauntered to the edge of the clearing. She could hear his voice only indistinctly, thrown casually back over his shoulder. "Oh, you know the old tale of the Radley blood being tainted blood. I don't know the details of the legend, but it's common gossip in the village."

Annot tossed her fair head proudly. "Aye, and that's all it is, gossip. There's nowt wrong wi' Radley folk. We're good hard workers, all on us, and just as good as t' next man. I'll have nowt said agen my folk."

Dorian turned, smiling at her display of pride. "True enough, Father says your father is one of the best workers in the new mill, now he's got over his disappointment of no longer being an independent hand-loom weaver."

"Aye, and that's no easy pill to swallow, I can tell thee. It near broke me dad's heart losing his independence. The cloth he wove were t' finest as ever went into Huddersfield Cloth Hall. He were proud of it, and rightly so. Still, he's got over it now, and he's a right good worker, one o' t' most loyal thy dad's got, but it wouldn't a stopped him coming up to t' Hall and demanding tha had a beating. It were all me mam could do to stop him giving me a right good thrashing."

"I'm glad he didn't, Annot. He could possibly have harmed my future son, and my father will forgive all if he has a De Lacy grandson to soften the blow. Possibly even Mamma will relent then too." He folded his arms about her again. "But come, Annot, we are wasting time. Let us lie here in the shadows and talk of when you come to live at the Hall."

"Me? Live at Brackenroyd Hall?"

"Of course. You must give up your work at the mill right away—after our two fathers have talked tomorrow—and move in with us. Then, at the right time, we shall be married."

"Not right away?"

"No, not yet. Papa suggests you could learn our ways a little first, and learn to know us all."

Annot laughed, a bitter little laugh. "I see. I'm to learn how to use the cutlery properly and talk nice, am I, before I'm fit to wed thee? They've to see whether I can be schooled right, like a pony for the master's children to ride. If I'm biddable and learn easy, I'll do."

Dorian's smile was amused. "Well, you must admit, little one, you could do with having some of your rougher points fined down. But don't worry, you'll become as fine a lady as Mamma or my sister, Sophie, I'm certain of it. Come, now, we're wasting time again."

And drawing her down into the shadows, he silenced her protesting mouth with kisses. Fern's vision of the embracing couple melted and vanished. Somewhere out in the night a dog howled at the moon, and Fern stirred in her sleep.

The vision shifted and changed. Annot was entering the door of a small stone cottage, and Fern recognized it as one of the little cottages near Brackenroyd church, those with a long row of windows on the upper floor. Fern had learned that this well-lit upper room used to contain the hand-loom weaver's prized loom in the old days before the mill came with its power looms and drove the independent weavers out of business. Annot stepped into the flagstone living room, where a woman was busy at the black-leaded oven range, stirring the savory-smelling contents of a large pan over the fire. On the deal table behind her a huge brown earthenware bowl held a mound of dough, left to rise. The woman looked up anxiously.

"Oh, Annot lass! Thy father's fair vexed tha were out so late. He's nobbut just gone out hisself to look for thee."

The girl smiled and sniffed. "Oven cake. I can smell tha's been baking oven cake, Mam. Where hasta hidden it? I could just eat a lump wi' butter on."

"Butter, is it? And where dosta think money for butter comes from, wi' thee giving up work an' all and soon an extra mouth to feed? Don't thee let thy father hear thee, vexed as he is."

"He'll not be mad wi' me long, not when he hears t' news."

"What news?" Her mother left off stirring the pot and straightened, wiping greasy fingers on her apron. "What news can there be to straighten this mess, I'd like to know?"

Annot found the oven cake, left to cool on a ledge in the back scullery. Clogs clattering down the two steps back into the living room, she broke off a piece and began to eat it, butterless. "How'd tha feel if I telled thee I were to be wed?"

"Wed? Who to? Who'd have thee now?"

" 'Appen Dorian de Lacy."

Her mother's eyes goggled. "Him? He'll never wed thee, tha great fool. His sort just take their pleasure o' the likes of thee and then wed some titled woman. The most thy father can hope for now is to get him horse-whipped—though that's far from likely—and 'appen a mite o' money to tide thee over."

Annot sat on the edge of the table. "Dorian says his dad's decided he has to make an honest woman of me, so we're to be wed. Me dad's to go up to t' Hall tomorrow."

"Never!" Mrs. Radley flopped into a spindle-backed chair, overwhelmed by the news. "Eeh, fancy that! Who'd a thought it? Our Annot mistress o' Brackenroyd. Well, I never did!"

It did not take long for Mrs. Radley's amazement to resolve itself into excited anticipation, but Annot's father was less eager to be mollified by his daughter's announcement when he finally returned.

"Art tha sure, lass? Canst be certain t' lad's not having thee on?" he grunted suspiciously, but on Annot's assurance that he was to be summoned to meet the master of Brackenroyd on the morrow to settle it, he abandoned his aggressive stance on the hearth, and seating himself, began to fill his clay pipe with shreds of black tobacco.

"Just think on it," murmured Mrs. Radley happily. "She'll be able to ring t' bell while t' maid fetches her tea to her, and ride about in a fine carriage just like Mrs. de Lacy does. What a grand life it'll be for her."

"Art satisfied, Father?" Annot asked.

"Mebbe. I'll think on it while I go down to t' privy," he replied, and rising and taking a large key from a nail by the mantelshelf, he went off through the scullery and out of the back door down the yard, his clogged feet clattering on the stone setts as he went.

"He'll be content once it's settled wi' t' master," Mrs. Radley pronounced confidently. "Shift thissen, Annot, side them dishes out o' t' way, and lay a place for thy father. When he's a bowl of this good stew inside of him, he'll think kindlier on it."

Fern's vision of the cottage parlor faded and was gone. Pictures began to flash before her eyes like the pages of a magazine, flicked rapidly by an unseen hand. There was Annot mounting the steps Fern recognized as Brackenroyd Hall; a pudgy-faced woman dressed in black, presumably the housekeeper, taking Annot's bundle of clothes to the kitchen and solemnly burning them all; a lady of middle age accompanied by a haughty young woman, both surveying Annot coldly, the one through gold-rimmed pince-nez and the other with an openly amused smile. The older woman turned away and left the group, the expression on her face registering disdain and extreme distaste.

Sobbing echoed in the bedchamber. Annot lay sprawled across the bed, knuckles pressed into red-rimmed eyes and her face contorted with weeping. Fern, sitting in the bed, could have reached out and touched her.

"They hate me! They despise me, but I'm just as good as them," the girl wept.

"Of course you are. Don't upset yourself," Fern soothed, but the sobbing continued.

"I hate 'em, and if it weren't for t' baby I'd go away. But I've noan got anyplace to go. What'll become of me? I hate 'em all, same as they hate me."

Fern reached out to pat the girl's convulsed shoulder, but touched nothing. Annot wept on, unaware of her. Then suddenly the door opened, and a shaft of light entered the room from a candle. It was Dorian, dressed in a brocade dressing gown, who carried it. He laid a finger warningly to his lips, his handsome face seeming Machiavellian in the candle's light.

"Hush, Annot," he whispered as he laid the silver candlestick on the night table and sat beside her on the bed. His hand caressed her shoulder. "Hush, love, or they'll hear."

She sat up sharply. "And what do I care? They've nowt but scorn for me and my common ways, and I doubt they'll interfere wi' what tha wants to do in t' middle o' t' night. After all, they'll say, tha's going to wed me any road."

His hand ceased its caressing, and his face grew gloomy. "Yes, Mamma and Sophie have accepted that."

"Well tha doesn't look too happy about it."

"It's not that, love, it's Papa. He considers it high time I settled down and married and stayed home to learn the running of the mill."

"Well that's summat, if he's glad on us wedding."

"But hang it, I'll have to stay here in Brackenroyd permanently, don't you see? Papa thinks my seasons in London are far too extravagant, and in any case, I should be here to learn the business. What a bore, to live here all the year round! I understood him to agree to continue my allowance if I married you, but I didn't realize I wouldn't be able to go to London. There's precious little I can spend it on here."

Annot lifted her tearstained face, and Fern could see the dawning suspicion in her blue eyes. "Dost mean tha only agreed to wed me for t' brass? Oh, no, Dorian, tell me tha loves me! Tha telled me tha did down in t' wood!"

He brushed aside her pleading hand impatiently. "Of course I do, silly. But I'm annoyed Papa sees this as a way to pin me down. And even Mamma, who's usually as indulgent as mammas come, seems to concur with him."

"Aye, if she's forced to have me as her daughter-in-law whether or not, she'll profit from it some road," agreed Annot bitterly. "Well, I wish her joy of it, because there's none for me i' this matter, seemingly."

"Come now, my love, you take too harsh a view of the

business," Dorian said smoothly. "You forget you'll have fine clothes and servants and a carriage—and here's something which will soon be yours."

From his dressing-gown pocket he withdrew a small object and gave it to Annot. Fern could see a heavily chased silver ring.

"What is it? A wedding ring?" asked Annot.

Dorian smiled. "No, a betrothal ring. It's been in the family for centuries, I understand. A De Lacy always gives it to his new bride, and I've just persuaded Mamma to part with it so I can give it to you."

Annot turned it over curiously. "It's got writing on it. What does it say?"

Fern thought she could detect a faint grimace on Dorian's face at this reminder of his fiancée's ignorance. "It has twelve raised points, each carved into a letter. It spells *Amor Aeternus*. That means 'Love Eternal.' "

The girl's face softened, a gentle light of happiness lighting her features. "Oh, Dorian! How lovely! I'll treasure it forever—that is," she added, "till the day I give it to our son for his bride."

"Our son? You seem very certain it will be a boy."

"Aye, well," Annot murmured, cradling against his chest, "in five months we'll know, one way or t' other."

Dorian slid the ring back into his pocket, shrugged off his dressing gown, and leaned over to pinch out the candle. In the darkness Fern could hear Annot's contented sigh.

When Fern again opened her eyes it was dawn, and the great bed was empty save for her own slender figure. She reached out expectantly, as though touching the coverlet where Annot had lain could confirm the reality of her presence in the night. Had she really lain there, sobbing and then consoled by Dorian, or had it been only a dream of unusual intensity and verisimilitude?

No, it was more than a dream. Fern was certain of it. Annot, whose life had once brought her to this very room, had somehow come back, crossed the barrier of time and of death to reenact the events of her life for her great-granddaughter to witness. But why? There seemed no reason for it—yet. Fern had the uneasy feeling that there was more yet to be revealed before the meaning became clear. And Bruno must be wrong, for it was undoubtedly some kind of race-memory, some link with the past which brought such vivid dreams, -recollections, however one liked to name them.

She could hardly wait to tell him. Once he heard of the dreams, every detail of which remained indelibly clear to her, he must then at least begin to be convinced. She *must* convince him she was no neurotic.

As Fern washed and dressed, she glanced out of the latticed window. From the moorland path a solitary figure strode toward the house and paused below to look up. The look on his face was startling; a hunted, desperate expression glazed his eyes, which stared blindly upward. Fern drew back from the window quickly. It was Bruno, hatless and disheveled, his hair bedewed with mist. Behind him loped the wolfhound, Pharaoh. Suddenly Bruno turned away and strode around the side of the Hall, out of sight.

A few minutes later Cassie knocked and entered with the breakfast tray. Fern's curiosity was too great to be contained.

"Has the master breakfasted yet, Cassie? I see he walked out very early this morning."

"He's just come in, miss, in by t' kitchen door, soaked through. He's been out all night, seemingly, because his bed's not been slept in."

Fern snapped her lips shut. She had already overstepped the bounds of propriety in questioning Cassie about the master; curious as she was, she would ask no more, though she burned to know what he had been doing. Out on the moors all night in this freezing weather? Why? Then another thought crossed her mind. It answered the mystery of the dog whose howls had invaded her dreams—it must have been Pharaoh, chilled and miserable and longing for his bed by the kitchen fire.

"Did you hear a dog howl in the night, Cassie?" she asked, and then remembered the girl went home to the village to sleep and most likely had not heard it. But Cassie's usually amiable face had blanched. "Why, what's the matter? You look quite frightened."

"A dog in t' night? Not me, miss, nor do I want to hear it. Up on t' moor were it?"

"Presumably. But why does that frighten you?"

"Them's Gabriel's hounds, miss, so they say. Trouble to come to those as hear 'em. 'Scuse me, miss, have you done wi' t' tray?"

She could not leave the room quickly enough, so it seemed. Fern smiled. How ridiculously superstitious village folk could be. But she dismissed the thought quickly, for she was concerned about Bruno. His look had been so strange, and wild, that either he was disturbed by the strange happenings with Phoebe last night, or possibly he was ill. She hastened downstairs to find him and encountered Cassie just leaving his study. The girl laid a finger to her lips.

"He's fast asleep in t' chair, sleeping like a baby. I've lit t' fire, as he's still in his wet clothes, but I haven't the heart to wake him, he were so tired."

"Yes," Fern agreed reluctantly. "Let him sleep. I'll look in on him later."

But despite Fern's frequent peeping in on him, Bruno slumbered on all morning. Eventually the idea came to her that since she still had the key to the unused wing which Mrs. Thorpe had surrendered to her, she could look about there again, undisturbed. Satisfied that Bruno was still deeply asleep, Fern made her way to the ancient studded door.

Once again the chill air of damp and neglect struck her as she passed through into the stone-slabbed corridor, an atmosphere mingled too with sadness and decay. The dusty floor still showed signs only of Bruno's footsteps toward his laboratory. The door was securely locked, and Fern grew curious to know what lay within.

As she turned from the door, she noticed the dark wall beneath the gallery and the absence of Annot's portrait. Now, why should it have been removed? Undoubtedly it was by Bruno's order, but why? Fern felt a sense of perverse irritation. He had done it on her account, she was sure, and she would demand the reason just as soon as he awoke.

It was a relief to reemerge from the old wing into the warmth of the newer Hall. Odd, but it seemed always ominously cold in the old wing, a chill as of the grave. Fern shuddered at the silly notion and retraced her steps toward the study. Bruno was awake, seated at his desk. He looked up as she entered.

"I see you have been in the old wing."

It was a statement, not a question, and Fern felt resentful of the note of challenge in his voice. His face betrayed no wild signs of distraction or illness now.

"Yes, I have. How did you know?"

"There is dust on the hem of your skirt. Mrs. Thorpe is too able a housekeeper to permit dust elsewhere in the Hall, so it follows you have been in the old wing. Why?"

"Curiosity, that is all."

"But you found my laboratory locked. And I intend it to remain so, for it is dangerous for a layman to dabble there."

"Why have you removed Annot's portrait?" Fern's challenging look met a cool stare in return.

"For the same reason I appropriated the notes Amos brought, to discourage your obsession with the girl."

"Then you are deceived, Bruno, for I dream of her still." Fern's voice was almost triumphant.

"Still?" The thick brows rose in query. "Then your preoccupation with the subject is even deeper than I thought."

He looked down again at the papers before him, as if he had done with the topic, and Fern's protesting reply died on her lips. What was the use of arguing with him, since he was too cold and skeptical to begin to understand? He, devoid of feeling for any but himself—and possibly Luke and his family—could never understand her affinity with her past. Instead, she remembered his haunted look of the morning when he came home.

"You were out all night, I believe."

He looked up sharply. "That is no affair of anyone but myself. Do not seek to question me, Fern, for I will not be questioned."

"I was simply concerned for you. You looked so . . . strange, when I saw you through the window."

"It is nothing. I have many pressing matters on my mind. The mill, my experiments . . ."

"And Phoebe?"

His fierce look reverted to the papers before him. "Phoebe? No, to be sure. I shall isolate the cause of her trouble, but it will take time."

Fern was startled. "You do not mean to repeat an experiment like last night, surely? It was too much for her, and for Fabia."

"For Fabia, perhaps. She was a little startled, but the child is well and remembers nothing."

Fanny bustled in, apron and cap strings flying behind her. "Sir, the Reverend Amos begs leave to call on you."

Bruno rose from the desk, glancing at the mantel clock. "Amos, at this hour? He can scarcely have finished his lengthy Sunday sermon yet. Show him in, Fanny."

Fern could see by Edgar Amos' white, tight-lipped expression that he was tense, but whether with anger or with another emotion she could not tell. That he had come in haste was evident, for beneath his coat he still wore his cassock. Bruno nodded and waved him to a chair, but as Pharaoh uncurled his length from the hearth rug and came sniffing toward him, the young vicar remained standing.

"What brings you here so early, Amos?" Bruno inquired as he reseated himself behind his desk. Fern sat unobtrusively by the window.

"Dr. de Lacy, I have come to protest most vigorously on behalf of my parishioners Mr. and Mrs. Armitage about the incident here last night, and of which I understand you were the instigator."

Bruno picked up his pipe. Pharaoh began to growl at the vicar's angry tones, laying back his lips to bare his teeth. Amos twitched the hem of his cassock away nervously, taking a hesitant step backward.

"*Weg*, Pharaoh, still!" At Bruno's quietly spoken order the dog retreated sullenly to the hearth rug and lay down. "Forgive me, the dog understands only German," Bruno went on smoothly. "Now, please be seated, Amos, and tell me. Have the Armitages themselves protested?"

Amos sat gingerly. "No, they have not. But it is my duty, as a man of God, to protest on their behalf when you dabble with the unknown and bring them and their child into possible danger. They told me after morning service of what happened here last night, of their concern because they could not understand it, and I felt it was my duty to hasten here at once, to beg you not to repeat this experiment. You do not know what you are doing."

"But you do?" Fern had half-expected him to storm at Amos, but Bruno's voice was enigmatically calm.

"I know you succeeded in causing Phoebe to speak, but with the voice of a woman. I know there is something strange, something supernatural at work, and I entreat you not to experiment with an innocent child again. By dabbling so you could arouse elemental forces which you cannot control. There is much we do not know or understand, but to meddle with these supernatural forces can release evil powers which we none of us could combat. Evidently you have the power to evoke these forces, though I doubt you can control them."

Bruno's smile spread slowly. "You accuse me of witchcraft, is that it, Amos? You fear I may be a warlock or wizard, opposed to the strength of your church? You are talking rubbish, man, medieval superstitious rubbish. I am, as you know, a man of science, but I admit that science is not always concerned with absolute truths. In this fringe between the things we can understand and those we can't explain, between nature and the supernatural as you call it, lie many strange phenomena such as levitation, precognition, and hypnosis. What happened last night with Phoebe was certainly a phenomenon I have not encountered before, but there is assuredly a scientific, logical explanation of it. In time, I shall discover it."

"No good can come of it!" Amos' protest was almost a wail of despair.

"Good has already come of it. We have established that Phoebe is physically capable of speech. Now we must find what prevents her from speaking."

"It is not with her physical well-being that I am concerned, but her spiritual welfare," Amos shouted. The dog growled menacingly on the rug, but Bruno stilled him with a look.

"Forgive him, Amos," Bruno commented quietly. "Like many of us, he distrusts what he cannot understand."

Fern could feel her palms prickling. She felt acutely embarrassed by the hostility between the two men, but could not join the battle. After all, both men had valid points of argument.

"A little child such as Phoebe surely cannot come to harm, if such is your fear, if she is protected by her own innocence?" Bruno said after a pause.

Amos grunted. "Even the innocent suffer if evil powers are evoked. Innocence is no protection."

"I am not entirely convinced that malevolent powers were at work," Bruno went on, as if to himself. "Our view of the world is limited by the blinkers of our experience, and we must penetrate the fog of mysticism and superstition if we are to reach beyond. Possibly there is a scientific explanation for many so-called supernatural phenomena."

Amos looked surly. "It is possible, but not yet proven. All we know is that dabbling with these things produces dire results."

"And are you certain it was my presence which caused this ... manifestation, or whatever you may call it? Could it not equally well have been due to another's presence, say, Fern even?"

Fern's jaw dropped open in surprise. Amos too stared in bewilderment. Bruno lit his pipe slowly, as though savoring the moment.

"It is possible, I suppose," Amos admitted.

"No, no!" Fern cried in alarm. "You cannot blame me!"

"But you claim to have affinity with the past. If, as you

seem to believe, Phoebe's voice came from the past, why not attribute the reason to your affinity—and your presence?"

Fern was too stunned to answer, and since Amos was only blinking in embarrassment, too tongue-tied to come to her defense, she got up blindly and rushed from the room. Tears scalded her eyelids. How *could* Bruno blame her for the frightening event last night?

For almost an hour Fern paced her room, agitated and irate. It was this house that brought evil with it, she decided, its atmosphere which had affected Phoebe, or possibly Bruno himself in dabbling with unknown powers, as Amos stated. But not her, not Fern's fault, for she herself felt the power of this place, a victim of its strange emanations. It grieved her that either Bruno or Edgar Amos should believe her capable of bringing possible danger to Phoebe, although unwittingly.

At last she descended the staircase, calmer now, though still fretting, and saw Amos in the hall about to take his leave. He turned from Bruno, who reentered his study and closed the door, and saw Fern. His smile was weak and uncertain.

"I feel in need of a breath of air, and the sun is peeping out. Do you mind if I walk a little way with you?" Fern asked him.

"By all means, Miss Saxby. But do take care to wrap up well, for the wind is treacherously cold."

Fern fetched her ulster and gloves but chose to go hatless. The cold breeze whipped tendrils of hair loose from its neat coils, and Fern welcomed the unaccustomed feeling of freedom it gave her. Amos walked alongside in gloomy silence, measuring his stride to match hers. The gravel crunched beneath their feet as they walked. At length Fern broke the silence.

"Do you believe this occurrence to be of my doing, Mr. Amos?"

He shrugged his shoulders apologetically. "As the doctor says, you do claim an affinity with the past of the Hall. It is possible you are a contributory factor, though you may not realize it."

"Then you do believe Phoebe reverted to a former life? You believe in reincarnation?"

Blue eyes gazed at her blankly. "Who can say for certain? There is so much we cannot comprehend in this life. But I fear the consequences if Dr. de Lacy meddles. It is Phoebe's soul which is in danger—or her psyche, as he would term it. I am afraid, Miss Saxby. I sense danger, though I cannot explain it."

"And so do I." The words were out before Fern realized. They had reached the stone gate pillars surmounted by stone lions. Amos stopped suddenly.

"Go back to the Hall, Miss Saxby. It is bitterly cold, and you have no protection for your head. I would not wish you to catch a cold. Do go back."

Reluctantly Fern agreed. She would have liked to talk more with him, to try to clarify just what it was they both feared. Slowly she retraced her steps, then on an impulse turned off across the lawns, away from the direction of the moor.

A rose garden, now only a thicket of tangled thorny branches scoured by the winds, gave way to an enclosed garden bordered by a high yew hedge. Fern strolled through, unaware of the wind's keenness, and emerged into a glade of trees close by a lake. Beyond the trees a dark stump projecting from the ground caught her eye, and curiously she wandered toward it. Surely not a sundial, so far from the Hall?

It was a black-marble slab, with a few words carved in its glossy depth: "Annot Radley. Born 1798. Died 1815."

So Fern had found the poor creature who nightly invaded her dreams.

Chapter 7

The gong had already sounded for Sunday lunch by the time Fern regained the Hall, and Bruno was waiting in the dining room to place Fern's chair beneath her before taking his own seat at table. Fanny ladled out brown Windsor soup from the tureen and withdrew.

"I discovered Annot's grave in the grounds," Fern announced quietly. Bruno went on sipping a spoonful of soup. "Why did you not tell me it was there?"

"I supposed you would find it sooner or later. I could not prevent you," he replied coolly.

"If you could, you would have removed that too, like her portrait and the notes, I imagine." It slipped out. She had not meant to provoke him. Bruno sighed in sign of dissipating patience and then continued spooning his soup. For a few moments Fern ate in silence too.

"No doubt you think that removing all evidence of Annot will make me forget she ever existed, but it is not so. As I told you, I dream of her. I feel sure she comes back to me because she wants me to know something. It's not that I'm so obsessed when awake that I dream of her; it's more . . . more as if I were possessed than obsessed."

Bruno's spoon clattered noisily into his half-emptied bowl. "For heaven's sake, Fern, how long must this nonsense go on? You speak of possession now—influenced by all Amos' ridiculous primitive hysteria this morning about raising spirits, I've no doubt. How impressionable you are, a mere child at heart! Now, please cease this chatter about Annot before you too become hysterical. It's time, at twenty-two, that you became a mature woman, and especially if you are soon to become a wife."

Before Fern could answer, Fanny entered to remove the soup dishes and place a joint of roast sirloin before Bruno. As she laid the tureens of roast potatoes and carrots and Yorkshire pudding on the damask cloth, Fern watched Bruno's strong, dexterous hands as he deftly carved the joint. At last Fanny, her keen eye satisfied that all was correct on the table, bobbed a curtsy and disappeared. Bruno passed to Fern a plate of neatly sliced roast beef.

"You exaggerate, Bruno," Fern said calmly as she spooned carrots and potatoes alongside the beef. "I do truly dream of her, not wishfully, but it simply happens. And the detail of the dreams is so minute it can be no coincidence. I could tell you which cottage Annot lived in, the furnishings there, and a thousand other things I could not possibly have learned otherwise."

Bruno snorted disbelievingly. "It is no secret which is the Radley cottage. No one will live in it now, so disliked is the name, and Micklethwaite, who lives in the cottage adjoining, uses the Radley one as a pigsty. It is common knowledge, as you have no doubt heard."

"I knew no such thing. I have barely been into the village since my arrival."

"Village girls come to the Hall to work. You could have learned gossip from them."

Fern was irritated. "Do you think I have nothing better to do than make idle talk with the servants? I tell you I dreamed all this, but since you obviously do not believe me, let us leave the matter rest. What do you plan to do now about Phoebe?"

His dark eyes lifted from his plate, and a frown creased his brow. "Fern, it is not a wife's place to quiz her husband—or future husband—as to his actions. My affairs in my work are a private matter."

"Will you see her again?" She was not to be put down like a child so easily.

"I shall visit Luke this afternoon, to ascertain whether he is as disturbed as Amos represents over last night. Future course of action will depend on that."

"May I come with you?"

"No." It was a bold answer with no explanation. Fern felt hurt. He was cutting her out of not only the running of the mill, his work, and what he would do with regard to Phoebe, but now even out of his friendship with the Armitages, it seemed. He wanted her to share no part of his life. What a dismal prospect marriage to this man held out. No true union of minds, no affection, no companionship even. Inwardly Fern rebelled. Bruno, having now finished his dinner, sat back to await Fanny's arrival with the pudding, and as he sat in silence, he took an object on a chain from his pocket and began to swing it idly to and fro.

Fern's breath caught in a gasp in recognition of the object. It wasn't just that it was the bright shining thing he had swung rhythmically before Phoebe last night in the study; it was the heavy carving on a silver ring which brought back to Fern forcibly the vision of Annot and Dorian in the bedroom last night. Fern stared at it in fascination.

Bruno smiled wryly as he noted her rapt expression. Fern leaned forward in her chair.

"That ring—I have seen it before!"

He cocked his head to one side quizzically. "Yes, last night."

"And again—in the dream. Dorian promised it to Annot. Every De Lacy gave it to his new bride, he said."

"So you know the tradition. But he did not give it to Annot, but to the woman he did marry, my great-grandmother,

Sarah Ramsden. Someday soon it will be yours, Fern. I wonder where you learned about the ring?"

"I told you—in the dream. I saw it closely. It has twelve carved points which read *Amor Aeternus.*"

He frowned and slid the ring back into his pocket, just as Fanny entered with a huge steamed pudding and a bowl of custard on a tray. Fern waited until the door had closed again behind the maid before pursuing her advantage. Bruno was obviously impressed by her knowledge of the ring.

"So you see, from my dreams I am learning about Annot. She was brought to this house on trial, as it were, to be trained as a lady before the wedding could take place. I hope further dreams will reveal just why she became so unhappy that she killed herself."

Bruno pushed back his chair and rose from the table. "I want no pudding. Please excuse me. I am going now to see Luke Armitage."

Fern looked up at his face, but it was set and enigmatic. "Do you begin to believe me now, Bruno?"

He turned as he reached the door and his look was ominous. "I do not. Such detail as you have related is fully reported in old Thomas' notes, which Amos brought."

"But I have not read them, remember, you took them from me."

"They lie on my study desk. You could well have read them this morning while I slept. No, I am not convinced, Fern."

And before she could utter a startled denial that she could resort to such subterfuge, he was gone. Inwardly Fern fumed. How could he believe her capable of sneaking in and reading furtively while he slept! Pushing away her plate of pudding, Fern rose and ran out after him, burning in protest. He was in the hall, pulling on his caped greatcoat as she came up to him.

"And the ring, Bruno? How could I have known the wording on it?" she asked defiantly.

He turned and stared fixedly at her, his dark features solemn and implacable. "The dining table is eight feet in length. It would seem you have remarkably keen eyesight,

94

young lady. But the way you stared at the ring told me more."

He withdrew once again the glittering silver ring from his pocket, and again Fern stared at it transfixed. Bruno's eyes bored into her face. "It fascinates you, does it not, Fern? You are so suggestible, I could hypnotize you within seconds now."

She tore her gaze from the ring and glared at him. "You could not! I would not let you!"

He laughed, a hollow, mirthless tone. "You are so impressionable, my dear. There exists between us a rapport which I have never found before in a patient. We are very alike, Fern, you and I. Such a close affinity between hypnotizer and hypnotized does not occur often, but when it does, we recognize it, we medical men. It comes closely akin to hysteria in the patient."

"Again you accuse me of being hysterical," Fern cried, almost tearful in frustration. "But I am not. I am as sane and balanced as you are."

He picked up his riding crop from the hall stand, glanced at his reflection in the oak-framed mirror above, and strode toward the front door. In the passage he turned. A veil of angry tears was misting Fern's eyes.

"And this hysteria I spoke of, we know it has a sexual basis," Bruno added quietly, as an afterthought. The door opened, admitting a draft of icy wind, and he was gone. Fern stood aghast. For some moments she was too stunned to move. Had she heard aright? Anger and resentment gave way to a flood of shame and embarrassment.

She grew conscious of hot, sticky palms and of Fanny's approaching footsteps as she reappeared through the green-baize door leading down to the kitchens. Fern avoided the maid's curious gaze as she passed her to go to her own room. Two thoughts thundered in her brain: one, that Bruno believed her attracted by him, and two, that he had scorned her sufficiently to speak of a matter to which no member of polite Victorian society ever even remotely referred—sex. She did not know which insult to fume against most.

How dared he be so blatant! It was a measure of the man's

arrogance that he thought he could talk to her so coarsely and that he could believe her physically attracted to him. What a crude, ill-mannered oaf he was! Fern speculated how Lydia Hastings would have dealt with him, but in the presence of such a vapid, colorless woman he probably would not have felt the need to provoke with such crudity. In the Hastings household it was, as in any good Christian home, tacitly understood that sex was never mentioned, and even objects which could have a sexual connotation, such as the legs of tables and pianos, were discreetly draped. How, against such a background of polite prevarication, could Bruno be so monstrous as to speak to her of her sexual attraction to him!

Fern paced her room angrily, torn between fury and shame. Was he perhaps right in his judgment after all, and she was attracted to him? Scornfully she rejected the idea. It could not be true. He had nothing about him to appeal to a woman—no chivalry, no warmth, no tenderness. And how could one be drawn to a man who made it evident he found equally no appeal in her?

The dismal Sunday afternoon passed slowly, raindrops pattering incessantly against the windowpane. Fern declined Fanny's offer to bring up afternoon tea, and as the evening drew on she watched the great lumbering night clouds advance slowly over the mountain edge. Bruno still had not returned. Angered and disconcerted as she was by him, Fern felt the vast Hall empty and lifeless without his great vibrant presence.

Fanny came again to draw the heavy velvet curtains closed and replenish the fire, picking coals elegantly from the brass coal scuttle by the hearth with carved brass tongs.

"Will that be all, miss?" Fern nodded her thanks and dismissal, and Fanny bobbed and withdrew. With a sigh Fern decided to prepare for bed. Washed and nightgowned at last, she looked at her reflection in the dressing-table mirror. Hair unbound and the voluminous folds of the white nightgown ethereally pale in the candlelight, she looked young and defenseless, and inwardly she felt dreadfully alone. Her wide eyes stared back at her thoughtfully. Sleep was far away yet.

Rising, she donned her woolen dressing gown, and taking the candle, she went down to the library in search of a book.

As she reached the gallery she heard the front door open. Looking down over the parapet, she saw Bruno, greatcoated and hatless. The candle's light caught his eye, for he glanced up.

"Fabia has a mind to go shopping in Bradford tomorrow. I promised her you would accompany her. Malachi will drive you both down," he said quietly. Fern came down the stairs quickly, snuffing out the candle, and came to stand before him as he doffed his coat. Shopping, she thought, but with no money. Since sending her money in London, Bruno had offered no more, and she was reluctant to mention the omission. Having hung his coat on the hall stand, he turned to face her, his dark head silhouetted in the light of the solitary oil lamp. Fern shifted uncomfortably beneath his gaze.

"I shall furnish you with money." It was as if he had read her thoughts, and Fern was embarrassed. "I propose to allot you ten pounds per month, if that will suit you."

"It is generous, Bruno, thank you."

But already his eyes had lifted from her face and were turned toward the study. Having dealt with the matter of an allowance for her, he had already forgotten her. Politely he waited, but Fern was not ready to be dismissed.

"Were Luke and Fabia well? And Phoebe?"

"Perfectly."

"They were not disturbed, then, as Amos thought?"

"Not at all. He exaggerated, but then, he is a highly emotional man."

"Is Luke happy for you to continue your work with Phoebe, then?"

His eyes flickered down to her face, "He is, but I am not— yet. I deem the moment not quite ripe, and moreover, I sense Fabia was a little troubled, though she says nothing. But if you will excuse me, Fern . . ."

Already he was stepping around her toward the study. Reluctantly Fern bade him good night and remounted the stairs, her book forgotten. Perhaps, after all, Bruno was showing consideration, arranging a shopping expedition for her and Fabia, but his authoritative manner of announcing it, combined with his complete uninterest in her, would seem to deny it.

Fern slept a deep and dreamless sleep that night, and when next morning dawned bright and crisp with a mellow hint of spring in the air, she began to enjoy the prospect of the day's outing. Malachi drove her in the trap down to the village to call at the schoolhouse for Fabia, who was as excited as a child as she climbed into the trap and sat alongside Fern.

"Was it not kind of Bruno to suggest we spend the day in town?" she said happily as the trap made its way along the cobbled village street. Fern was watching the curtains twitch as they passed, and some women even looked up from scrubbing and donkey-stoning their front steps to stare dourly. No doubt, to them Fabia in her best gray flannel and Fern in deep-green velvet were hardly dressed for a workaday Monday morning.

"Luke has given me money to buy gloves for Phoebe and a length of flannel for a nightgown," Fabia was saying excitedly. "Poor little thing, she feels the cold so. I feel such a lady, driving into town with you to buy them instead of making them myself. Luke is so kind. And Bruno too—is he not the gentlest and most considerate of men? You and I are lucky indeed."

The village slipped away behind them as the trap mounted the moorland road up and away from Brackenroyd. The road that ran along the scar afforded a fine view of the valley below, and Fern gazed about her in wonder. The wind blew cold over the brow, and she drew the rug gratefully over her knees and Fabia's.

"Have you ridden along this road before?" Fabia inquired. "It gives one a splendid view of our valley. See, there is the Hall on the far ridge, and there Fox Brow, Ellen Stansfield's home."

Fern's eye was caught by the mill in the valley below, on the river's edge. From here it looked huge, ranks of slate-gray roofs marking out the textile-machinery buildings, blackened by the grime from its chimneys. Above it she could see the river's silver-gray ribbon threading between the curves of the mountainside till it flattened out in a vast gray expanse, hemmed by a wide dam.

"That's Bilberry Reservoir," Fabia explained. "And just above it, you can see Dr. Briggs's house."

The road twisted away from the valley and across the moor, across great tracts of winter-browned heather and through a tiny hamlet where chickens squawked in the roadway in protest at the trap's passing. Fabia was amused by the woman, her forearms white with flour from the baking she had evidently been wrenched from, who shooed the chickens fussily back into her yard.

"That's what I should be doing now, baking, and not jaunting off on a day's holiday." She chuckled happily. "Oh, I am so grateful to Bruno and Luke—and to you too, Fern."

Fern smiled. It was odd how often Fabia referred to Bruno's kindness. Evidently she saw him in a very different light from herself. Or it could be Fabia's own warmth and kindliness which elicited similar response in him, she reflected. Perhaps her own agressiveness was at fault that she had found no such gentleness in him yet.

"Phoebe is happy too," Fabia chattered on. "She is to have tea with Edgar. Funny, but they get on well together, which is odd when you consider how shy she is, and he too. But Bruno is her idol. She adores him and seems truly happy when she's in his company. I'm so glad, because she doesn't have a very happy time at school. The other children find her odd because she doesn't speak. At one time she was teased unmercifully, but now they just leave her alone. She's a very lonely child."

She relapsed into silence for a moment, pondering the problem. Fern instinctively reached for her hand in tacit sympathy. Fabia's back straightened.

"It's a pity she has no brothers or sisters, but it does not seem to be God's will. Nevertheless, I am glad she has Bruno. She seems to prefer adults' company."

Bruno's, and perhaps Edgar's, but not mine, thought Fern sadly. She still remembered the sting of the child's shrinking from her touch. It was a hurtful memory, for it was said children were perceptive creatures.

"Bruno is optimistic he can help her," Fabia went on. "Now he knows she can hear, he is certain he can teach her a new method of communication recently devised, a means of conversing by sign language with the hands. He says it is being successfully used in Germany, and will be of great advantage to her until she learns to speak. He is so sympathetic, so kind . . ."

There, again, she was maintaining his consideration. Either there was a facet to his personality Fern had not yet discovered, or Fabia was besotted with him, and as she was obviously so in love with her husband, it was hardly the latter.

The trap jolted on, the horse's hooves clattering rhythmically on the road, and as Fabia relapsed again into silence, Fern drew in lungfuls of the clean, sweet air, pure and free from the smoke of the valleys, reveling in the sense of freedom the high moors gave her. Frowning hills, stern and rugged, overlooked vast undulations of heather-clad moor. The solitude and silence gave an air of powerful strength to the place. Mountainous and bare of habitation for miles, the moors were her native home, she felt, intoxicating in their solid majesty. After some miles when little was to be seen but dry stone walls lining the road and the expanse of Malachi's broad back, the road began to dip down, and an occasional farm or cluster of cottages was to be seen, and then it descended more steeply, and more houses came into sight, larger and more imposing, often with their own large gardens.

"We are in the outskirts of Bradford now," Fabia pointed out. "There, down in the valley, you can see the town."

And indeed Fern could see it, its great gray mass spreading in the very depths of the valley. The houses alongside the road were impressive, the solid mansions of prosperous merchants who had amassed their wealth from the area's woolen trade mainly. Fabia spoke of the town's history.

"Worsted, such as your mill produces, is manufactured here, and Bradford is renowned for it, though many mills do produce mohair and alpaca and silks too. Just see how many mills there are."

It was true, for they were riding by many gray, gaunt buildings, mills and warehouses, where men in clogs and aprons bustled about to the accompaniment of a background of whirring machinery. But soon the cobbled mill streets gave way to the broad clean streets of the town center. Fern recognized the railway station where she had first met Bruno.

"The church of St. Peter," Fabia indicated in Forster Square, "and there is our new town hall with its tower which is an exact replica of the campanile of the Palazzo Vecchio in Florence. There's the technical college—the Prince and Princess of Wales came to open it only last year. Almost all the buildings are but newly built. Is it not a fine town?"

Fern could not but agree, for its civic buildings were most impressive, and the many shops and banks and hotels were equally grand. Malachi, given orders to take the trap to an inn yard until they were ready to return, helped the ladies to dismount and drove off. Then the delight of shopping could begin.

Into every large emporium and small private shop in the main streets they went, exclaiming with admiration at the new French millinery in the Misses Drake's establishment, the caps and bonnets and headdresses for weddings, the gloves and cambrics and mantles, the sprigged muslins and luscious velvets. And finally they found the prosaic flannel Fabia sought. Having purchased that and some wool to knit Phoebe's gloves after all, she pronounced her errands completed and inquired what Fern required.

"I would like to buy gifts, for Phoebe and you," Fern said. Despite Fabia's protests, she insisted, and as Fabia firmly declined a pretty flower-patterned porcelain potpourri bowl, Fern persuaded her at last to accept some sewing silks, a sheet of pins, and new cutting shears.

"And for Phoebe, what shall I buy?"

"Really, she has no need of anything, Fern—beyond new clogs, that is. But of books and toys she already has sufficient, truly."

"Then I shall buy the clogs, and a length of muslin for a Sunday frock." And Fern was not to be dissuaded this time. As they both fingered the assortment of muslins in the emporium, Fabia sighed.

"Oh, look at that pretty violet-gray silk. It's exactly like a gown Ellen used to wear, before she retired into isolation. Poor Ellen. I think the wild Yorkshire countryside was alien to her. She came from Wiltshire, you know, and I think our moors frightened her a little. She changed so much after Arthur died."

"Did you know her well?"

Fabia shook her head. "I was new to Brackenroyd when she was widowed. Now she will see no one. Her old maid-housekeeper, Hepzibah, looks after her and occasionally comes to the village, but Ellen never goes out except in the evening, alone on the moors, and she runs home if she is seen. Bruno is the only person who can talk to her. He has an uncanny knack of getting through the barrier of those who are . . . handicapped in some way."

Like Phoebe, thought Fern. He can penetrate her cautious reserve, and that of the eccentric Ellen. If his manner is so efficacious with lame dogs, why does it not extend to ordinary people like me? Perhaps if he thought me helpless too, in some way, he would try. The bizarre notion of feigning the neurotic he believed her to be flashed through her mind. How foolish of her, to consider shamming madness in order to attract his attention!

To wind up a pleasant afternoon, the two ladies sipped tea from willow-patterned china cups in a little tea shop, nibbled hot toast and powdery sponge cakes. Finally the time came to return.

"It would be useful to have a little fob watch," commented Fern as they made their way to the inn yard.

"Then why not buy one?" Fabia replied.

Fern was shocked. "Did you see the price in that jeweler's? Thirty-eight and six for a lady's gold watch, and two pounds for a gentleman's. It's very expensive."

"But you are wealthy now. Two pounds is little enough on

your income," Fabia remarked calmly. "To us it would be a prodigious sum, two-thirds of what Luke earns in a week, but value is relative to one's income."

"True," Fern admitted. "But I am not used to wealth. Nor am I yet legally entitled to it."

"When are you and Bruno to be married?" Fabia inquired, tilting her head and gazing frankly into Fern's eyes. Fern hid a blush.

"I don't know yet. Soon, I expect."

And the thought of her marriage occupied Fern's mind throughout the homeward journey over the darkening moors. Bruno had made it clear he would not ask her to marry him again, but would leave the approach to her. The time had now come, it seemed, to make that approach. Until she was truly mistress of Brackenroyd, her position would remain as nebulous and ill-defined as it had been as the Hastingses' governess. Only as his wife would Bruno listen to her, take notice of her. Until then she was of no account.

In the village Fabia climbed down from the trap, promising to take Fern to the clogger's shop in the morning to order Phoebe's new clogs. Her face shone with happiness.

"It's been such a lovely outing, Fern, I've enjoyed it so much. I'm longing to tell Luke and Phoebe all about it. Thank you so much."

Fern envied the young woman's radiance, the light, eager step as she hastened indoors, waved, and closed the door behind her. She could visualize Luke's welcoming smile and the eager conversation that ensued. How lucky was Fabia, warm and secure in a happy marriage. Fern signaled to Malachi to drive on.

Brackenroyd Hall stood huge, sentinel-like, at the head of the drive, lugubrious and forbidding. No lights shone at the windows. Bruno must be out yet. As Malachi drew up at the wide, shallow steps, Fern waved to him to drive on around to the stable yard. It would be cozier to enter the Hall by a warm, lighted kitchen than by a desolate front vestibule. The pony began to canter under the arch into the stable yard, anxious for his feed and a warm stall. Malachi reined him in by the kitchen door just as Bruno emerged, caped and spurred, his tall figure silhouetted in the doorway against the lamplight within.

"Mein Herr?" Malachi murmured in query. Fern heard Bruno bark words of command in German, and the grooms-man nodded. Bruno turned to Fern.

"I wanted to talk with you, but that must wait now. I have business to attend to. Will you ride with me?"

Taken aback by his sudden desire to want her conversation and to have her company, Fern forgot her fatigue. "Gladly," she replied.

"Then change into a riding habit, quickly."

He strode off to the stables, Malachi following with the pony. By the time Fern returned, he was waiting in the yard alone, holding Phantom and Whisper by the reins.

"Mount up," he said tersely, and leaping into the saddle, he headed for the archway. Fern decided to ignore his lack of courtesy in not helping her to mount. She was too curious to know what he wanted to discuss, and what his errand was. Judging by his urgent manner, she thought it must be grave.

She followed him at a canter down the drive, and at the great stone gateway he turned, not down toward the village and the mill, as she had expected, but up toward the moor. That way lay nothing but Fox Brow, and then only the moors. What trouble could lie in that direction? Despite the steepness of the track, Bruno was urging Phantom on, and Fern was hard-pressed to keep Whisper up close behind him.

"Where are we going?" she called out at last, but Bruno's reply, thrown over his shoulder, was lost on the wind. Reaching the brow, he veered off the track across the heather, slowing a little. He was glancing back at her, to see if she was still with him, and then for no apparent reason he reined Phantom in to a canter. Fern rode alongside him.

"Is there trouble, Bruno? Can I be of help?"

She could see his expression in the gathering gloom only dimly, but it was clearly taut and resolute.

"Trouble enough. I've had Mrs. Pickering in my study this last hour."

"Mrs. Pickering?"

"The wife of one of my workers—*our* workers. You wanted to know the problems of running a mill. This is one of them. It's not just ordering and manufacturing and record keeping and buying and selling, but human problems too. Mrs. Pickering's family is half-starving."

"Because of the low wage we pay?"

He snorted. "The wage is uniform with what all the local manufacturers pay. It's Pickering himself. He drinks half his money away at the Woolpack. His wife tells me she stands at the inn door pleading with him for money for food, and many other wives are there after their husbands too. I'll not have it. I won't have starved families laid at my door. And since you are joint owner of the mill, I thought perhaps you too would like to help me persuade the men to see reason."

Fern was bewildered. Why, then, were they galloping up onto the barren moors at night? The Woolpack lay in the center of the village, and the men's cottages too. Bruno was watching her intently in the waning light as they rode. Before Fern could frame a question, her riding crop slipped from her hand.

"Oh, my crop! I've dropped it." Instantly Bruno reined in and dismounted, holding Phantom by the rein as he turned to stoop and search. Fern too dismounted to look. In a moment he found it and handed it to her in silence. Fern looked up at his face and saw the cool lantern in his eyes beginning to fade and be replaced by a light, a gleam of pleasure she had seen reserved only for the Armitage family hitherto. And then suddenly, without warning, high on a windswept hill, he stepped forward, dropping the rein and taking Fern in his arms. Without a word of preamble he kissed her, long and eagerly. Instinctively Fern responded. It was the first time anyone had ever kissed her, apart from Mamma, on the cheek, and it was an exciting experience.

His broad back under her fingers gave her a glow of delight. All her previous dislike of him, intense as it had been, melted with the passionate kiss. His touch evoked such a longing sensation that Fern was in ecstasy.

He stood back at last, his dark eyes raking her face. For a moment Fern could only gaze at him in wonder. How suddenly one could change one's whole view of a man, given the right motivation.

"Well, Fern, are you angry with me?"

"No, Bruno."

"Then how do you feel?"

"Reassured. I thought you hated me."

"Hated you? Hate is a primitive emotion."

"Well, scorned me, then. Now I can ask you what I decided today I would ask you. The time has now come, I think."

"Then ask me. What is it?"

"You said you would not marry me until I asked you, when I was ready. I am ready now, Bruno. Will you marry me, soon?"

It could have been imagination, but Fern fancied she could see the fire in his eyes die away. Once more the cool detachment took its place.

"Very well. I shall ask Amos to publish the banns at once. In a few weeks the wedding can take place. It is your privilege to name the date."

How cold, how unemotional he had suddenly become again! He spoke as if it were a legal or business transaction he was arranging, not a wedding. Fern began to feel confused and angered by his sudden, unforeseen changes of mood.

"Come, we waste time," he cut in sharply, taking her elbow to help her to remount. "We should be up on Thwaite moor by now."

He too remounted and turned Phantom's head toward the moor, up and away from Fox Brow. Sullenly Fern rode beside him, her mind turbulent and perplexed. Now she was contracted to him, this enigmatic, changeable, unpredictable creature. Of her own volition she had been misled into inviting him to be her husband.

Already he was spurring Phantom on ahead, his bride-to-be forgotten.

Chapter 8

The moon was venturing a pallid face over the horizon of crags before they reached the place Bruno sought. Fern caught a glimpse of the vast, expressionless surface of Bilberry Reservoir below in the valley as they galloped. Its inscrutability, and the silence and desolation of the moor, gave the moment a strangely unreal, dreamlike quality. Bruno, riding ahead, suddenly raised his hand and drew up. Fern did likewise, dismounting as he did.

He tilted his head slightly, listening. At first Fern could hear nothing but the moaning of the wind over the heather, but then other sounds drifted to her ears. Voices, men's voices, hushed but excited.

Bruno advanced slowly along the plateau to a ridge of gray crags, Fern following him. Beyond lay a hollow encircled by rocks, and within its bounds some twenty or so men crouched in a ring, their expectant faces illuminated by lantern light. All of them, cloth-capped and still wearing their working corduroys, stared fixedly into the center of the ring, where two gamecocks circled each other warily. Fern could see the light gleaming on the cruel steel spurs attached to the birds' ankles.

"Get at 'im, sithee," one of the men growled at his bird impatiently. Another laughed hoarsely.

"Tha's not fed 'im enough ale, lad. He's not fighting mad."

Bruno's sigh was angry. "So Mrs. Pickering was right," he muttered, as if to himself. "What's not spent on ale is wagered on cockfighting. I'll not have it."

Instantly he strode down the slope into the center of the circle, lifting the birds with a booted foot and tossing them apart. Both cocks' eyes glittered malevolently at the intruder but seemed to deem his spurred and booted feet a dubious proposition. Both retreated sulkily, while their respective owners, seeing the cape-clad figure that had swept down like a vengeful vulture in their midst, scooped up their birds and stowed them away in wicker baskets. All eyes stared fearfully at the master.

"Your cock may not be fighting mad, Enoch Drake, but I am," Bruno said quietly. "This is my land, and I will have no illegal activities here. You all know the law. You know that cockfighting has been illegal these thirty years and more. The magistrates would have no mercy on you if they knew, but I prefer to maintain the law on my land. I shall not tell them, provided you all give back the wagers you have laid tonight and give the money instead to your wives. There shall be no more cockfighting here. Take your birds and go, quietly."

Murmuring, the millhands rose and began packing their belongings. One, his corduroy jacket already grease-grimed and now bespattered with blood, growled in vexation. "I told thee we should a posted scouts on t' hill. Nobody'd listen to me."

Bruno turned on him. "Scouts or no, I would have found you and stopped this. Get home to your wife and children, Ben Pickering, and waste no more of your wages on ale and cocking. I'll hear no more excuses next time your rent is overdue."

The men moved off sullenly to tramp homeward across the moor, taking their lanterns with them. By the moonlight Fern could still see the evidence of their meeting, the strewn feathers and dark patches on the turf that marked the death of many birds. Their corpses were gone, no doubt to fill the village stewpots on the morrow.

Fern and Bruno rode home in silence, passing the gaggle of sullen-faced millhands on the way. Fern made no comment about the incident. Bruno was evidently unpopular with the men for spoiling their sport, but he had been right to protect the law and the village women. She felt grudging respect for his action, but still smarted to think how he had inveigled her into proposing marriage.

They rode on till the Hall came in sight, its gaunt turrets outlined against the moon. By night it wore a shrouded, secretive air, and with its windows all in darkness, it gave a sense of uneasy, waiting silence. Once again Fern felt that strange sense of familiarity mixed with apprehension.

"Who built the Hall, Bruno?" she asked as they cantered up the drive.

"Ralph de Lacy, Dorian's father."

Oddly, Fern shivered. It was the name "Ralph" that had caught her unawares, again with that strange feeling of half-recognition. "Ralph?" she queried.

"The last of many Ralphs in the De Lacy family tree. The name goes back for centuries. I rather think it was a Ralph—or Rafe, as it was spelled and pronounced then—who built the original old Hall."

Her gaze moved to the old wing, protruding until it half-buried itself in the cliffside. That was where Bruno's laboratory lay. Someday she must discover its secrets.

Once more in the stable yard of the Hall, Bruno helped her dismount. "Are you tired, Fern, or shall we talk over supper?" he inquired. She looked up at him, trying to gauge his expression, but it remained inscrutable. Well, she *was* hungry, and Bruno seemed to want to be forthcoming for once.

It being Fanny's evening off, Mrs. Thorpe served supper herself, with Cassie's somewhat gauche help. As she finally withdrew, Fern saw the older woman smiling contentedly to herself. No doubt she was glad to see what appeared to be dawning companionship and closeness between her charges, the new master and his lady.

After supper Bruno saw that Fern was comfortably seated in a deep armchair by the fire. He offered her wine, which she declined, and poured himself a glass of port. Then, taking up a position, feet astride with his back to the fire, he sipped the port in silence for a few moments. Fern waited to discover what he wanted to discuss.

"First, our wedding," he said at length. "Since you wish it to be soon, Amos shall read the banns at once. Shall you go to the church on Sunday to hear the first reading?"

"Indeed, I shall be glad to. And you too?"

"Of course, we must be seen together." He paused for a moment. "What kind of wedding would you like, my dear? The traditional white wedding, I presume?" Without waiting for her reply, he continued, "But not many guests, I think, since we have few friends and no relatives. A ball in the evening, perhaps, for the local worthies if you like."

That would be pleasant, thought Fern, a chance to decorate and enliven the Hall, filling it with gay company and laughter. That was what the old house desperately needed to chase away the shadows.

"Then I shall arrange the guest list and entertainment for the ball, and you the buffet and decoration. You must also visit a dressmaker to order your wedding gown and trousseau. The bill may be sent to me."

He was so practical and so prosaic about the affair, as if it were of no more consequence than arranging the delivery of some bales of wool, but Fern waited patiently to see how the conversation would develop. She would not hinder it by interrupting.

"We shall not go away after the wedding, for there is much to be done at the mill. Later, perhaps, if you feel in need of a holiday." For the first time he looked down at her. "Are you comfortable, Fern?"

"Perfectly, thank you."

"Then I beg you will join me in a glass of wine." And without waiting for her answer, he put down his glass of port on the mantelshelf amid the porcelain figurines and crossed to the sideboard behind her. Fern heard the cabinet door opened, and the clink of glasses.

"Canary? Madeira?" he asked.

"A small glass of Madeira, thank you."

In a moment he returned to offer her the glass and picked up his own. Then he seated himself opposite her, crossing his legs and leaning back in the chair.

"Now, let us talk. We know so little of each other, Fern, and I feel this must be rectified, as we are soon to be man and wife. Tell me about yourself. About your childhood, your family."

It was not easy to talk with those keen dark eyes leveled critically at her across the rim of his glass, but as Fern began, hesitantly at first, to speak of her parents, her schooling, the shock of their sudden death, and her change in circumstances, she began to feel more at ease. He did not interrupt to question, but occasionally nodded as he took a point and his somber eyes registered interest. Gradually Fern felt more and more that she wanted to open up to him, to establish an intimacy hitherto nonexistent. At last she reached the arrival of Mr. Lennox's letter and the new prospect of Yorkshire and marriage. Here she stumbled a little in embarrassment and fell silent. Bruno sat nodding reflectively.

"I see. And tell me, did you feel you had any *rapport* with Yorkshire before Mr. Lennox contacted you? Did your feelings of affinity with this place arise only when you came here?"

"They did. I had never had a chance to visit Yorkshire before, but it is with Brackenroyd only—the Hall and the village—that I have this feeling."

"Interesting," Bruno commented. "Now, tell me of your dreams—no, seriously, I do not mean to mock you. I honestly would like to know in detail what you have dreamed."

Fern regarded him earnestly. It was true there was no hint of mockery in his eyes, only an honest air of inquiry. Very well, then, if he was anxious to atone for his past disbelief, she would give him the opportunity. To meet halfway in compromise would be a better start to marriage than mutual distrust.

Every detail so far as she could remember of the dreams of Annot she recounted, and again Bruno listened thoughtfully as he sipped his port. When Fern had finished, she realized that without noticing she had drained her own glass while talking, and Bruno now rose in silence to refill it. Having done so, he sat opposite her again.

"And have you always dreamed, throughout your life?"

"I don't think so. I'm not aware of doing so before I came here."

"What else have you dreamed of? Other dreams, not connected with Annot?"

"Unimportant ones, I suppose. I forget them at once. Except last night's—I did have a silly dream then."

"What was it? I'd like to know."

"Oh, Mrs. Thorpe had a lot of colored balls of wool, and they were all in a tangle. I was helping her unravel them. And yes, there was a funny kind of gargoyle on the wall, and it had Malachi's face. I can't remember anything else, except that a dog kept barking."

"A dog? Any particular dog?"

"No. I never saw it in the dream. I just heard it."

"I see. Are you afraid of Malachi?"

Fern blushed. "No, I don't know him. You and he always speak in German, and I don't understand, but I'm not afraid of him. Why should I be?"

"Why indeed? He is quite harmless, I assure you, despite his bulky appearance and none-too-handsome features."

He fell silent, and remained so for some minutes. The clock on the mantelshelf gradually began to tick ominously loud in the vacuum, and as Bruno still did not speak, Fern wondered whether he had had enough of conversation and she should leave.

Suddenly he spoke. "Was it you or Mrs. Thorpe who needed help?"

"I beg your pardon?"

"To unravel the wool. Was it *your* wool, and Mrs. Thorpe was helping you?"

"No. I was helping her."

"And what colors were the wools?"

"Oh, I don't know. Red and blue, I think, and perhaps yellow."

"Primary colors. Are you afraid of dogs?"

Fern began to feel irritated. "No, I am not. I think I dreamed of the dog because there is often a dog barking at night near here. Cassie says it's Gabriel's hounds."

He laughed shortly. "Does she indeed? And do you know the legend of Gabriel's hounds?"

"No."

"Are you sure? It could be significant if you do."

"I tell you I do not. What is it?"

He leaned back thoughtfully. "This area is rich in Norse legend, since the Norsemen did come here, you know. It is one of their gods, Odin or Woden, who is said still to roam the Yorkshire moors with his dogs, the soul-thirsty Gabriel hounds. Perhaps you fancied it was your soul they were after, Fern."

Fern sat up angrily. "I did nothing of the kind, since I tell you I did not know the story. In any case, I don't believe it."

"Don't you?" His smile was frankly mocking. "I thought you believed in everything supernatural, communion with the dead, reincarnation, and all."

"And what if I do? We don't have to see and have proved to us all that we believe in. Edgar would agree with me in that."

"I'm sure he would." His smile lingered still, as though provoking her to go on.

Fern, angered by his cool scorn, went on. "You believe in the existence of electricity, don't you, because you've seen its effects. But you've never seen it. Does that make you doubt its existence?"

"Touché, young lady. You are quite right."

Now he was humoring her, as one would a petulant child. Fern rose, putting down her empty glass.

"I am tired. I think I shall go to bed now." He rose politely as she made for the door. In the doorway a belated thought came to her.

"Bruno, why did you say it was significant if I did know of the Gabriel's hounds legend?"

"Because in dreams we reveal what we truly are and worry about. You have told me much of yourself through your dreams."

Fern's eyebrows rose. "Do you mean you asked to hear of them only to analyze them and find out about me?"

"Yes. You are an excellent subject for research. When I have had the opportunity to consider it, I shall tell you the significance of the balls of wool and Malachi the gargoyle. Sleep well, my dear. I think you will dream well tonight."

Fern was so astounded and angered by his impudence that she slammed the door and marched furiously up to her room. The cheek of the man! Professing personal interest in her, and all the while he was only using her as a guinea pig for his research!

"I think you will dream well tonight." Now, what had he meant by that? That she was so incensed that a further dream would be born out of frustration and fury? Ah, well, she really was too tired to fret over his meaning any longer. The day in town and the ride over the moors must have really exhausted her, for her eyes could barely stay open.

Sleep must have come quickly that night. Either that or time suddenly sprang back with the rapidity of a recoiling spring. Fern was afterward never quite certain which. She only knew that in the darkness the door suddenly opened quietly, revealing a bulky figure outlined by the light of the candle in her hand. It was Annot, her eyes reddened and her face crumpled in misery. She put down the candle on the night table and flung her weight, increased now by advanced pregnancy, across the foot of the bed, where she began weeping noisily. Fern would have reached out to touch the shaking shoulders, clad now in finest merino wool instead of workaday serge, but the miserable figure had no substance.

Again the door opened. A chambermaid, trim in black

gown and starched apron and cap, carried in a jug of steaming water, which she set down on the marble washstand.

"Go away," Annot sobbed. Looking up through tear-fringed lashes, she saw the maid. "Oh, it's thee. I thowt it were Mrs. de Lacy, come to tell me off again. I can't do nowt right for her, Rose. She hates me."

"Not at all, miss. She wants you to be more ladylike, that's all. Breaking bread into your soup just isn't done in polite company. She only drew your attention to it in order to help."

The maid's tight lips confirmed her own disapproval. Annot sat up, reaching for the hem of her elegant gown to wipe her tearstained face. Rose clicked her tongue and fetched an embroidered handkerchief from a drawer.

"Then she shouldn't a told me so in front of all t' others. She could a said it in private, but I think she enjoys making a fool of me. Dost know what she said tonight, after dinner as we sat by the fire? 'Reach for the pole screen over there, Annot.' I fetched what she were pointing at, a little embroiderd thing on a frame perched on t' top of a pole, and put it by her. 'No, it's for you, your face is so red,' she said. Now, what were that meant to mean? How were I to know that ladies put it in front of them, to shield their faces from the fire? I thowt she meant me to do some stitching on it, though it were all done so far as I could see. She tittered and looked at the gentlemen as much as to say what a fool I were. No wonder Dorian don't talk to me much now."

"She meant well," Rose reassured as she poured water into the bowl. "And Mr. Dorian is kept busy by his father over the mill. I'm sure you're exaggerating."

"I am not! They hate me, all of 'em! I think even Dorian's sorry he let 'imself in for marrying me now. They all want me out. It's my bairn they want, all to themselves, but they shan't have 'im. I'll die first."

"Now, come, there's no point in upsetting yourself, though it's common in your condition. Let me help you prepare for bed."

"I'm ready for bed."

"Not without a wash you aren't. Don't you know all polite people wash before bed?"

"There's too much fuss over washing and scenting and curling, if tha asks me. If they paid more heed to being nice to folk, they'd do better. There's no honesty or a mite of human kindness in any of 'em. I'd much rather be back wi' my own folk."

"And that's where you'll end up if you don't shape. Now, come." There was a hint of compassion in the maid's voice. Annot rose reluctantly to let Rose help her undress, but even as the gown was lifted over her head with some difficulty she was still murmuring.

"They hide me whenever any of their grand friends come. They're ashamed of me, but I could stand all their scorn if Dorian stood by me. But he's grown cold, Rose, I know it. He no longer seeks me out. He wants no more of me."

Rose made no answer. Annot lifted huge eyes to her, mutely begging her to deny it.

"He'll not wed me, I'm thinking. I'm nearing my time, but there's still no word of a wedding. If it's a lad I bear, happen he'll have me then, eh, Rose?"

The maid compressed her lips, unwilling to be drawn into voicing an opinion. As she went out, Annot sighed, splashed some water on her face from the bowl, and dried herself. In the voluminous folds of her lawn nightshift the telltale bulge was less conspicuous. Annot surveyed her reflection in the mirror thoughtfully, then seemed to make a decision.

As she took up the candle and went out, Fern's curiosity mounted. She followed the spectral figure along the corridor to where Annot was tapping on a door.

"Enter," Dorian's voice invited. Fern watched the girl rush to his bedside, where the young master, already nightshirted, was about to climb into bed. She too, like Annot, saw the unwelcoming surprise on his handsome face. He looked very young and rather ridiculous with his tasseled nightcap flopping over one ear.

"Annot! What are you doing here?"

"Aren't tha—you—glad to see me? You never come to my room now." Her arms were held out invitingly.

"It . . . it isn't proper," he blustered, flapping his hands in bewildered uncertainty.

Annot shrank back, rebuffed. "That's not what tha used to say, Dorian."

He drew himself up proudly. "Father has made me see reason. We must wait till we're married."

Large eyes rose hopefully. "When, Dorian? When will t' wedding be? The bairn'll be here afore we say us vows, if we wait much longer."

His eyes flickered away in embarrassment. "I don't know. When my parents decide, I suppose. But get back to bed now, Annot, or you'll catch cold. And listen—there's a step on the stairs. It could be Father! Go, Annot, go!"

"Shall I come to thee later?" she whispered at the doorway, her pointed little face still alight with hope.

"No, I don't want you here. Go, quickly."

But it was the coldness in his eyes that daunted her. Fern could see clearly the misery in Annot's face as she turned, rejected and forlorn, to leave. Fern stood aside in the doorway to allow her to pass, forgetful of the wraith's insubstance.

Back in the bedroom again, Fern lost sight of Annot. She climbed into bed, and once again time seemed to lose its rational course. The wail of a newborn child pierced the night air and faded; fluid figures came and coalesced and vanished. Sounds filled the air, voices lowered on a sob and voices raised in dispute. Through all the confusion Annot's wraithlike figure, now slender again and bowed, moved slowly.

Fern rose from her bed and followed the forlorn figure of Annot downstairs. In the parlor the De Lacy family sat in solemn conclave, Mr. de Lacy behind the table, Mrs. de Lacy seated apart with her back half-turned, and Dorian standing downcast and irresolute by the window. Another gentleman, middle-aged and portly, sat beside De Lacy, his pince-nez focused on the girl who entered.

Fern stood behind Annot and felt the girl's vulnerable misery. The looks bestowed on her were solemn, critical, and

117

inimical. It was evident a family conference had been in progress up to her entrance. Only De Lacy senior granted her a brief smile.

"We have again been discussing the position, Annot, and wish you to know what we have decided," the old man said gently. His wife darted him an impatient look before cutting in.

"It is settled. Dorian is to marry his cousin Sarah. Her father, Mr. Ramsden here, is in agreement."

The old gentleman nodded, and Annot's face burned angrily. "And what of me, and of my bairn? What of thy promises that Dorian would wed me?" she demanded.

"Now, come, my dear, you must have seen for yourself by now that it would never work. Your way of life and my son's are very different," De Lacy began to point out.

"Tha didn't seem to take much account o' that before!" Annot exploded. "But I'll not stay where I'm not welcome. I'll take t' baby and go in t' morning. That's if Dorian is of a mind wi' thee."

Her look of appeal met Dorian's silent back.

De Lacy stirred to speak, but his wife was too quick for him. "You can leave the child with us. You are not in a position to support him, and you know he will be well cared for here."

"Not I. He goes wi' me. I'm not given chance to see him now while t' nurse keeps him to herself, so there'd be precious little chance of me seeing 'im if I left 'im to thee. He's my son, and I'll keep 'im."

"Now, don't be rash, Annot. He'd have far more opportunities with us than with you."

"I know it, and I'm grateful for the offer, Mr. de Lacy, but he goes wi' me."

"Let's discuss that tomorrow. But in the meantime, be assured that you will not suffer. We shall see to it that you have a regular income, small but adequate, so that you do not starve."

"There's no need o' that, Mr. de Lacy. I'll not be pensioned off. If Dorian no longer wants me, I reckon I'm well

118

shut of him. I wish Mr. Ramsden's daughter joy of him, 'cause I no longer want him."

Dorian's face, pink and sheepish, turned briefly from gazing at the blank windowpane. Annot turned to go, her head held high, ignoring the flutters of protest.

Fern, full of approval of the girl's proud independence, followed her out. They were a thoroughly nauseating lot, the De Lacys; a haughty, disdainful mother, a well-meaning but malleable husband, and a weak, selfish son. Annot was well rid of them all.

Satisfied voices were congratulating themselves in the parlor. Amalgamation between the De Lacys and the Ramsdens was undoubtedly to the mutual benefit of their trade, both families being woolen-mill owners. No wonder Mrs. de Lacy wore a complacent smile as Annot left, a disreputable potential daughter-in-law now happily replaced by a wealthy one.

"That bitch'll not have my William," Annot was muttering as she climbed the stairs. "That Sarah Ramsden can toil for an heir for 'em, they'll not have my son."

Determination jutting her little chin, Annot took a cloak from her bedroom and went along the corridor to a farther room. She opened the door softly. Over her shoulder Fern could see a candle burning on a side table, a great wicker cradle, the low fire in the fireplace encircled by a huge mesh fireguard, and beyond the chenille-covered table a cot where a nursery maid lay sleeping.

Annot advanced stealthily to the cradle and bent over it. Then, cautiously, she lifted the sleeping child and bundled him in one of the cradle blankets and crept to the door. The baby stirred and whimpered, but Annot laid a finger to his lips, which he began sucking noisily. The sleeping maid did not move.

Out of the house and away Annot sped, Fern following close. Down into the village the girl ran, holding the child close to her breast. At the cottage alongside the church she stopped, knocking at the door imperatively. After a moment Radley appeared in his nightshirt.

"Annot, lass, come in," he said in surprise.

"I've no time, Father. Take t' baby and ask me mam to get 'im out o' Brackenroyd. Take him to cousin Ida's i' York, or somewhere safe. The De Lacys won't 'ave him, tha mun see to that. Promise me."

"Aye, we will. But what of thee, lass?"

"Don't fret for me. But take care o' William. That's all I ask."

And just as suddenly as she came, she was gone. Fern could feel no breeze though she saw how the wind ruffled the churchyard trees, bending them like eerie figures in the moonlight. Annot, to her surprise, was directing her steps back toward the Hall.

To the lake, that's where she was heading. Fern, knowing the girl's destiny, shuddered fearfully but knew that she could not change what was to happen. The girl's footsteps left imprints in the frost-speckled grass as she walked purposefully through the copse of trees and down to the lake's edge. There she paused and looked back to the house; then, sighing deeply, she dropped her cloak on the lakeside and stepped slowly in. Fern watched, petrified. Powerless to change fate, she stood as Annot's small figure slowly receded, step by step. At last, long hair floating on the water, her head disappeared. No sound broke the silence. Save for a few bubbles on the surface and a forlorn cloak at the water's edge, there was no longer any trace of Annot Radley.

Fern felt sick, nauseated by the De Lacys' inhuman treatment of the poor girl, which had led to this final, irrevocable act. Tears gushed to her eyes, tears of anger and frustration. Then, through the tears she saw a figure on the far side of the pool, watchful and silent. It was a woman in white, pale and spectral, and as Fern looked at her, her anger changed to horror. It was no living creature, she knew instinctively, but some spirit who came to witness a Radley's humiliation, a being somehow connected with Annot—and with herself, for the figure looked at her from hollow eyes, filling her with terror.

Fern shivered violently, the sensation of a foglike substance invading her nostrils and lungs returning with terrifying insistence as it had once before, choking and menacing. In a crazy sort of way Fern felt drawn to the creature, though she was repelled by her, and felt she could not resist walking around the lake toward the fearful thing. But before she could move her feet, the vision began to fade, slowly, like morning mist dissipated by dawn sunlight. As the last vestige disappeared, a dog's cry echoed distantly, its howl lingering faintly and charged with foreboding. Fern awoke suddenly, to find herself in bed, the blankets over her head, but she was shivering like one in an ague. What—or who—was the frightening figure in the dream who came to watch Annot die?

She could not wait to tell Bruno of this latest dream, of how Annot was driven to her death. He listened intently.

"Now the story is ended, will your preoccupation with your great-grandmother cease, I wonder?" he asked at length.

"It is done, Bruno. You can restore her picture, and the notes if you wish. But there is still something amiss. Would you—to please me—have Annot's grave opened?"

"Opened? Why?"

"I don't know. I just feel there is some final ... mishap, of some kind, to be put right."

"She cannot be buried in the churchyard, you know."

"I know."

He sighed deeply. "Very well. If that will put an end to your obsession, I agree."

He was so reasonable, so patient, that Fern could not bring herself to tell him of the other creature, the one whose presence was far more terrifying than ever Annot's had been. He would think her even more neurotic if she spoke of this new visitation, and since the wedding was so near, perhaps it would be best to keep silent. With luck she would dream no more.

Bruno's expression was puzzled that night at dinner. "I had the gardeners dig up Annot's grave today," he commented at last over dessert. "She is now reburied, close by, and I think you need fret for her no more."

Fern laid down her spoon. "Then there was something wrong. What was it, Bruno?"

"She had been buried face-downward. Why, I do not know,

but it seems your misgiving was not unfounded. Now I hope you will be content."

Fern smiled her gratitude, though inwardly she burned with anger. Not at Bruno, but at the inhumanity of the earlier De Lacys. Not content with humiliating and maltreating Annot, they had subjected her to this final indignity. No wonder the poor child's restless spirit had roamed here, pleading to be restored to face her Maker, though denied a churchyard grave. Poor Annot. Poor maid, rest in peace now, Fern thought. The Radleys will come into their own soon. After the wedding, a Radley will inherit what you and your son, William, were denied.

She looked across the table at Bruno. A smile lighted his dark eyes, for he knew he had pleased her by indulging her whim about the grave. She smiled back. Marriage to this man would have its pleasant side, after all.

Cassie was bubbling with excitement as she helped Fern prepare to go to church on Sunday morning. "Tha mun look thy best, miss, to go to t' spurrings," she said excitedly.

"Spurrings? What's that?" Fern asked.

"Why, when t' vicar calls t' banns for thy wedding. We call it spurrings."

And it seemed as if all the village showed Cassie's excitement, for the little gray-stone church was crowded. Word had evidently got about that De Lacy banns were being read. Pale spring sunlight flickered into the gloomy church interior through the high arched windows. It was God's benison on their union, Fern thought optimistically, as, led by Bruno's firm arm, she took her seat in the high-backed family pew. The brass plaque on the end of the pew announced "De Lacy" proudly, affirming it as the seat of honor of the family who gave the village its patronage and protection. Curious faces turned, unobtrusively, to survey Fern and her straight-backed escort, the glint of inquiry in the villagers' eyes belying their stolid expressions.

"If anyone knows of any impediment why these two should not be joined together in holy matrimony ..." Edgar Amos' voice intoned, and for a moment there was an interrogatory silence. Fern half-expected the ghost of Annot to sidle from the shadows to upbraid the De Lacy who now sat in the family pew; then she dismissed the silly notion. Annot now lay content in her woodland grave.

Outside the church porch afterward Bruno stood in the sunlight and chatted amicably with a still-cassocked Amos. Fern smiled at the villagers as they filed out past the group, though no smile was vouchsafed her in return. Only a few desultory, assessing stares flickered over her and away. Two elderly ladies in Sunday bonnets stood, heads together, whispering.

"Every inch a Radley, that one."

"Not so loud, Emily. She'll hear."

"Better-looking, happen, and walks well. What's that tha says, Nellie?"

"Lower thy voice, love."

"She'll never hear. And there's a sight more she'll never hear an' all."

"How dost mean, Emily?"

"About t' other one. He'll never let on to her about t' other."

"What other, love? What's tha talking about?"

"Tha mean tha hasn't heard? Well, I never! Fancy thee not knowing about her! I thowt all t' village knew. Well, come on, else us roast'll be burnt up in t' oven."

They moved down toward the lych-gate, out of hearing, but Fern had overheard. What did they mean? Another woman? Did Bruno have another woman on his mind? Then was their marriage only to carry out old Thomas' will, after all?

Fern felt the hot rush of blood in her throat. She stared at Bruno furiously, resenting the calm way he chatted with Amos, as if all was well and straightforward. Was he too, like Dorian once before, simply toying with her while all the time he loved another? She must demand the truth from him just as soon as they were alone.

Fern could not wait until Sunday lunch was over. Angrily she told Bruno what she had overheard outside the church and demanded an explanation. Bruno smiled indulgently.

"Rubbish. You should know better than to eavesdrop on

old maids' gossip. There's no truth in it at all. Speculation such as that passes idle moments entertainingly for such as the old Misses Hirst. I daresay Emily was simply teasing Nellie, pretending she knew more than her sister, that's all. Now, let's talk of our wedding plans."

Mollified, and satisfied that he was speaking the truth, Fern entered into discussion of the ball for the guests and the ball for the tenants and millhands which was to follow on the next evening. Luke, Bruno told her, had agreed to give Fern away at the wedding service, and Fabia to act as her matron of honor.

"And Phoebe should be a bridesmaid too," Fern suggested.

Bruno shook his head. "She will not. We have asked her."

Fern was surprised. "Little girls usually welcome the opportunity to dress up. Why not?"

He shrugged his broad shoulders. "It seems she has not taken to you, for some reason."

"You mean she dislikes me. I feel it, and yet I don't know why, for I like her immensely."

"Feelings need not necessarily be mutual. If she does not feel warmly toward you, for whatever reason, it would be better to accept it and leave well alone."

So that was that. Phoebe would not be a bridesmaid, but Fern still felt hurt that she could not communicate her warm feelings to the child, though Phoebe showed her love of Bruno openly. Still, as Bruno advised, best wait and let matters take their course.

The ensuing weeks were fully occupied for Fern with visits to the dressmaker to order her trousseau, with Fabia's help in the choice of materials and patterns, and to the shoemaker and the haberdasher in Bradford. Choosing shoes reminded her of her promise to buy clogs for Phoebe.

"The village clogmaker has the pattern for Phoebe," Fabia told her, and it was while Fern stood in his tiny shop, flag-stoned and low-beamed, that she saw the beshawled village women putting their heads together and whispering while they waited for the clogmaker to heat up new irons. She feigned not to notice, watching instead the clogger's slow, sure movements as he sought among his cardboard patterns, and then, having found Phoebe's, he brought forward a sackful of wooden blocks, roughly shaped.

"What'll it be, miss? Sycamore dost fancy, or alder or beech? All on 'em's hard-wearing."

Fern looked at him in bewilderment and heard the women's snickers. The old man's leathery face watched her with a kindly enough expression. "What does Mrs. Armitage usually order?"

"Beech, as I remember." He selected a block and swept his stock knife along its length, nodding in satisfaction. "New leather for t' uppers shall it be, or mill leather?"

"Oh, new, of course." Again the women behind sniggered. The old man explained.

"I'm only asking, as most folks prefer leather from t' carding machines in t' mill. That's waterproof, dost see, having soaked up so much oil."

"Oh, I see. Then I'll have that, and thank you for explaining. How long will they take to make?"

He paused for thought, calculations wrinkling his weathered brow. "I'll have 'em on t' stithy this aft. Tha'll not be wanting brass toe caps, I take it. Metal clips on tomorrow, and then t' irons; say Friday morning. Will that suit?"

Fern was glad to escape the little shop with its clutter of knives and benches, tanning horse and rollers, and array of metal and gas brackets. It was not its smoky closeness but the mocking smiles of the women she wanted to flee. They ridiculed her for her ignorance of what was vital to them; but why did she fear them instead of trying to befriend them? Their faces, gaunt from struggle and worry, wore distinctly hostile looks. And she had clearly heard the name Radley spat out in a tone of scorn and hatred as she left.

Chapter 9

Fern gazed out of her bedroom window, her heart seeming to knot with excitement. It was her wedding day. The first faint glow of morning sunlight was blushing through the fine veil of mist that blanketed the river, and the very air seemed to hold out a promise of fine weather. With luck the sun would shine on her nuptials, an omen of happiness and joy.

Already Brackenroyd Hall had taken on a festive air, groomed for the day. The dining room and the library had been decorated with hundreds of wax candles in silver sconces and in the chandeliers, mirrors gleamed in every alcove and recess to reflect their glow, and garlands of flowers hung from every vantage point. Tonight the ladies and gentlemen would dine and dance here in honor of the master of Brackenroyd's wedding. The servants, now greatly increased in number for the event, hurried busily about their duties in preparation; from below, Fern could hear their laughter and the clatter of dishes. A wedding had brought Brackenroyd Hall to life again, revived it to the bustle and joyful activity it had needed.

Gone now was its former gloom and silence. With its new-found activity Fern had felt her own spirits lift over the past week. Annot's memory now lay at peace, no longer troubling her sleep, and if Fern felt an uneasy twinge on recollecting the other, shadowy figure, she brushed it quickly aside. Of late no more dreams had troubled her. Sleep had been deep and restful. And after today, her nights should be always content and secure, with Bruno at her side.

She smiled to herself as she thought of the room she had had prepared for their bridal chamber, a grander and more spacious room than the one where she had slept hitherto. The finest tester bed in the house, with its fluted pillows and laven-der-scented hangings and coverlet, now stood there awaiting them, Persian rugs on the floor, chairs upholstered in gold satin, and tawny velvet curtains at the high windows. On the walnut dressing table candles in silver candlesticks waited to light their wedding night, glittering on the cut-glass bottles and pierced silver trays. Scented winter roses and hothouse hyacinths would make the chamber fragrant. The cheval mirror, supported by two gilt cupids, would reflect their union.

Her reverie was interrupted by an excited tapping at the door. She turned as Cassie entered, her eyes glowing and wisps of fair hair escaping from beneath her cap.

"We're fair throng down in t' kitchen, miss, wi' so much still to be done, but I were dying to see t' wedding dress, so Mrs. Thorpe said I could come and take a peek, so long as I didn't touch. That's if you didn't mind, she said."

Her mistress smiled, and crossing to the bed, she lifted the swaths of tissue which protected the creation. Fanny, as the superior maid, had been appointed lady's maid and would no doubt be vexed if she heard Cassie had been allowed to touch the gown. Nevertheless, Cassie's fingers stretched out despite herself as she cried out in admiration.

"Oh! It's beautiful! It's lovely! You'll be the bonniest bride t' village has ever seen!"

And indeed it was. Yards of creamy damask clustered over a satin undergown, the overskirt lavishly trimmed with cream lace, the bodice demurely high-necked and tucked. Fern declined to notice Cassie's work-roughened fingertips as she caressed the luxurious folds.

"And here is the cap I am to wear also," Fern said, turning to lift from the dressing table the little cream bonnet of silk, again trimmed with the lace and scattered with feathers. Cassie's fingers flew to her mouth in breathless admiration. Her sighs and squeals of delight were immensely satisfying to the bride. A light tap on the door preceded Fanny's entrance.

"Heavens above!" the maid exclaimed in horror. "What *are* you doing, Cassie?"

"It's all right, Fanny," Fern reassured her. "Go now, Cassie, back to your duties. Soon the dressmaker will be here, and she and Fanny will dress me. You shall see me before I leave for the church, I promise."

Madam Fixby, the dressmaker from Bradford, and Fanny were deft and sure in their buttoning and pinning, repinning and final stitching, but as they grew more and more excited as time passed, Fern felt herself growing oddly more detached from the frenzy. Bruno too would now be preparing to go to church, down in Luke Armitage's little schoolhouse. He had driven down early this morning while Fern was still in bed, leaving word that he would send Fabia back up to the Hall in the coach. The next time Fern would see him would be before the altar, where he and she were to plight their vows of constancy and love. . . .

Fabia arrived, aglow with excitement and more attractive than Fern had ever seen her in the new gown of palest blue silk Fern had chosen. Fabia leaned against the doorjamb, breathless in admiration.

"Oh, Fern, you look beautiful!" Fern looked at the reflection in the pier glass. Indeed, the froth of lace, the creamy luster of the damask, needed no enhancement with jewelry. The demure cap nestling on her piled gold hair was truly becoming. She felt as radiant as a bride should.

She picked up the little white Bible she had elected to carry, and cast a final look about the chaotic bedroom before she left. No more would she return to this room at night alone, a maiden, vulnerable and helpless. No more a prey to irrational dreams born of apprehension. By tonight she would be a wife. Bruno's wife. The thought was a very pleasant one.

Luke was waiting in the vestibule, and Fern warmed to the glow of admiration in his eyes as he helped her and Fabia into the coach. The sun, which had slipped briefly behind the clouds as they rode, burst out again magically as they drew up at the church, lighting its old gray stones and the few curious onlookers who clustered at the lych-gate.

As in a dream Fern let Luke take her arm and lead her into the gloom of the church. The pews were crowded, but Fern noticed no one but the tall breadth of the man who waited by the foot of the altar steps. His back, powerful and solid, made her surge with an emotion she could not define, save that it was a most pleasurable sensation. Edgar Amos, standing a head taller than Bruno at the top of the steps, seemed like a haloed saint where the sunlight from the high windows caught and held his sandy head. The whole scene was unreal to Fern, a tableau whose characters were but lifeless puppets.

But music played, and Amos spoke. Fern heard her own voice speak words, and Bruno too, and then they were turning to go. Bruno's hand cupped her elbow, and slowly, slowly they were moving out. In Fern's ears rang the sound of Amos' voice.

"I now pronounce you man and wife."

So it was done. Now at last she was Mrs. de Lacy and mistress of Brackenroyd. Now nothing could ever take that away from her. She glanced up at Bruno, saw his stern, strong profile as he looked straight ahead, and was happy. A fine match indeed, as the old lawyer Lennox had said. Handsome, clever, rich—what more could one want of a husband?

Respect, perhaps; love, even? Well, that would come. There was all the time in the world now to win his esteem and affection. Fern bowed her head graciously to the villagers, acknowledging their cries, but whether the sounds were of affectionate congratulation or simply grudging admiration at the sight of a personable couple, one could not tell. Still, there was time enough too to win the villagers.

Bruno had never been more charming than tonight, she reflected later as their guests swarmed about the Hall, raising their glasses in toast to a lovely bride and exclaiming at Bruno's good fortune.

"Damn pretty wife you've got yourself," Fern heard one grudgingly admiring millowner remark to Bruno, his own jaded wife prattling incessantly to her daughter nearby.

"Indeed," Bruno rejoined, smiling at her proudly. Serenely Fern moved among her guests, poised and self-assured, smiling contentedly with her attentive husband at her side.

"Your wife adds grace and beauty to the Hall," Sir George Radborne commented to Bruno as he twisted the tips of his waxed moustache appreciatively. His lady wife bowed her head graciously in agreement. "An excellent mistress for Brackenroyd," Sir George added speculatively.

Bruno guided Fern through the throng of guests, introducing them to her with the utmost charm.

"I should like you to meet Dr. Briggs," he said, pausing to bow to an elderly bewhiskered gentleman, who rose, putting aside his wineglass to bow over Fern's fingers.

"Charmed, my dear. Brackenroyd must count itself favored to have acquired a mistress as delightful as yourself. May I present my wife?"

He indicated a fragile-looking lady seated on the velvet sofa, who bowed and inclined her head. Dr. Briggs murmured in Fern's ear, "Forgive her that she does not rise to meet you, Mrs. de Lacy, but I fear she is none too well. A bad chest, you know. But she was determined to come to your wedding."

"I am honored, Dr. Briggs."

"But if you would permit us, I must take her home very soon. You see how her color is mounting."

Indeed the lady did seem rather flushed and unduly bright about the eyes. Fern was at once concerned for her.

"You must take her in the carriage, Dr. Briggs. I shall ask Bruno to instruct Malachi to bring it around at once."

Bruno was quick to understand and act. Swiftly and unobtrusively Dr. Briggs and his wife left the reception, the doctor promising to send word of his wife's welfare in the morning.

The other guests, unaware of the lady's indisposition, continued their toasting and merrymaking throughout the evening. Fern was amazed how the mountains of food laid out on buffet tables, the legs of beef and mutton, the eggs and spring chicken and pigeon and game pies, seemed to disappear with bewildering swiftness. But it was warming to hear the lively chatter to the background of music.

"A governess, did you say?"

The shrill voice, raised in disbelief, cut through the general hum of conversation with the sharpness of a whip crack. Fern involuntarily turned toward the voice. A gaunt-faced woman, sparkling in diamonds and velvet, stood openmouthed as she interrogated her companion. Bruno touched Fern's elbow lightly and steered her away.

Fern tugged her arm free, her cheeks flushed with embarrassment, but before she could utter a word of protest, Bruno forestalled her.

"I know what you would say. But she is of no account and not worth the trouble to argue with. She is a snob."

"But one of your friends, I presume, since you invited her," Fern argued. "She does not think me worthy of you—or of Brackenroyd."

"She is no friend of mine. Simply the wife of one of the local magistrates, and since I invited most of the local dignitaries, she was included. Henceforth she will not be on our visiting list. Come, let us have a glass of champagne. I have not yet toasted my lovely bride."

Unresistingly, Fern let him lead her to the table. Despite her cheeks still flaming with anger, she felt warmed by his protectiveness. He raised his glass, his eyes resting on her over the rim.

"To you, Fern, the loveliest mistress Brackenroyd has ever known. May you find much happiness here."

"And you," Fern whispered. Bruno, inclining his head, kissed her lightly but lingeringly on the cheek. Fern's day of happiness was complete.

Carriages had been ordered for midnight, but by the time the last laughing guests had made their final congratulations and farewells, the grandfather clock in the hall was preparing to strike one. Fern hung happily on her husband's arm, smiling and radiant. The footman closed the door behind the last guest.

"Shall I lock up now, sir?"

"Yes. It is time for bed. Come, Fern."

Together they mounted the wide, shallow staircase, Fern bemused with contentment. At the doorway to their bedroom, Bruno paused, opened the door, and stood back.

"Go now and sleep well, Fern. Tomorrow will be another busy day."

She looked up at him, startled. It was difficult to read from his expression just what he meant.

"Aren't you coming to bed?"

He shook his head, his eyes no longer alight, but dulled, as if with fatigue or worry.

"I have matters to attend to. It will be late before I retire, and I would not wish to disturb you. I shall sleep next door."

Fern stared, unable to hide the hurt, the disappointment in her eyes. His expression softened.

"Tomorrow we must tour all the tenant farms, to receive their congratulations, as is the custom. And in the evening we must attend the tenants' ball. You need to rest well and be refreshed. Good night, Fern."

Abruptly he turned and left her, and hesitantly Fern went into the room she had prepared so lovingly. Fanny came, her pretty face now looking rather weary and hollow-eyed.

"Go to bed, Fanny. I can undress myself," Fern said. "Wake me early in the morning."

Alone again, Fern sat miserably on the bed, fingering its fine coverlet. How ironic for a new bride to be left to sleep alone, even if there was a door connecting her bedroom to the one where Bruno was to sleep. She rose and crossed to the door. From beyond she could hear his footsteps as he paced the parquet floor. Why had he left her alone? Surely not to work on his papers—was there some other reason he would not reveal?

Perhaps he sensed she had married him only for Brackenroyd. Or perhaps he loved another woman, as the two old sisters at the church had implied. Maybe he was tormenting her by his changeable ways, appearing affectionate one moment and cold the next, so as to confuse her. But why?

Fern turned away from the connecting door. She was not going to open it and beg his company. Slowly she undressed and prepared for bed. The sprigged dimity nightgown, specially bought for tonight, had somehow lost its charm, and as Fern hung her magnificent wedding dress away in the closet, she sighed ruefully. Bruno might be trying to teach her a disciplinary lesson in denying her his company tonight, but nothing could alter the fact that she was now rightfully and truly mistress of Brackenroyd. Nothing could take that away from her.

She lay in the great canopied bed, trying to find pleasure in planning what she could now do. Now she could alter or refurnish the Hall, now she could insist on taking a share in the responsibility of running the mill and the estate; but somehow these speculations brought less joy than she had anticipated. Somehow it seemed barren joy without company. The room grew chill as the fire burned low, and Fern felt lonely.

As the firelight dimmed and the room grew dark, Fern began to shiver. It was strangely, unaccountably cold. And the chill had a damp feel to it, clinging and unpleasant. She huddled lower among the blankets and closed her eyes tightly, willing sleep to come. But as her mind began to dull into the half-world between waking and sleeping, the damp chill seemed to grow into an insidious fog, wreathing its way into her nostrils and clamming her throat. Fern gasped for air, moaning.

"No, no, I don't want you!"

Recollection returned. Once before she had experienced this strange sense as she waited to see Annot's story reenacted. And then, as now, she had rejected the horrifying vapor that had threatened to invade her. Why did she fear the miasma so? Was it because its cold, clammy sensation made one think of death?

Terrified, Fern rolled out of bed and stumbled across the

room to the connecting door. There, her hand on the knob and her mouth already open to cry out Bruno's name, she paused.

It was the feel of death; she was certain of it. And yet, in some strange way the sensation was not one of menace. It was more of pleading, of entreaty. She had longed for company—but of the living, not the dead. But if it were the dead who came so persistently and urgently, there must be a reason. She had upheld, had she not, the power of the past even in the face of Bruno's scorn?

Fern made a momentous decision. She would fight the pervasive power no longer. Purposefully she climbed back into the great bed and lay back, relaxing the tension in her muscles and consciously baring her mind of antagonism. Brackenroyd held a strange, secretive air of past tragedy, part of which she had learned in Annot's story, but there was more that still haunted the gloomy old mansion, and its power would not be broken until the truth was known.

The chilly sensation returned, more slowly and insidiously now, less clamorous than before, as though it was aware of her new compliance. And this time as the haze filled her nostrils and throat it no longer brought with it the terror she had felt before. Closing her eyes and breathing slowly, Fern gave herself up completely to the invading mist, feeling it seep and spread throughout her body. A dizzying sensation made her mind reel; she felt as though she were spinning through a vortex, wheeling through space and losing count of time, being sucked down, down, through a black void.

Later, aeons later, it seemed, the strange sensations eddied and died away, and Fern lay bemused, her eyes still closed. When she opened them at last, it did not seem at all strange to find herself lying, not in the huge tester bed, but amid the long grass at the edge of a cornfield. She stared up at the deep azure sky above where the birds swooped and sang, and felt inexpressibly content. Leaning up on her elbow, she gazed downhill where the village lay, peaceful and broodily content in the summer sun. She had better return home before Mother grew angry at her absence.

Brushing the flecks of grass from her cotton skirts and gathering up the basket of eggs beside her, she began to descend the little track that ran down between the fields of ripening wheat and oats, noting as she did the thin, poor quality of the crops this year. Frost in May followed by the long drought in June had rotted many of the fields already; pray heaven the weather would not turn wet before harvest, or there would be little bread in the village again this winter.

In Brackenroyd's main street she passed a number of her neighbors, women outside their cottage doors busily plucking a chicken for the evening meal when their menfolk returned from the fields, or fetching their washing in from where it hung over fragrant rosemary bushes to dry. They all smiled or waved a greeting as she passed. At the gate of her home, right next to the little gray church, she turned in. Of course, Mother was at market today. The cottage would still be empty.

She dawdled in the garden, savoring the scent of Mother's treasured sweet briar roses from which she made her own toilet water and metheglin, admiring the tumble of honeysuckle framing the doorway. She loved the flowers in the little garden, the violets and gillyflowers, the marigolds and primroses, but not half so tenderly as she nurtured her own little plot of herbs in one corner.

Mother had been quick to spot her daughter's clever ways with herbs, years ago, and she had seen to it that the girl learned the arts of making simples and recipes from old Mother Uttley, whose wisdom and knowledge of cures for ills was known far and wide. Mother Uttley, her myopic old eyes peering closely but not unkindly as she supervised, had taught the little maid all she knew, and the girl was grateful that there was one skill she could now perform well.

The fragrance of her own plot filled her nostrils. Lavender, alive with humming bees, vied with sage and rosemary. Rosemary—dew of the sea, the curate had said it meant. What a beautiful name. Marjoram, sweet-scented geranium, its leaves smelling of mint; clove gillyflowers—all had their part in her life, either to preserve and make into jelly like the violets, or

135

to candy, like the rose-petals, or to form essential ingredients in her simples and compounds for treating afflictions such as the cough or a bellyache. Even her family, who considered her inept and slow at all else, acknowledged her now as a mistress of the art of making potions. The whole village found occasion to seek her help from time to time, and she was glad. No written recipes did she keep of her mixtures, nor did she use Culpeper's herbal, like they said Mistress de Lacy did up at the Hall—before she died, that was, God rest her soul—for she could neither read nor write, but she was proud of her one skill nonetheless.

Unlatching the cottage door, she went down the two steps into the flagstone-floored parlor. The fire was burning low, and she replenished it with firewood to keep the iron stewpot slung over it still at a simmer. Pulling off her white-linen cap, she let her hair fall about her shoulders, savoring the aroma of meat in the pot mingled with the scent of the herbs hung in clusters on the low beams. She seated herself on the high-backed bench, and as she did so, a marmalade cat crawled out from beneath, stretching her four paws delicately.

"Come, Tibb," murmured the girl. The cat leaped obediently onto her lap, kneading her knees with its paws before circling around and around and settling itself to sleep. It was a cozy room, wooden platters on the dresser nestling cheek by jowl with jugs of creamy milk and ale, pieces of salt pork hanging from hooks against the whitewashed walls, a leather bucket of water by the door, fresh-drawn from the spring.

The girl shifted the unwilling cat from her lap. As she lifted the basket of brown eggs from the floor and placed it on the oak table, a knock came at the door. A woman's flushed face peered around the edge.

"Oh, tha's come home. I'm that glad, as I wanted thee to make a salve for me, if tha would."

The girl indicated the high-backed bench by the window, and the woman eased her bulk gratefully onto it.

"It's our Will, he has a bad rash on his face, that spotty he won't go out. Canst make us an ointment that'll clear it? I've no wish to pay good pence to t' apothecary if tha can help.

He's starting to pick at them spots, he'll not leave the scabs alone. I fear he'll end up badly pockmarked, and it'd be a shame, such a good-looking lad."

He was quite handsome, the girl reflected as she took pots and jars from the press and took down the pestle and mortar from the dresser. But too vain for a fieldworker, though perhaps all youths were self-conscious of their looks. Will was . . . what? Seventeen? Four or five years younger than herself, but already the focus of many a Brackenroyd lass's eye. Swiftly she pounded, milfoil and bugle, samile and a dash of wine, while the woman's eyes roved curiously around the parlor, missing nothing.

Strange, thought the girl, but people always seem to treat those with a disability as if they were simple or even weren't there. But perhaps it was not surprising, in the circumstances.

The door opened again, and a pretty girl entered, her dark eyes darting quickly from the girl to the woman.

"Oh, Phoebe, I just came to ask thy sister to make me a salve for Will," the woman said quickly, as though to explain her presence. The girl at the table looked up and met her sister's gaze. There was in Phoebe's eyes the hostile look, the guarded, distrustful look which had always been there.

"Oh, aye, that's all she's fit for."

The girl continued to pound in silence, as though she had not heard. The woman took it as a cue.

"Poor thing," she clucked, shaking her head sadly. "She's allus been a bit queer, hasn't she? Such a shame, thy mother being such a good woman an' all, to be burdened wi' a simpleton. Still, she has thee, and that's a blessing, Phoebe. Yon poor lass'll never get herself a husband, I'm thinking, but I doubt tha'll have any trouble in that direction."

Phoebe's smile was sardonic. "She's not so daft as she makes out, that one. She's sly, she is. Many folk mistake her quiet ways for gentleness or madness, but she's all there, if I'm not mistaken."

"Aye, well, thy mother dotes on her, and that's a fact. But folk often do favor the runt of a litter. Dost recall Mistress Sykes and her little clubfooted, squint-eyed lad? She near died of a broken heart when he died, and he one of eleven too."

The girl never raised her eyes while they spoke across her, nor did she feel rancor at their words. It was true her mother was fond of her, and would be as fond of Phoebe if her sister's tongue was less vicious and hurtful. But why did folk always behave thus, shouting to poor old blind Hawthorne as if he were stone deaf instead of acutely sharp-eared, and talking of her in her presence as though she were a stone statue instead of only short of the one faculty?

She scraped the greasy unguent out of the mortar and scooped it into a little pot. The woman stopped prattling and came to take it from her.

"Thanks, love. Is our Will to put this on his face . . . tonight? Every night?"

The girl nodded vigorously. The woman turned to Phoebe. "Pity though, isn't it? She's a bonny lass, and very capable wi' her herbs and things. Pity she's not right." She tapped her forehead significantly.

None of the women had noticed the door open, nor the kindly faced woman in the doorway whose expression darkened as she overheard. They all started when she spoke, quietly but emphatically.

"My daughter is perfectly well, mistress, neither simple nor to be pitied. She is a gentle, well-behaved, and dutiful child, and a blessing to us all."

The visitor flushed. "I'm sorry, Mistress Radley, I'd no wish to offend thee. I were simply sorry for thee, one daughter so bright and clever, and the other—"

"The other just as clever, just as beloved, but the good Lord chose, for what reason we cannot tell, to keep her silent. That's all that ails the child, mistress, and I'd thank you to remember it."

Snatching up the pot of salve, the neighbor fled, her stammering protests silenced by Mistress Radley's firm manner. The mother stood by the door after she had gone, surveying her two daughters.

"I'll never know why it was the Lord chose to grant me just

the two daughters, the one who chatters overmuch and the other who has never spoken a word."

Phoebe turned and began to take down the plates from the dresser, while her sister cleared the table of her herbs.

"But I know this," Mistress Radley continued in a gentle tone. "I love thee both greatly, and I wouldn't have either of thee otherwise. Now, come, sharp about it, or thy father'll be home afore we've his supper ready."

Father came home from the fields, work-weary and aching, when the sun sank too low for work to continue. But despite his weariness, he found time to commend his wife and daughters for their care and concern for him.

"I'm a lucky man, wife," he grunted as he pushed his chair back from the table, patting his replete stomach in satisfaction. "Never had man a comelier nor a more capable wife, nor two bonnier lasses. I'll wager not King Charles himself is better cared for nor I am."

Mistress Radley chuckled softly. "That's true, husband. I'll wager Queen Henrietta Maria never made her husband a down mattress such as I made, or if she did, it were no softer nor warmer."

Phoebe yawned and said she was going to bed. Her sister sat by the fire, mending a rent in her homespun green kirtle. Her mother put the last of the platters away on the dresser, lit a tallow candle from the fire, and touched the girl's shoulder.

"Come, Catherine. Time for bed, lass, if tha's to be up early in t' morning."

Obediently she rose and put the mending aside. In the bedroom she undressed quickly in the dark so as not to disturb Phoebe, and climbed into bed alongside her. In the gloom she heard her sister mutter, "I wonder what goes on in thy mind, Catherine? I've seen that look in thy eye—tha's hiding summat, I know it. But what's the use of asking thee what it is—tha couldn't tell me."

Catherine lay back, smiling to herself in the darkness. Phoebe rolled over and propped herself up on her elbow.

"But I wish I knew what it were. Is it a lad, Kate? Hast thee a lad?"

Catherine closed her eyes, and Phoebe fell back with a sigh.

"What use if you had?" Phoebe grumbled on. "He couldn't get a word out of thee, no one can. No, it can't be a sweetheart, for who'd find joy in a dumb puppet? I would to heaven I knew what went on i' that head o' thine. I know one thing—tha's not daft, as the villagers all think. Tha's cunning, more like, knowing far more than folks think. What more didst learn from Mother Uttley, Kate? Did she learn thee how to make cows miscarry, or women even? Did she learn thee any spells?"

Catherine shook her head firmly, but Phoebe was growing excited with the idea.

"Tha can cure warts, and wi'out touching them who has the warts, too. Wouldn't it be just as easy to cure or harm some-one else wi'out touching them, wi'out being near them, even? Was it you made Mistress Banforth miscarry last spring?"

Catherine sprang up, shaking with denial; she had no words to utter. She could hear Phoebe's laugh.

"Tha could have done it, Kate, for she beat thee in the contest for baking a cake at the fair. Tha were ill-pleased, I recall. But I didn't think as tha had the power to get thy re-venge. Well, I never. Tha's in a fair way to becoming a witch, I'm thinking, after Mother Uttley's learning thee."

Catherine's fierce desire to deny the vile charge burst into anger. Involuntarily her hand rose, and she cracked it across Phoebe's cheek. Phoebe swore and grabbed at her hair, and the tussle would undoubtedly have become a fight if their mother had not entered to bid them good night.

In the darkness after she had gone, Phoebe burrowed down under the rough woolen blanket, muttering as she did, "Tha'd better take care, that's all I can say, Catherine Radley, if ever the witchfinder comes this way. He'll find thee out for cer-tain."

Catherine turned to face away from her, trying to rid her heart of the dreadful feeling she had toward her sister. It was not charitable to hate, but Phoebe was so cruelly provoking. She must try to pray, to become calm and forget the hurtful lies, to realize it was difficult for anyone to understand when she was unable to tell them anything.

Phoebe had been so far from the truth in her wild guesses about her ability to cast spells, and yet so near the truth. She had seen something in Catherine's eyes which had betrayed her secret. Catherine's anger melted instantly as she remembered. It was difficult to keep the light out of her eye, the bounce from her step, when she felt so happy.

But she would hug her secret to herself for some time longer yet—how could she do else, when she had no voice to reveal her confidence? People would just have to guess at the reason for her happiness, and it was odd that Phoebe had been so quick to guess aright.

It *was* a lad—a man, rather. She had been up in the copse gathering firewood when he found her, and he had addressed her politely and with a warm smile that creased the corners of his eyes. He had taken her silence for maidenly modesty and been the more charmed, she could tell, and without invitation he had gathered and bound the wood for her, bidding her sit and rest on a fallen tree trunk while he did so.

"What is your name?" he had asked at last when she made to go. Shaking her head, she had turned and moved to the edge of the clearing. "No, wait, tell me," he had ordered, and there was urgency in his voice. "Then I shall find out for myself," he had said, following her to the edge of the wood. Then she had turned frightened eyes on him, fearful lest he accompany her into the village and set idle tongues wagging. He had grasped her wrist, sensing her fear.

"Do not fret, I shall not embarrass you. But I did not know Brackenroyd held so fair a maid, and now I have seen you, I must know more of you. Will you tell me who you are?"

Shaking her head, she had run down the crags, stumbling under the bulky weight of the firewood, hearing his voice behind her on the wind. "I shall find you, little one. And discover your name. We shall meet again."

Breathlessly she had fallen at last by the edge of the cornfield, hidden in the long grass. And there she had lain until it was time to go home, finding pleasure in recalling the deep timbre of his voice and the laughter lines about his dark eyes. And finding pleasure in knowing that he had found her desirable. She was certain she would see him again, for there was determination in his laughing words. There was a strength, a purposefulness about the handsome young man that made it inevitable.

He did not know her name. It was odd to realize now, in the stillness of the night alongside Phoebe's snoring figure, that neither did she know his. Everyone knew everyone in Brackenroyd, but he was a stranger, no common fieldworker or weaver. Strangely, she had not until this moment questioned who he was, but simply accepted his arrival in her life as inevitable. He was here, they would meet again, and he would still desire her.

A roseate cloud of happiness settled over Catherine as she neared the edge of sleep. Then, just on the brink, she started back into wakefulness. Somewhere out in the night a dog was howling pathetically at the moon, and in that instant she knew. With a sudden flash of insight she foresaw that the supreme happiness that would come with this dark stranger would be shattered at its zenith by the hand of death. It was to come. It was inevitable. Gabriel's hounds had sounded the knell.

Chapter 10

She opened her eyes, trying to banish the stab of apprehension and the prevision of tragedy brought on by the dog's cry. She stared about her in confusion. Dawn glimmered through a high leaded window, not a narrow cottage slit, illuminating a bedchamber of great beauty and taste. No Phoebe snored by her side; there were only the luxurious brocade hangings of the great bed.

It took some moments to orient herself. She was Fern, not Catherine. Fern Saxby, or rather Fern de Lacy now. And yet it was difficult to accept. But a few moments ago, it seemed, she had been simmering with frustration, yearning to deny Phoebe's accusations, and trying to quell her anger with thoughts of the man in the copse.

The man. Fern sat upright, startled. He had been the image of Bruno, tall and powerful of build, piercingly dark-eyed and black-haired. The same aquiline nose and dignity of bearing, he had been Bruno to the life, save that his was a kindlier, gentler expression. Was it all a dream, then, where Bruno, the last person in her thoughts before she slept, had played so prominent a part? Was it all a dream of wishful thinking, Bruno transformed to the sympathetic, understanding man she would like him to be?

It could not be. In the half-light of dawn she still felt more of Catherine in her than Fern, could still feel the mute girl's dismay and frustration. And she remembered the sensations of last night as she yearned for company and that dank, cold chill had enveloped her. It had been no dream. Catherine had come back, had possessed her body.

Hesitantly she rose from the bed, reaching for her dressing robe, half-minded to pursue her day normally as Fern and yet half-reluctant to dismiss the gentle Catherine. It was a hard choice to make.

"Bruno."

She had spoken his name before she was aware of it, and reproached herself inwardly. There was no need to call on his advice, for he would dismiss her silly dreams as yet more evidence of her instability. Nevertheless, she crossed to the connecting door.

"Bruno?"

There was no answer. Fern tried the handle, but the door would not yield. It was locked. Angrily she turned away. How foolish to think of approaching him when he was obviously so determined to keep her at arm's length.

Footsteps approached. It would be Fanny with early-morning tea, or possibly Cassie with jugs of hot water. Fern opened her bedroom door and saw Fanny, tray in hand.

"Put my tea down here, Fanny, and I'll take the master's in to him."

She ignored the girl's inquiring glance, taking from her the tray with its china pot and cream jug and the pretty patterned cup and saucer, and watched her set down the other tray on her nightstand.

Fern followed her into the corridor and waited till the maid had retreated downstairs, then tapped at Bruno's door. When no answer came, she entered quietly. Bruno lay sprawled, fully dressed and fast asleep, in a chair by the fire. But it was not the fact that he was dressed that startled her, but that his bed was still neatly turned back awaiting its occupant. He had not been to bed at all, and what was more, his breeches were mud-spattered, mud-caked riding boots lay on the hearth rug before him, and he still clasped a riding whip in his hand. Asleep, he looked vulnerable and carefree. Fern felt a maternal glow of affection and pride.

"Bruno, are you awake?"

She spoke softly, but he awoke at once, his sunny sleeping expression retreating rapidly into a clouded, suspicious look. He half-raised the whip in his hand before he mastered himself; then he dropped it to the floor and raised his arms to her. Fern would have run to them had not the tray in her hands impeded her. Slowly he lowered his arms and shook his head slowly, like one who has drunk too heavily the night before.

"God, what a night," he muttered hoarsely. "Such dreams, such nightmares."

Fern bit her lip, reluctant to speak of her own visions, but she saw the opportunity to score off him.

"Dreams are for those with a problem, you tell me, for those who have not yet found themselves."

He looked up sharply, his eyes glowing under their bushy brows. "And you think I have no problems? Did you in your sublime innocence believe you had the sole monopoly of problems? I too have mine, wife, and you are not the least among them."

His voice was so venomous, so full of spite and scorn, that Fern shrank. She banged the tray down sharply on the table beside him and rushed from the room, fuming with anger. How could one please such a man! He was cruel, unpredictable, and vicious! In his sleep he had looked so defenseless and human that she had been induced to feel a warmth for him she had not believed possible, but with a few malicious words he had killed off that feeling at birth. She felt cheated.

He appeared later in the dining room for breakfast, having changed now from his mud-stained clothes into a Norfolk tweed suit, but he still looked perhaps a trifle paler than usual, she thought. He ate morosely and with diffidence. Fern began to feel concerned; perhaps he was not well.

"Did you not sleep well last night, Bruno?"

"Why do you ask?" The words were sharp, brittle, and defensive.

"I noticed your bed had not been slept in. Did you ride out early this morning?"

"I did not. I rode all night. But I would prefer, madam, that you do not question me. What I do is my own affair and none of yours."

Fern was stung beyond endurance. It was useless to feel concern for this insufferable man. "Very well," she replied in level tones that belied the tumult inside her, "I concede that your affairs are private, and I claim the same right for myself. Henceforth I will not confide in you, nor expect you to do so in me. Is that how you would like it?"

He shrugged his shoulders. "As you will; it is of little interest to me. You have all you wanted now. You are mistress of Brackenroyd."

"You are right." She knew her eyes flashed fire and hoped he would register the extent of her anger and determination. "Quite right, I have all I want in Brackenroyd. It is mine now, equally with you, and no one can take it from me."

"No one but death," he countered quietly, and Fern felt the heat in her blood die into a chill. Death, he said. For a second or two she lay once again in a narrow truckle bed alongside Phoebe, feeling the threat of death overshadowing her happiness. With a wrench she returned to the dining table. Laying aside her damask napkin, she rose.

"Are we still to ride around the tenant farms this morning, as we planned?" she asked coldly.

"No need for you to go," he answered with indifference. "I shall say you are indisposed but that you will attend the tenants' ball this evening."

"As you will," Fern said, and swept back the heavy portiere that covered the doors. Outside she regretted letting him dictate the morning's program. Perhaps it was intentional to keep her from meeting the farmers this morning, to keep alive the locals' evident distrust of her. She would have done better to insist on going, to make their acquaintance and begin to break down resistance. In future she must take care to evaluate Bruno's schemes more carefully.

But there was still the ball tonight. There was still chance to befriend the farmers and start to win them over. And Edgar Amos would be there, so she would have one ally.

Oddly enough, Fanny came into the kitchen, where Fern was discussing the fare for the ball with Mrs. Thorpe, to announce that Reverend Amos was abovestairs.

"He said he called only to leave a message, but I thought perhaps you might like to be at home to the reverend, madam."

"Quite right, Fanny. Bid him sit in the parlor a moment. I shall come directly."

Amos rose quickly as she entered, and she could see that his keen eyes had noted something amiss, the way his sandy eyebrows twitched as though to rise in question before deciding it would be impolite. Calmly she bade him be seated again.

"I hope you will forgive my intrusion on the very first day of your wedded life," the vicar said. "I came really only to apologize, since I fear I shall not be able to come this evening. A sick parishioner has first claim always on my time."

"Which is as it should be, but I am sorry I shall not have your company."

He smiled uncertainly, though she could see he was pleased at the compliment.

"You see, I fear I have a long way to go to befriend the local people, and your guidance could be invaluable to me."

"I am at your disposal at any time, Mrs. de Lacy. That is, at any time other than today."

"I thank you." She paused a moment, considering how to speak. Then, impulsively, she rushed on. "Why do they hate me so? I know they do. I hear them. I heard them in the clogger's shop. They said the name Radley as if it were poison. Oh, Edgar, what have I done that they should hate me so?"

She was pleating folds in her skirt nervously as she spoke, hating herself for being so sensitive to their scorn and for pleading with a comparative stranger for help. It was foolish, too; he would wonder why she turned to him and not to her husband.

He was looking at her sadly. "I do not know, Mrs. de Lacy, but I fear you are right. For some strange reason the name of Radley has always been loathed here, but not because of you. It existed long before you came. I never knew why, nor has anyone been able to tell me. Only, rest assured it is not you personally they dislike; now you are a De Lacy, possibly they will forget."

"But that is not enough! I want to know the reason."

He hunched his shoulders, spreading his hands in defeat. "There is much we would know but which is denied to us. We must learn to accept."

How weak he was, how ineffectual compared to Bruno. Instantly she regretted the comparison. Regaining her composure, she changed the subject.

"Do you have parish registers in the church, Reverend? How far back do they go?"

He nodded, evidently more at ease on this subject. "Indeed we have, and very interesting many of them are, too. I'm afraid I don't know how far back exactly records were kept, for many of the older registers have been put away in cupboards in the vestry and are somewhat dusty and dilapidated. In what period were you interested?"

Fern felt the muscles tighten in her throat, but she appeared calm as she spoke. "I believe there was once a Catherine Radley in the time of Charles I. I wondered if perhaps you might have a record of her birth . . . and death."

He was frowning dubiously. "I doubt that our records go back so far, but I shall most certainly check for you, Mrs. de Lacy. But another day, if you will permit, as I must be on my way to the sick lady now."

"Of course." Fern rose to escort him to the door. "By the way, who is the sick lady you are to visit?"

"Mrs. Briggs, the doctor's wife. She's very poorly, I understand, but then, she was always delicate, so we must not lose heart."

Poor lady, thought Fern after he had gone. She had looked

ill last night; it was to be hoped the indisposition was not serious.

In an effort to lighten her mood, and because the sun was shining again, Fern decided she would not stay indoors but go out in the cold fresh air. Perhaps she would find Fabia at home. She sent Fanny to fetch her cloak, electing to walk rather than ride. Nearing the schoolhouse, she saw Fabia and young Phoebe just coming out of the front door.

"It's so lovely, we decided to go and pick pussy willow—catkins, that is," Fabia said as she tied Phoebe's bonnet strings.

"May I come with you?"

"We'd be delighted, wouldn't we, Phoebe?" The child ventured a hesitant smile and took hold of her mother's hand. Fern fell in step beside them as they walked uphill toward the moors, leaving the village behind. She was grateful for Fabia's reticence, for she did not inquire why Fern was not doing the rounds of the tenant farmers with Bruno.

Above the village the fields stretched away into the purpling distance, interlaced by gray-stone walls, and here and there a copse or two. Pale-green buds on the trees seemed to glow with translucence in the soft spring sunlight, and Fern felt content and free up here. Fabia too was lighthearted.

"I know the best place for catkins—in Catsgrave Copse, down by the stream. Come, Phoebe, I'll race you there."

Laughing, they all ran. The heather sprang resiliently beneath Fern's feet, the breeze blowing back her hair and catching in her throat till she was breathless. They stopped, gasping, at the edge of a thick clump of trees, and Fern could see the glint of the sunlight on the stream rippling through the woods. Fabia was right. Heavy sprays of catkin hung, limp and yellow, in profusion.

Both women started forward, but the child hung back. "Come on, Phoebe, for we haven't much time," her mother urged, but the child still clung to her hand, pulling back. Fern waited, wondering. "Come on, Phoebe," Fabia pleaded.

The little girl began to whimper. Fern knelt by her side. "What is it, Phoebe?" she asked softly. The child's moans ceased at once, her eyes growing round and suspicious. Fern touched her arm, but the child leaped back, her dark eyes now angry and hostile. Fern felt a shudder of fear run down her spine, for the eyes that glared were those of the other Phoebe. For a second Fern lay again in that truckle bed and saw the eyes and felt the tearing fingers at her face. The eyes were flashing still . . . and they were the eyes of the child.

Numbly she rose and turned helplessly to Fabia.

"I'm sorry, Fern. I don't know what's come over the child," Fabia said in some embarrassment. "Perhaps she's sickening for something, in which case it would be as well to take her home."

She pulled a few sprigs of catkin from the nearest trees. It was a quieter, more thoughtful party on the homeward journey, and Fern began to wonder. They had all been so high-spirited just a few minutes earlier; was it her influence that happiness always seemed to turn sour so quickly? What was the malign influence she brought that caused the village folk to resent, even hate her, and a poor dumb child to fear her? The memory of those eyes recalled the night Bruno had attempted to hypnotize Phoebe, and the child's words.

"I didn't mean it to happen, I swear to God I didn't!"

Fern knew now, it was the other, older Phoebe who spoke, the one now dead for three hundred years. What had the other Phoebe done that she now repented?

It all seemed so clear now. Catherine was returning through Fern, and Phoebe through the child Phoebe—but to expiate or complete what?

Banishing useless speculation, Fern tried instead to talk to Fabia of other matters. How was Luke faring, she asked, and affairs in the school.

"He is somewhat hard-pressed at the moment, since one of his pupil-teachers has the influenza, but he'll manage," Fabia told her. At once the idea came to Fern.

"Then perhaps he would allow me to help for a time. I am not inexperienced in teaching."

Fabia tried to hide her pleasure behind a show of politeness, protesting it would consume too much of Fern's time, and she mistress of the manor too. But Fern would not listen. Besides, the idea had advantages; if she could not easily get to know the adults, the children of the village at least would be accessible. And in studying the faces of other children in order to learn their names and ways, perhaps she could shut out the picture of Phoebe's face, contorted with hate and fear.

Luke was more than grateful, and it was soon agreed that she should come to the schoolroom in the morning. "But are you sure Bruno will agree?" he inquired.

Fern felt resentment stiffening. "I agree, Luke. That is all that matters. Bruno's opinion does not enter into it."

She saw the surprise on his good-humored face and wished she had phrased her answer more diplomatically. He would feel sorry for his friend, married to a shrewish, self-willed woman, his bride of only one day. Still, this was as Bruno wished it to be. In time all the village would learn that each was independent of the other.

In fact, it was that same evening that the villagers were first made aware of it. The Hall once more was crowded with well-wishers for the master's marriage, but this time the guests were not the landed gentry but tenant farmers, the Hall servants, and the millhands and their wives. As before, the Hall shone with candlelight and decoration, and the tables were loaded with food just as generously as the previous night, but the toasts were drunk in ale and beer and not in wine. Fern wore, not a magnificent gown like last night's, but a decorous violet day dress, high-necked and beruffled, with a diamond brooch at the throat, which was a gift from Bruno.

"Be the gracious lady, Fern, charming but distant," Bruno murmured as he offered his arm to lead her down the staircase. Below, she could see the heads turn, and the subdued talk died away as they descended. The men nearest the stairs raised their heads in a sketchy salute to their master. Behind them she could see the wives peering curiously over their men's shoulders, appraising her gown and assessing the diamond before staring shrewdly at her face. Now, if ever, was the opportunity to meet them and attempt to disprove any preconceived notions they had about her. Mentally she rejected Bruno's advice to remain aloof.

"This is Fearnley, the mill manager," she heard Bruno say, and turned to greet the stocky man who was shifting uncomfortably.

"How do you do, Mr. Fearnley."

"Oh, aye," he grunted, growing pinker and obviously more ill-at-ease in the unaccustomed surroundings.

"I trust affairs at the mill are running well?" she went on, anxious to get him to talk on matters he knew about.

"Aye, none too badly."

"Perhaps I shall come in soon and see for myself," she said with a smile, and saw at once the way his gaze slid to the master. Bruno frowned.

"How is Mrs. Fearnley now?" he asked the manager.

"Fair to middling, sir. She's over t' influenza, but now t' bairn has it. He'll be right again soon, though."

"I hope so. I'll see you in the office in the morning."

Bruno turned away, leading Fern with him. He introduced her to several more people, but Fern found no opportunity to talk with them. Bruno was quick to intervene and to lead her away. Finally, exasperated, she dropped his arm. Bruno's dark brows rose in question.

"I wish to talk. I see Mrs. Iredale over there by the window, the woman who lost her child soon after I came. I want to talk to her." Fern had not intended her voice to sound so sharp, for several people were within earshot.

He shook his head. "Unwise, my dear. Come to the dais, where I will respond to their toast. A few more polite words with a few of them, and then we can leave quietly." He took her arm firmly.

"But I don't want to leave!" She shook off his arm, aware that now several more curious ears were straining to listen.

"Do as I say, Fern." His voice was low, but there was no mistaking the tone of command, the tone that implied he would not be disobeyed. Rebellion flared in Fern. She would not be dictated to like a child who does not know how to behave. She glared at him equally forcibly.

"I shall talk to whom I please. And I shall inspect the mill if I wish."

"Do you intend to make a spectacle of yourself in public, madam?" The voice, still low, was charged with icy anger, but Fern was not to be cowed. Her anger matched his.

"I do not, but it seems you will force it upon us both if you continue to dictate to me. Now, let go of me."

"I will not. We shall talk of this later."

Without another word he gripped her arm so fiercely that Fern could have winced with the pain. Forcefully he propelled her across the room to the dais, helped her to mount the steps, and then pulled out a chair for her to sit. Short of creating a scene by running from the room, there was little she could do. Defeated, Fern sank into the chair, but inwardly she fumed with rage. He would hear more of this later; he would not humiliate her thus again.

In a blur of anger she heard Bruno call for the beer tankards to be replenished, heard Fearnley's stumbling words of congratulation to the master of Brackenroyd and his lady, and the subdued cheer followed by silence as the throng emptied their glasses. The atmosphere was markedly different from last night's, when a gaily dressed company had chattered without restraint. Tonight's company, soberly dressed in their dark Sunday best, were emphatically more reserved, more subdued. Was it only that they felt a little ill-at-ease in the grand Hall, or was it more than that?

Bruno rose to respond to the toast, his quiet, authoritative voice betraying none of the anger of a moment before. The villagers listened in respectful silence, and Fern could see in their eyes no hate, no resentment of the master.

After he had done, he led her away. Fern went without protest. It had been a very tiring day; not physically, but emotionally she felt drained, too tired to argue more. At her door he left her.

It was Cassie who brought her late cup of hot chocolate, her eyes glowing.

"It were a lovely ball, miss ... madam. I'll always remember it." Her eyes misted in reminiscence.

"I'm glad you enjoyed it, Cassie."

"Shall I tell thee why, madam? 'Cos Tim Butley asked me out wi' him, on me next evening off. I'm that proud he asked me, 'cos every lass in t' village fancies Tim, they do."

Fern smiled at the girl's radiance, glad for her. To Cassie, marriage to a good worker like Tim must seem the ultimate in contentment. If only she knew what marriage was for a woman. Whatever stratum of society she lived in, it seemed it meant only blind obedience and submission, if continual warfare were not to ensue.

Two days married, and already so cynical! Fern could have laughed if the situation were not so tragic. Here she was, bound to a domineering man who evidently liked her no more than she liked him.

And yet . . . As she undressed for bed, Fern mused about the laconic man with the dark ways she had married out of need. In some ways he was so attractive. If only he were not so silent, so uncommunicative, and so determined to rule her. Well, he would not. Tomorrow she would start work at the school with Luke, trying to live life her own way.

Suddenly the connecting door opened, and Bruno stood in the doorway. Fern pulled her dressing gown hastily about her, covering the delicate nightgown. He did not come forward, but stood there, seeming to fill the whole doorway with his height and breadth. He had not yet changed from his evening suit. Deliberately Fern sat in a chair with her back toward him.

"Fern," he said quietly, "I wish to make it plain that there must never again be a repetition of tonight's performance. However the situation may be between us, it must appear to others that there is harmony. Henceforth, therefore, I must insist that you do not cross me in public."

"Then do not make it necessary for me to do so."

He sighed deeply. "My dear girl, I am not anxious to dictate to you, as you seem to think, but simply to guide you. It is evident you do not know how a lady behaves when among others of a lower station. Tonight I only wished to save you from your own impulsiveness and ignorance."

"And how do you know how English people behave, living most of your life in Germany?" Fern flashed back.

"Because good manners and social etiquette are basically the same in both countries. I am not angry with you, Fern, only disappointed. But I believe there is a book I have heard good report of, which might help you. It's called *A Manual of Etiquette for Gentlewomen*. I shall order it for you when I go to town."

How dare he patronize her! Fern rose from her chair and faced him. "I am no common servant girl, to be schooled to become what you wish. No finer gentleman existed than my father, and I learned long ago that manners basically are consideration for others, something which you do not seem to comprehend. I would have done better to ignore you tonight, to inquire how that poor woman Mrs. Iredale fared."

"That would have been foolish, and you know it. Have you forgotten already how she resented your coming to her house?"

"Only because of some superstitious rubbish the villagers believe about the Radleys, and how am I ever to disabuse them of the idea if you try to prevent my talking to them?" She could not resist smiling as she went on to tell him her news. "But you shall not prevent me. Tomorrow I start to teach in the school, to help Luke. I shall get to know the children, at least."

To her surprise, he nodded and smiled. "A good idea. It will help to keep you occupied. Good night, Fern."

Stepping back, he closed the door, and Fern heard the key turn in the lock. So be it. She had no wish to have his company in her bed. And what was more, she felt she had scored a minor victory in refusing to capitulate. He had not argued long.

Fern slept a deep and dreamless sleep that night. In the morning she rose early, ate breakfast from a tray, and prepared to go down to the school. The morning was fine and clear, so she decided to walk, wrapping up well against the cold in a warm ulster and muffler. As she closed her bedroom door behind her, she saw Cassie outside Bruno's door.

"The master don't answer when I knock, madam. Shall I go in?"

"Give the tray to me. I'll take it in, Cassie."

Gladly the girl relinquished the tray and scuttled off. Fern tapped lightly at the door and went in. Bruno was not there. Nor had his bed been slept in. She put down the tray on the night table and left.

Curiosity nagged as she walked downhill toward the village. It was no business of hers, admittedly, since they had agreed to go their own ways, but where was Bruno? Neither last night nor the previous night had he slept in his bed. Was he sleeping elsewhere in the Hall, or was he out, and if so, where?

Outside the school, a gaunt gray-stone building, some boys played marbles in the small playground while a cluster of girls, the bigger ones holding the smaller ones by the hand, stood gossiping by the door. Fern smiled and spoke to them as she passed, but they only stared, openmouthed, too overcome to reply. She found Luke in his classroom.

"I'll show you your classroom," he said, leading the way to a smaller room with somber half-tiled walls and rows of iron desks. In the corner a huge iron stove belched intermittent gusts of smoke. Behind a single high desk on a dais, evidently the teacher's desk, stood a row of cupboards and a high blackboard on a swivel easel.

"In there you will find materials and chalk and all you require. The children's slates are in a slot at the front of their desks. The class monitor will be able to show you where everything is." Luke sounded abstracted. Evidently he had much on his mind, but Fern assured him she would be able to manage quite well.

"Arithmetic first, after prayers, then spelling and handwriting. After playtime, geography and drawing. This afternoon will be singing. I'm afraid we have no piano, but there is a tuning fork in your desk. Then, history and reading before school ends at four."

It sounded quite a heavy program, but Fern was looking forward to seeing the children. At last a whistle shrilled in the yard. Looking out of the window, she could see the children lining up quickly into neat files, and then chanting a song as they marched in step to the rhythm into their respective doorways—the boys at the east door, the girls at the west.

She took off her ulster, hung it on the peg behind the door, and sat up at the high desk to await her charges. In a moment they came, no longer singing but marching silently to their desks, where they sat and eyed her expectantly. Row upon row of pale, solemn faces stared at her. Fern bade them good morning pleasantly and introduced herself, but not a flicker of emotion crossed their blank faces. Boys on one side of the room, of all ages, and girls on the other in neat white smocks over their dresses, they all sat uniformly still and emotionless. Fern felt dismayed. She was glad when a bell rang to summon them to the hall for prayers.

After a simple service consisting only of a hymn sung in lackluster voices, a reading from the Bible by Luke, and the Lord's Prayer, the class marched back to the classroom. Slates clattered out from the desk slots as Fern began writing sums on the blackboard. Not a child attempted to talk to its neighbor or disrupt the lesson in any way. It was unnatural. Fern found it hard to comprehend. But then she noticed the thinness of the little bodies, the gaunt, gray look, and some of them were even barefoot. Poor things, they looked too hungry and cold to think of mischief.

During the spelling lesson they began to appear more alive, possibly because the warmth from the stove was beginning to thaw out their cold little bodies. The morning passed without event, and at noontime she went to eat with Fabia in the house.

"Some of them even have no sandwiches for their dinner, Fabia, and some are barefoot. Are they really so poor?"

Fabia was careful. "The wages at the mill are not handsome, and most families have several children to feed and clothe. It is not easy."

"But I will not have them starve! Could we not give them hot soup, Fabia? If there are no facilities here, I could get

157

Mrs. Thorpe to make it at the Hall and send it down. They must have something nourishing to eat."

"Soup would be marvelous," Fabia said, and Fern could hear the careful note still in her voice. She was anticipating Bruno's opposition, perhaps. Well, if he was responsible for the children's hunger, through not paying their fathers sufficient wages, he was not going to interfere in her attempt to rectify matters.

"Then I shall see to it tomorrow, and clogs for the children who have none," Fern said stoutly. And she would, whoever might try to oppose her.

"There is one thing," Fabia said slowly. "The villagers may not welcome what you plan—they are a proud race and may well construe your actions as charity."

"Charity? What does it matter what one calls it? They surely will be glad to see their children shod and fed."

Fabia nodded. "They would welcome it, but you must be careful how you do it, for fear of offending them. They would sooner see their children cold and hungry than accept charity from ... from ..."

Her voice trailed away. Fern eyed her questioningly. "From a Radley, is that what you would say?"

Fabia nodded. "From the mistress of Brackenroyd is one matter, for they have been accustomed for centuries to protection from the master and his family. But from a Radley is another matter. I don't know why this age-old resentment of the name, but it is undeniably there. So I would caution you to take care."

Her advice was sensible, thought Fern as she returned to the school. A lone child sat at her desk in the classroom. There was something vaguely familiar about her face, solemn and wide-eyed.

"Have you had lunch?" Fern asked pleasantly. The child shook her head. "I seem to know you—have we met before?" The child stared without answering. "What is your name?"

"Elsie Iredale, miss."

Iredale. Fern could not remember one name from so many she had called out from the register this morning. Iredale. It was Joss Iredale who had lost a little girl just after she came—yes, this child here now had been lurking in the corner when Fern had gone to the cottage. She smiled.

"How is your mother now, Elsie? Has she recovered from the shock of your sister's death?"

A shadow crossed the child's face, and she scowled. "My mam says it's 'cos of you that Aggie died. She says when there's a Radley in t' village there's allus trouble, same as it's allus been for hundreds of years. There's a taint in thy blood, miss, me mam says."

Other children trooped into the room, relieving Fern of the obligation to reply. She felt shocked and hurt. The older people of the village were evidently passing on their distrust of her to their children, and the task of befriending them was not going to be easy after all.

It was during the afternoon's lessons that she became gradually aware that these were not all the same children who had been present during the morning. She still could not fit many names to faces, but the faces were different now; she was sure of it. She asked Luke when school at last was ended.

"You are right. Many of the older children go to work half-time and attend school half-time. Those from the age of ten up to thirteen work in the mill either in the mornings or in the afternoons and come to school half a day only."

"So that is why they look so tired! It is too much for them!"

Luke shrugged. "Unfortunately, in most cases it is an economic necessity. There is nothing we can do."

There must be something we can do, Fern argued inwardly as she made her way home. These poor, exploited children, made to work and freeze and starve without any hope of bettering their lot; it was appalling. Robert and Sarah Hastings, despite their father's coldness toward them, would never have to suffer the privations of these poor Brackenroyd children.

Over dinner she poured out her arguments to Bruno, who listened in impassive silence. At length he laid down his dessert fork and smiled at her in compassion.

"You want so much to be the benevolent mistress of Brackenroyd, don't you, Fern?"

"I can't bear to see their suffering!"

"Well, let me tell you, yours is not the way to overcome it. By your impulsive recklessness you could ruin all."

"You mean only to exploit them, to grow fat and wealthy from them, is that it? Well, I will not stand by and let you."

"Listen to me." His voice was icy cold. "You are young, inexperienced, and hotheaded. Let well alone, and do not interfere. I have told you that the mill and the welfare of the workers is my concern alone, and I repeat once again, do not meddle in what you do not understand. No, do not argue with me." He raised a peremptory hand to forestall her angry reaction. "You think you can change the world, but you cannot. Children of ten may work half-time—it is the law. I appreciate your concern for them, but you cannot, and *shall* not, change matters.

"Madam, I say it for the last time. Mind your own business."

Chapter 11

Edgar Amos squatted in the vestry among a pile of decaying registers.

"Drat those mice," he muttered as the ledger he was about to dip into crumbled into pieces in his hand. He laid it aside and withdrew another from the dark recesses of one of the huge cupboards.

The pale spring sunlight filtering in through a high window was suddenly blotted out by a shadow. Amos looked up interrogatively. A huge black shape silhouetted against the window made him start, till he recognized the voice.

"Amos?" It was the master, greatcoated and muffled against the chill breezes. Behind him lurked that great ugly dog. "I am on my way down to the mill. Will you walk with me?"

It was typical of the man not to explain his reason, but Amos agreed nonetheless. One did not readily offend one's patron, so he fetched a muffler and trudged along beside De Lacy, endeavoring to match the length of his stride. The dog sniffed suspiciously at his heels, and Amos wished the creature would not stare at him so malevolently from its great yellow eyes.

For a time they marched in silence. Amos was cold, and wondered if the master would broach the reason for seeking him out before they reached the mill, for it was not far. At the mill gates De Lacy stopped, staring at the waters of the river.

"Why are you not wearing an overcoat, Amos?"

The vicar smiled apologetically. "It is thin and fraying at the cuffs, but I cannot afford a new one."

"Then order one. Send the bill to me."

He would listen to no thanks. Strange, thought Amos, how the man could be so observant and concerned, and yet at other times so brusque, even callous.

"Soup is to be sent down from the Hall to the school today for the children," the master went on quickly. "I want you to see Luke Armitage, to tell him I sent it."

"That is exceedingly thoughtful of you, sir."

"Fern's idea, not mine. But the villagers would not accept it from her. You are to let it be known that it is the master's wish."

"Very good." Amos could not help feeling grudging admiration for the man. In an odd kind of way he was trying to protect his wife, but he was so gruff, so lacking in polish. His foreign upbringing, no doubt.

De Lacy turned to face him. "You're not a bad fellow, Amos. Intelligent and well-read. It's a pity you're in the church. It cannot be very satisfying for you to minister to a lot of primitive, superstitious people like the Brackenroyd folk."

"They are good people, sir, hardworking and honest." Amos was quick to defend his parishioners against a newly arrived foreigner.

"But superstitious, nonetheless. Was it not your great man of last century, Edmund Burke, who said that superstition was the religion of feeble minds? I agree with him. By the way, what were you doing in the vestry when I called?"

Amos was irritated by the change of subject before he

could retaliate, but did not show it. Instead he replied courteously, "Mrs. de Lacy asked me to see if I could find reference to a Catherine Radley in the seventeenth century. I was checking the records."

De Lacy's handsome face darkened into a scowl. "So, she is still besotted with her family history. She would do well to leave it alone."

The vicar saw his chance to score. "But was it not also Edmund Burke who said that a people not interested in its past was not worthy of its future? There I agree with him."

"Touché," the master admitted with a hint of a grim smile. "But to be interested is not the same as to be obsessed."

Without another word he turned and marched into the cobbled mill yard, but he could not rob Amos of a feeling of triumph as he retraced his steps toward the school. Just for once De Lacy had not got the better of him. The feeling of superiority in this encounter gave him a more charitable outlook toward his benefactor, and he mused as he walked that the master was not such a hard and heartless character after all.

Luke Armitage, the schoolmaster, smiled broadly when he heard of the master's gift of soup for the children. Amos felt content at being entrusted with news that brought such happiness, and the gray little valley seemed to glow under the benison of spring sunshine as he made his way back to the vicarage. A young woman was waiting on the doorstep. He recognized Lucy, Dr. Briggs's maidservant.

"Begging thy pardon, Reverend, but the doctor asks will you come at once. The mistress is very bad, sinking fast, the doctor says."

Poor soul. Amos half-ran with the girl up the hill to where the doctor's imposing stone house stood in its neat gardens, but it was too late. Mrs. Briggs lay still and white, her amiable features placid in death. Her husband and sister clung to each other, the one mute in shock, the other sobbing noisily.

"So sudden," the doctor said shakily. "A chill, and then, without warning, it became pneumonia. Nothing I could do. Nothing."

Amos performed his duties, consoling and making arrangements for the dead woman's funeral, and then left the family to mourn alone. His return to the vicarage this time was infinitely more thoughtful and less lighthearted than it had been this morning. Heavens! It was dusk already, and he had eaten nothing since breakfast. Mrs. Crowther would be flapping anxiously about him like a mother hen over her chick when he reappeared. Then he must notify the master of Mrs. Briggs's death and arrange for the burial. Ah, well, his research to find records of Catherine Radley could wait for another day.

Radley. An anxious thought struck him. It was highly likely that the villagers, shocked as they would be by Mrs. Briggs's demise, would shake their heads and venture to say, once again, that sudden death and the return of a Radley to Brackenroyd were no mere coincidence. Poor Mrs. de Lacy. She was going to find life here difficult for a long time yet.

It was not until the day of the funeral that Amos saw Mrs. de Lacy, and he was struck by her pallor, greater than was usual for one who was not actually a relative of the deceased. He was waiting outside the church door, despite the drizzling rain bespotting his starched cassock, to see the cortege arrive, and he could not help noting the young mistress's appearance as she dismounted from the first black coach behind the hearse. The master helped her and Mrs. Briggs's sister out, then Dr. Briggs, looking older and frailer than he had ever done. For a moment Mrs. de Lacy stared at the black-and-silver hearse, her black-crepe veil thrown back from her face, before lowering it and entering the church.

In the mild, misty rain the bearers lifted the highly polished coffin with its gilt mountings from the hearse, the four black horses with their black plumes, limp with rain, stamping their feet and snorting steamy breath.

Up the steps and into the church the bearers moved, slowly and majestically. Behind the coffin followed the family, in deepest black and the women heavily veiled. Amos took his place to begin, catching a brief glimpse of the De Lacys in their pew, both standing with heads bowed.

"I am the resurrection and the life, saith the Lord ..." Amos spoke the words of the service, feeling the reverence and solemnity of the occasion adding a new weight of importance to his little church. Dr. Briggs was evidently deeply moved, his bulky frame shuddering slightly as though it were a battle to restrain his tears.

"For man walketh in a vain shadow and disquieteth himself in vain; he heapeth up riches and cannot tell who shall gather them ..."

That would make a good text for a sermon to preach for such as De Lacy. The rich man filling his coffers, but to what end?

He was aware of thin cambric handkerchieves dabbing at reddened eyes, of the gentlemen's shining top hats and silk cravats, of the lurid patches of colored light on the mourners' faces, cast by the stained-glass windows above. It was a melancholy occasion indeed, and he felt genuinely sorry for the old doctor.

The service over, he led the file of black figures out of the church behind the coffin. Rain was still falling on the sodden turf and the heap of newly dug soil by the grave. At the gate Amos could see the waiting coachmen and the horses stirring restlessly, anxious to return to the dry warmth of their stables. The mourners made a silent circle about the grave.

"For as much as it hath pleased Almighty God of his great mercy to take unto himself the soul of our dear sister here departed," Amos intoned, "we therefore commit her body to the ground. ..."

Dr. Briggs scattered a handful of earth on the coffin, and while Amos spoke the final prayer, the other mourners cast sprays of spring flowers. He saw Mrs. de Lacy sway suddenly, as if to fall, but the master caught her elbow, supporting her while the file moved slowly away.

It was not altogether surprising when Amos heard the next day that Mrs. de Lacy was not at the school as she had been the past week, but as the pupil-teacher was now recovered and back at his post, she was no longer needed there. Still, it might be as well to pay a visit to the Hall; the lady might be indisposed, and he must not neglect his pastoral duties.

Mrs. de Lacy was reclining on a chaise longue in the parlor when Fanny showed the vicar in, flashing him a quick smile with her pert dark eyes as she bobbed a curtsy and withdrew. Mrs. de Lacy laid aside a book she had evidently been reading and motioned him to be seated. She was still unnaturally pale, and her usually lively eyes were distant and cool. Amos sat in the leather chair next to the fire, rubbing his hands to the blaze.

"Are the children at the school eating their soup, Edgar?" Mrs. de Lacy asked in a lackluster voice.

"Indeed, and are relishing it."

"I am glad of it." The uninterested tone in her voice could only indicate either that she was not well or that she was aware that the gift of soup was her husband's gesture, no longer hers.

"How is Dr. Briggs?" she asked next. "I fear his wife's death has been a terrible blow to him. He must have loved her deeply."

"I have no doubt he did, but he is a very Christian gentleman. He will find solace in knowing they will meet again."

"In the hereafter, or in another life on earth?" The question was bald, but he could see the gleam of interest which now enlivened her eyes.

"Either is possible. Love is an abiding power."

"Then if you believe love can be reborn from one generation to another, is it not possible that hate, equally strong and enduring, can continue too?"

Her eyes glowed now, with the unnatural gleam of fever. Amos tried to parry her question, unsure how to answer.

"Is it this house that makes you think such thoughts, Mrs. de Lacy? Brackenroyd Hall has a powerful, intense, atmosphere. Evil memories are mingled with happier ones, and a sensitive person such as yourself could well suffer a kind of malaise, a sickness of the spirit, as a result."

"But I asked your opinion—can hatred linger on and come back?"

"Come back," he echoed thoughtfully. "You mean, like a ghost, *un revenant,* as the French say? I would prefer to think not. A body is laid to rest at death, and it is to be hoped the spirit remains at rest, in peace, forever."

Her eyes relapsed into an interior reverie. Suddenly Edgar remembered the reason for his visit. He sat forward to catch her drifting attention.

"I have found a reference in the parish records to the lady you inquired about," he said eagerly. At once Mrs. de Lacy sprang to life, her face registering rapt attention, and the gleam revitalizing her eyes again.

"Catherine? You found her?"

"Well, I found an entry for a Catherine Radley in the 1642 register. It was the only Radley of that name, although of course the name Radley appears frequently over the years."

"That is the Catherine I sought. What does it say of her?"

"It was very brief, an entry regarding her death." He raised his eyes ceilingward in an effort to recall the exact words. " 'Catherine Radley, departed this life Lammastide, the first day of August, 1642.' There was no mention of her age, but no doubt as I go back in the records, I shall uncover the date of her birth."

"It was 1620, for she was twenty-two when she died."

He regarded her in amazement, but she was cool and collected. There was no sign of feverishness about her pallid face, and yet how could she know? Before he could ask her meaning, the portiere across the door rattled back along its bamboo pole, and Bruno de Lacy stood there.

"Ah, deep in conversation, I see," he said, advancing to the fireplace and turning his back upon it, standing legs astride the better to enjoy the warmth. "What were you discussing?"

"Ah, whether love can surpass death, conquering it to be reborn," replied Amos, anxious not to betray the mistress's concern over this Catherine Radley. De Lacy would only sneer yet again.

"Philosophical speculation, which, unfortunately, can be neither proved nor disproved, and therefore a waste of time," the master pronounced. Amos saw Mrs. de Lacy's gaze fasten on his handsome, dark features with an air of distaste. There did not seem to be an atmosphere of perfect connubial bliss in the Hall; perhaps he had best make his farewells and return to his study, where Sunday's sermon lay half-written on his desk.

Declining Mrs. de Lacy's invitation to stay for tea, he made his farewells and went out into the darkening April afternoon, glad for once to leave the Hall. It was, as he had said to Mrs. de Lacy, an oppressive, powerful atmosphere that clung to the very fabric of the Hall, but he had never been so conscious of it as now.

Fern sighed and sank back on the chaise longue after Amos' departure. Bruno offered her a cup of tea from the silver tray, eyeing her thoughtfully.

"You look tired, my dear. Are you not sleeping well?"

Fern put the cup aside and closed her eyes. "I sleep deeply, but I do not feel rested." It was true; deep sleep blanketed her mind, with no dreams to disturb her, but the lassitude by day was unaccountably strange.

"You've been overdoing things, with the school and the house to run. A change might be good for you, a month by the sea perhaps."

"No!" With a feeling near to panic, Fern sat upright. She could not leave Brackenroyd now. She was needed here; she felt it. Catherine needed her, though she had not yet come back.

"As you wish." Black eyes surveyed her levelly. "I shall go down to my laboratory to work now until dinner." Bruno laid aside the china cup and went out.

Fanny came to draw the curtains, light the gas lamps, and clear away the tray. Fern heard her skirts swishing through the doorway and the door closing. She lay, languid and limp, only her mind at work.

She *must* stay in Brackenroyd Hall, for Catherine's sake as well as her own. Somehow she felt intuitively that only by learning Catherine's problem could she resolve her own. It was imperative to stay, not to let Bruno drive her out, however oppressive and enervating the Hall's atmosphere.

The clock on the marble mantelshelf ticked on. It was nearing time for dinner, and she really must make the effort to raise herself and go upstairs to change for dinner.

Out in the corridor Fern had to pass the iron-studded door to the old wing. It was ajar. Bruno was down there at work in his laboratory. It occurred to Fern to go and warn him of the time, so, pushing the door open, she followed his dusty tracks to the old low-ceilinged hall and to the door in the corner under the minstrels' gallery.

That door too was ajar, but before Fern's hand could reach for the iron handle, a sudden chill came down over her, enveloping her like a dark cloak. She shivered. It could be the dampness of the age-old wing, or a sense of premonition ... or the feeling that came before with the advent of Catherine; but whatever it was, it was chilling to the very heart, and she felt afraid. Clutching her cashmere shawl closer about her shoulders, Fern paused, hand on knob, as the iciness grew, filling the murky shadows of the Hall. Opaque forms seemed to glow under the gallery, faint murmurs came to her waiting ears, and her fear grew into terror.

Fern pushed the door open sharply, anxious to see Bruno's reassuring shape, even though he might be angered at her interrupting him. But the low chamber with its wooden shelves and a bench was empty. She closed the door behind her, relieved that the menacing chill had not followed her in here.

But there was still that sense of weariness. She sank onto the stool beside the bench and breathed deeply, to quieten the thudding of her heart. On the bench stood a row of bottles and jars, all neatly labeled. Belladonna, digitalis, opium, laudanum, aconite, hemlock. Hemlock. For an instant she saw herself again in a flagstoned kitchen with a pestle and mortar, pounding a compound for a neighbor's abscess on the leg. Just as quickly the glimpse faded.

The door opened sharply, and Bruno stood there, scowling. "What are you doing here?" he demanded. There was hostility not only in his eyes but in his aggressive stance, feet astride.

"I came to fetch you for dinner." The excuse sounded as weak as her voice. His frown showed he did not believe her.

Fern felt angry with herself for sounding so guilty, and decided that, weak as she felt, attack was the best method of defense.

"Why do you have drugs here, Bruno? For what do you use them?"

The scowl darkened, his brows meeting in one long dark line. "For my work."

"But you are not a doctor of medicine. You told me your work is on the human mind."

"So it is. These drugs are capable of producing hallucination, and it is their effect on the human mind I am studying. Come, it is nearing time for the dinner gong."

She let him lead her away. This time the cold did not permeate her bones as she recrossed the old hall on his arm. It was only that night as she lay in the great four-poster that the thought suddenly came to her. How could she be so slow? It must be this strange weariness which had benumbed her wits, so that she had not thought of it before. The drugs in Bruno's laboratory—on whom had he been testing them? Unlike medical researchers with their corpses to dissect, he had no human brain at his disposal to experiment upon. The effect of hallucination on dogs or cats would be impossible to record, since they could not speak. So on whose brain was Bruno experimenting?

Of course. It was clear now. That was why he suffered Fern to come to Brackenroyd to share his inheritance. That was why he endured her as a wife. It was *her* mind he was tampering with! Hence, surely, the inexplicable lassitude, the tangled dreams. Fern felt fury mounting, chasing away the weariness and lack of interest. Then another thought struck her.

But were drugs the cause of Catherine too? No, no, that she could not believe. Catherine was no figment of a disordered brain; she was certain of it. Catherine was her own brainchild; no, more than that, *she was* Catherine.

How could she be so sure? Amos had confirmed it, had he not, by finding the entry in the records exactly as Fern had foretold? But the other dreams, the tangled balls of wool, and even the story of Annot—those, now she remembered it, had followed upon accepting a drink from Bruno before bed. That was how he had done it!

One doubt lingered. She could not thrust from her mind the memory of his eyes over the rim of a glass, warm and kindly, as he toasted his new bride on their wedding day. And that same night Catherine had come.

Torn with doubts and anxiety, Fern tumbled out of bed and tried the handle of the connecting door. It was locked. Out in the corridor she knocked angrily on Bruno's door, again and again. No answer came. To further furious banging, Mrs. Thorpe's anxious figure appeared. Fern turned on the plump woman in the arc of light thrown from her upraised candle. She looked curiously unfamiliar in dressing gown and gray hair fastened up in rag curlers. The woman's blue eyes sought hers in concern.

"Can I help you, madam?"

"I want to speak to Mr. de Lacy, but I cannot make him waken."

Mrs. Thorpe smiled wanly. "He is not there, madam. He is . . ."

"In his laboratory?"

"No, madam. He is out."

"Where?"

The woman's gaze shifted uncomfortably. Fern grew irritated. There was too much of a conspiracy of silence in this house.

"Where is he, Mrs. Thorpe? You must tell me. I am the mistress."

"Yes, madam. But I feel I should honor the master's confidence."

It was too much. Fern's patience snapped. "It is I who should have his confidence, Mrs. Thorpe, not you. I am concerned for his welfare, and I should know where he goes. Will you tell me?"

"Very well." There was distinct reluctance in the older woman's voice, but she gave in. "He rides often at night up the moors. He goes to Fox Brow."

"To Fox Brow?" Fern echoed in surprise. "That is where Ellen . . . Ellen . . ."

"Ellen Stansfield. Yes, madam."

Fern had to check her tongue, to bite back the impulse to ask why he went there. It was improper to discuss reasons with a servant. Thanking Mrs. Thorpe, she returned to her own room thoughtfully.

So it was to the young widow Ellen Stansfield that Bruno rode out every night. Fern could hear again in memory's ear the two old ladies outside the church.

"He'll never let on to her about t' other one." The other woman. It must have been Ellen all the time, and probably everyone in the village knew about it, except the mistress of Brackenroyd. Fern smoldered more and more. What kind of man was she married to? Not only did he drug her to use her brain for his experiments, but he betrayed her with another woman behind her back!

Her palms grew sticky as fury grew. She would not go back to bed until he came home; then she'd buttonhole him and have it out with him. And she would not be brushed aside by his cold, suave manner. This time they would have it out completely, openly, and honestly. She had had enough of his distant politeness, his urbane way of sliding out of matters he did not wish to discuss.

Odd, she thought, as she sat waiting in her dressing gown for dawn to bring him home, ironic even, that he has been using me while I thought all the time I was using him to validate my claim to Brackenroyd. All along we have been using each other under a thin veil of apparently respectable marriage. Both of us were frauds, but he at least knew what I was after. He never gave me the advantage of knowing what he sought from the marriage—a guinea pig in me, and a mistress in Ellen.

Before daylight Fern went to Bruno's room, withdrew the key from his side of the locked connecting door, and inserted it in her own side. Now she was mistress of the situation, she could dictate when she would speak to him, and this time he could not evade the answers she sought.

Her eyes were beginning to droop from sheer fatigue when at last she heard a movement in Bruno's room, and instantly she was alert. The first streaks of dawn were peeping through the gaps of the bedroom curtains. She sat still for a moment, listening and composing her thoughts.

He was not trying to creep stealthily, undetected, to bed, judging by the bumping sounds he made. Fern stood up, cold but determined, to challenge him now before he slept, now while he was fresh from his guilty rendezvous. Taking a candle, she grasped the key in the door, turned it, and opened the door, mentally girding herself to face the cold, uncompromising anger he would undoubtedly show at her demanding intrusion.

In the gloom beyond the reach of the candle's light she could not see him at once. There was no figure on the bed, no light in the room. Only a harsh, heavy breathing indicated his presence.

"Bruno?"

She held the candle higher, and saw the gleam of his eyes from the far corner. He staggered forward into the arc of light, and for a moment she thought he was drunk.

"Bruno, are you all right?"

He stared at her, and Fern's breath caught in a gasp. His clothing was disheveled and dirty, his black hair wildly disarrayed, but it was the wildness in his eyes that startled her—wide and staring, as if in disbelief, his mouth agape. At this moment he looked more animal than man, half-crouched as though about to spring. Fern stepped back involuntarily as a low moan escaped him, a piteous, haunted sound like a creature in pain.

"For pity's sake, what is wrong, Bruno?" she cried, but the moan changed to a growl, a sound so full of menace she was terrified. Then she saw the look in his eyes, fierce and intense, the pupils so enlarged they seemed to devour her, and her determination crumbled. As she stepped back through the door, slamming it and turning the key, she heard his weight crash hard against it on the other side, and his voice moaning and sobbing.

Shaking with fright, Fern slumped against the door. The other door—she must lock that too, in case he should try to reach her that way! Having done so, she sank on the bed, still shivering, and listened to the sounds from his room. After some minutes the moaning died away and there was silence.

It was hard to believe it had not been a dream. Bruno, always so remote and aloof, always so coolly in command—was it possible he could be that growling, half-wild thing beyond the heavy door who had seemed about to kill her? He must be drunk. There was no other possible explanation for his behavior.

He was sleeping now; she could hear his deep, stertorous breathing. Presently Fanny's footsteps approached, and Fern heard the clatter of the tea tray on the table outside the door. Fern composed herself for the girl's entrance.

"Morning, madam." Fanny's smile was bright as she poured amber tea into the china cup. "Mrs. Thorpe says I'm not to waken the master, as he has not slept. Will that be all, madam?"

"Tell Mrs. Thorpe I shall not be down until lunchtime, and after that I shall be going out."

"Yes, madam."

Fern had decided. First she would sleep, for she was exhausted, and later she would go up to Fox Brow herself, to meet Ellen Stansfield. If she could gain no answers from Bruno, perhaps she would learn from Ellen just what was going on.

It was a beautifully crisp, clear spring day when Fern at last made her way up the moorland path toward Fox Brow. She had dressed simply in a merino day dress and a hooded cloak, which now blew back from her shoulders as the mischievous breezes high on the moor whipped and played about her. Smoke curled from the low chimney above Fox Brow's dilapidated roof; its mysterious owner was evidently at home. Fern pushed open the latched gate and walked up the grassgrown path between neglected flowerbeds to the front door, its paint blistered and peeling.

Fern tapped at the door and waited, framing in her mind

174

the questions she must ask of this woman. But the person who came in answer to her knock was not at all what she had expected. Ellen Stansfield was undoubtedly once fair and desirable, but though still young, her beauty had fled.

"Come in, child, I have waited long for you." The voice was low and musical and with a warmth that touched a chord of memory. Fern followed the woman in, staring at the cloud of graying hair about the fine-boned head, admiring the graceful movement of her limbs. In the flagstoned parlor Ellen turned, her pale-gray eyes aglow but with a distance in them that made her seem abstracted, ethereal almost.

Fern stared, undecided now what to say. It seemed downright impertinence to accuse this gentle, vacuous character of duplicity, of alienating Bruno's affections. Ellen came closer, her thin gray gown seeming to float behind her, and she laid her fingertips on Fern's shoulder.

"I knew you would come, sometime. I'm glad you have come at last." The words trembled on the air, tenuous as gossamer. Again Fern felt the tingle of a half-remembered recollection, then lost it.

"I had to come, Mrs. Stansfield."

" 'Ellen,' please. Pray be seated." She indicated a well-worn armchair by the low fire, where a tabby cat glared at Fern before leaping down and surrendering the seat to her. Ellen sat opposite and held out her arms to the cat, who leaped gratefully onto her lap. She smiled at Fern. "Why did you come, child?"

"Because of my husband," Fern blurted out.

"You love him, do you not, and would like to know if he loves you?"

"I don't know ... Well, yes, I suppose so. I cannot understand him, but I know he comes to you at night. You must know him well."

"I do, indeed I do. He comes because he does not understand himself. But he will. Now you have come back to Brackenroyd, all will be resolved." There was a satisfied sigh in Ellen's voice, but Fern was puzzled.

"*Back* to Brackenroyd?"

The pale-gray gaze smiled on her again. "Oh, yes, you have come back, as I knew you would. You too have the gift, child, and if you do not know the reason yet, you surely will do so soon."

Fern began pleating folds in her skirt nervously, unsure how far to believe or trust this strange woman. But there was no one else in Brackenroyd in whom to confide.

"Bruno is strange, Ellen. Cold and unemotional, and yet he seems to have unaccountably violent ways at times. Why, only today I thought he would kill me."

Ellen smiled that faraway smile again. "Love takes us in strange ways, child."

"Love?" Fern sat upright, startled.

"It is a heat in the blood which cannot be cooled. It always appears fierce, sometimes even seeming like hatred in its violence, but it is still love in disguise. Indifference is more to be feared, for where there is coolness, there is no love."

"Are you trying to say Bruno loves me?"

"Did you ever doubt it?" The gray eyes met hers levelly. Fern sat clutching the arms of the chair in disbelief. Ellen leaned forward. "But you must have patience, child, for death must come before all is made plain."

"Death?" Fear clutched at Fern's heart. Already the villagers blamed her for the death of the Iredale child and Mrs. Briggs; surely there was not more to come?

"Death came once, long ago, and interrupted the play. Now the long interval is nearly over and the story can be resumed," Ellen was saying softly, gazing into the embers of the fire and stroking the purring cat in her lap. "Have patience, puss, it will not be long."

Fern rose to go, half-afraid of the eerie gloom where this half-mad woman murmured to herself and crooned over her cat like some medieval witch. Witch. That was it. The snatch of memory came back again—Ellen reminded her of old Mistress Uttley, who had taught Catherine the magic of herbs.

Ellen put down the cat and followed Fern to the door. "Do

not fret, child, all will be resolved, once death has visited Brackenroyd again. What you lost will be restored to you."

On the doorstep her thin fingers clutched Fern's arm. "Have you been to Catsgrave Copse yet?"

"No, that is, Fabia and I took Phoebe there to fetch catkins, but Phoebe would not go into the wood."

Ellen laughed softly. "That is not surprising. Phoebe will never go into the scene of her evil-doing, but you must go."

"To Catsgrave? Why?"

"Because that is where the story ended long ago and so must begin again. Have you not realized what its name means?

" 'Catsgrave' means 'Kate's grave.' Because that is where, Lammas night, many years ago, Catherine Radley met her end. That is where you must begin life anew, but only after death has come again."

Chapter 12

Fern refused to go to the dining room for lunch. She felt too confused, too puzzled and bewildered by her visit to Ellen Stansfield to face Bruno and possible interrogation.

It had seemed so clear before she had gone to Fox Brow. Bruno, it appeared, was being unfaithful to her, and added to that, he was planning some evil campaign against her. She was certain he had used his drugs on her, possibly to drive her mad with hallucinations or to render her physically weak, declining into ill health. Brackenroyd had been his goal, she believed, cheating her out of her inheritance by death or insanity, and she had hated him for it. Then the course had been clear—to fight rebelliously for her rights, for her inheritance and her husband.

But Ellen had undone all that, turning Fern's plans topsy-turvy. Fey, mystical Ellen was no husband stealer. And now that she too believed there was a kinship between Fern and Catherine, it put the lie to the idea of Catherine being only a figment of Fern's imagination fevered by drugs. And her words had strengthened Fern's feeling that Catherine's story was still to be unfolded and fulfilled.

Fern shivered as she recalled Ellen's words. "Death must come before all is made plain." Whose death? Fern's own, or someone else's? Bruno's, perhaps? To her surprise, Fern felt a shock at the thought of Bruno dying; it was impossible that so much power and vitality, so much repressed strength as his should be cut off.

It would be wonderful to be able to believe Ellen, that Bruno did really love his wife. If he did, he had a very strange way of showing it, Fern thought begrudgingly. And yet, if he did . . . She brushed idle speculation aside. If he did, he would say it and show it as other men did. Until then, she would not entertain the possibility.

But still she had a desire to see him. Mrs. Thorpe shook her head apologetically.

"He left straight after lunch. He was going down to the schoolhouse to see Phoebe, madam."

"Phoebe?"

"Yes, madam. He gives her a lesson most days, how to talk with her fingers, Mrs. Armitage says. Very clever man, Dr. de Lacy."

Fern had forgotten Bruno's intention to teach Phoebe the sign language of the dumb. Apparently he had not thought it important to mention to his wife that lessons were in progress—no more than she had told him of her teaching with Luke until after it had been arranged. For a newly married couple, there was little communication between them,

She must see him, if only to try to bridge the chasm that yawned between them, to try to establish some kind of amicable contact. Fern blotted out deliberately the impish thought that she wanted to see some telltale light of affection in his dark eyes.

Putting on her cloak, she followed him down to the schoolhouse. Fabia's blue eyes clouded as she answered the door.

"He's left, Fern. He was going to the mill. I'm so sorry you've missed him."

Not to be deterred, Fern trudged on toward the mill.

179

Crossing the cobbled mill yard to where a high double door emitted the noise of clanking machinery, she stopped and stared inside.

Even a layman could guess that this was the weaving shed, for a row of great iron looms hurtled and clanged, the shuttles flying so fast it made one dizzy to watch. Women in clogs stood, gray-faced and blank, before the great looms, and children too, some of whom Fern recognized from the school. Some of them, she noticed, had bowed legs, the result of rickets, and all of them looked weary and lifeless.

A man came striding toward her. Fern recognized Fearnley, the manager. He doffed his greasy cloth cap and jerked his head toward the next shed.

"Too noisy here. Come in t' mending shop," he bawled.

She followed him into the shed, where more women sat at tilted tables, poring over pieces of wool fresh from the looms. Fern could see they were examining the stuff for tiny flaws, repairing and drawing up those they found with extreme care. As they worked, men staggered in under the burden of yet more rolls of greasy cloth.

"From here t' stuff goes on to be milled and scoured," Fearnley told her with pride. "Would thee like to see, mistress?"

Assuming she would, he turned to lead the way, across the yard and into the scouring place. Lengths of wool in long iron troughs were being soaked in boiling-hot liquid and forked along mechanically till they reached great rollers, which squeezed the cloth.

"That's to get rid of t' grease," said Fearnley, "and in t' next room t' wool is dried."

In the drying room was a huge iron chamber where hot air was being blown through by a fan. The lengths of damp wool passed slowly over a series of lattices until it emerged dry at the far end. Outside the door Fern could smell the noisome vapor which arose from a series of vats.

"Grease from t' scouring, and sulfuric acid that is," Fearnley said, "to make into oil, and what's left t' soap manufacturers buy. No waste here. Wouldst like to see t' teasing shed now, or t' scribbling room? Or there's a load of fine cloths I can show thee in t' warehouse, meltons and worsteds and t' like?"

"Thank you, no, Mr. Fearnley, not now. I came only to find my husband."

"Oh, t' master's been and gone, half-hour sin."

"Do you know where he went?"

"Oh, aye. He were concerned over t' flow of t' water in t' river. He's gone up to t' reservoir to have a look."

Bilberry Reservoir—that was far away, too far to go on foot. Bruno was doubtless on horseback, so it was impossible to catch up with him now. Fern smiled her thanks and turned to go.

Catsgrave Copse; she could go there. It was not far, and the April afternoon was mild and sunny. Ellen had warned that a visit to Catsgrave—to Kate's grave—was essential.

It was a relief to escape from the thunderous clatter of the mill, with its powerful odors of grease and acid and its slimy stone floors, to the fresh, clean air of the moors. Fern breathed deeply, enjoying again the feeling of freedom that walking the crags always conveyed. She looked along the valley to where Bruno had gone, and in the mist she could just detect a glimmer of sunlight on the waters of the reservoir.

Farther along the crest she turned down toward the copse, led toward it by the bubbling moorland stream which wound its way down and eventually through Catsgrave. Fern followed its curving path to the edge of the copse, and paused.

Despite the mellowness of the afternoon sunlight and the luxuriance of the catkin-laden trees, the copse had a desolate air she had not noticed before. It was unnaturally still, no branches moving in the breeze. And no birds sang. Fern shivered. Perhaps it was the gray clouds slowly looming up from the east that stilled the birdsong, for they sensed the rain to come.

Just inside the wood there were a number of stepping-stones across the stream, and Fern noted as she stepped carefully across, the hem of her gown lifted high, that even the waters made no sound as they rippled past the stones. The

181

farther bank rose steeply to a small clearing, and here Fern stopped.

Tree trunks rose high all around, and in the deep-green and silent gloom the place had the air of a cathedral, only lacking in its sanctity. Fern sat on the grass, leaning against a fallen trunk.

This time Catherine came swiftly, a quick inrush that pervaded Fern's body without the fearful chill that had brought terror. Fern felt her gentle presence taking over and resigned herself contentedly to the usurper, for this was what she had sought. Too long had she waited for Catherine to return.

With her coming the birds suddenly found their voices again, trilling softly through the trees. A shadow fell across the faded blue of Catherine's gown, and she looked up. He was there, his black eyes dancing with happiness as he held out his hands to pull her to her feet.

"Cathy, my love, have I kept you waiting? My mare cast a shoe, and I had to take her in to the blacksmith and walk up."

No matter, she thought inwardly, for a glimpse of your beloved face I would wait a century. She held him back at arm's length to admire him, the broad strength of his body clearly revealed in the fine white shirt and dark-green breeches he wore. How soft and luxurious his shirt felt beneath her fingertips, far removed from the coarse smocks the villagers wore. Suddenly she felt ashamed of her own cheap, workaday gown, the faded cotton which was a hand-me-down from Phoebe.

"Cathy, I swear you grow more beautiful each time I see you," he was saying, drawing her close again to murmur in her ear. "How I failed to notice you in the village before I went away to London, I'll never know. Perhaps you were only a chrysalis then, a green young thing not yet grown to the beautiful butterfly you are now."

She nestled close, savoring his words. In all her life no one had spoken to her thus. Up to now she had been only a butt for criticism and scorn on account of her silence. Only now did she yearn for words to tell him how she loved him too.

"You are enchanting, Kate, and I would not have you otherwise. No, I know you would say you wish you could speak, but why yearn to be a chattering wench when you are so perfect as you are? We have no need of words, you and I, for we understand each other."

He cradled her close, and Catherine felt a glow of contentment and peace such as she had never known. That he loved her truly she did not doubt for a second; had he not, after their first chance meeting, sought out her name, as he promised, and waylaid her again, and again?

And he had told her his name. It had been a shock to discover he was Rafe de Lacy, son and heir to the lord of the manor. Only his constant reassurances that the gap between them was of no account had soothed her. He had sworn he would wed her and no other woman, but Catherine was glad she had no words to tell her family. They could never believe a rich landowner's son had honorable intentions toward a village wench.

Only Phoebe suspected that something new had come into Catherine's life, for she questioned sharply about her sister's sparkling eyes and lightness of step. But even Phoebe had lost interest in Catherine in the last few days, for she had found a beau of her own, a soldier invalided out of the king's army after a stray musket shot had injured his leg. Now she was too preoccupied to notice Catherine's frequent absences.

"Do your family know of me yet, Cathy?" Rafe's voice, tender and warm, invaded her musings. Catherine shook her head dubiously. Rafe smiled.

"Do not look so solemn, sweetheart, there is no sin in keeping it secret yet awhile. But I have told my mother about you."

Alarm leaped into Catherine's eyes. Mistress de Lacy would be sorely angered and might wreak her vengeance on the Radley family, perhaps even depriving them of the strip of land that was their livelihood. Rafe read her misgivings and pulled her down on the warm grass beside him.

"Have no fear, sweeting, for she is glad. She approves my choice, for your family is respected as honest and hardworking, and since my father's death she is anxious for me to wed and give her grandsons to bear the De Lacy name. Yours is good stock, Kate, and she and I will both be happy when you bear my sons."

Catherine reddened and buried her face in his welcoming arm. Rafe laughed, that youthful, buoyant laugh that never failed to fill her with happiness and optimism, and with his free hand he wound tendrils of her unbound hair about his finger.

"Your hair is spun gold, my lovely Kate. I adore your hair, as I worship you. See, I almost forgot—I brought a gift for you."

She looked up shyly as he held out his palm. On it lay a glittering silver ring.

"I had it specially made for us, Kate, with a message on it which betokens what exists between us."

She gazed into his dark eyes inquiringly.

"It is in Latin, and it spells 'Love Eternal,' for our love will outlast time, will it not, beloved?"

She nodded, gazing in wonder at the strange carvings on the ring's surface, then lifted her face for a kiss. He gave it, lingeringly and tenderly, then caught hold of her pointed chin.

"Now it is your turn. We are betrothed now, Kate, and you must give me a gift in return for the ring. I know! I will have a tress of your gold in exchange for my silver."

From his belt he withdrew a hunting knife, and before Catherine could protest, he cut off a curl from the nape of her neck. It lay, glistening in the sunlight, in the broad palm of his hand.

"I shall never, never part with this, Kate, I swear. And when we are old and gray we shall look at this curl and remember how our love began."

A tear hovered on Catherine's lashes. He was so gentle, so loving and kind, that she could never thank God enough for sending him into her life. A distant call on a hunting horn would have passed unnoticed, but Rafe sat up, alerted.

"I must go. Forgive me, Kate, but I must hasten. Will you meet me tonight? The old barn near the crossroads would be easier for you to reach than here?"

She hesitated. Until now they had met only by daylight,

here in the copse. The barn was too close to the village for comfort. But still, Rafe was unheeding of prying eyes. He saw no need for secrecy, so let it be. She nodded shyly, pouring love through her eyes.

He squeezed her close. "Tonight, then, soon after dusk. I shall not be late this time."

And he was gone, leaving her feeling bereft and the afternoon a shade grayer for his going. Catherine felt as though the whole encounter had been a magical dream. Could she truly believe her ears, that he had declared his love for her and that Mistress de Lacy actually welcomed the union? God was indeed merciful. And she had a silver ring as token of their betrothal—but no, it was not in the pocket beneath her kirtle. He had taken it with him. In the haste of his leaving, Rafe had pocketed it again. But no matter. Tonight he would give it her again. Catherine reclined against the tree trunk to enjoy the last of the afternoon sunlight before it would be time to go home and milk the cow for supper.

As the shadows lengthened, Catherine rose and wound her way upstream out of the woodland glade, skipping lightly across the stepping-stones and climbing uphill to the crags that edged the moor. Curling her hand above her eyes to shade them from the dipping sun, she could see the outline of the Hall against the skyline, its Tudor white walls and black timbers cradling against the moor's edge. Her thoughts lingered on her beloved, who by now was no doubt within those walls among his family, and her heart raced to think of him possibly speaking of her there now. She, a common villager, one day to enter that gracious Hall as Rafe's bride—it did not seem possible. She could not resist walking closer to it, to try to visualize the golden future he had promised.

Drawing closer, she could see beyond its walls the formal design of its grounds, the symmetrical knot gardens and precisely clipped yews bordering the gravel walks, so unlike her own garden, where plants grew in profusion, spilling over untidily and unrestrained. Cautiously she inched around the upper side of the Hall, where the great wing jutted out to bring itself in the hillside. On that side lay the stables and the mews, and the smell of new-mown hay drifted out deliciously to her nostrils. Impulsively Catherine opened the low iron gate in the wall and crossed to the barn. Inside, the scent of the hay was sensuous and soothing. She climbed the loft ladder and lay, luxuriating, in the warm depths of the hay.

The peace and stillness and warmth lapped about her like a comforting blanket, and Catherine must have drifted into sleep. Later she stretched self-indulgently and sighed, opening her eyes. A candle burned low in its holder by her side. Through parted bed hangings she could see the embers of a fire in the hearth and a paneled mahogany door. She sat up with a start.

Fern was in her own bed in Brackenroyd Hall. It was April 1883, cold in the small hours of the morning, not a summer evening in a barn. She furrowed her brow, trying to recollect. As Fern she had gone to Catsgrave Copse, but try as she might, she could not remember returning to the Hall again. It was confusing. Previously she had come back from that other life and continued this one where she had left off, but this time there was a gap in her memory. It was disturbing. What had she done in the forgotten interval? Had she seen Bruno as she intended, and if so, what had she said to him?

Bruno—Rafe—they were so alike in feature and yet so different in nature, the one so cold and unfathomable, the other so loving and candid. The one could make a woman seethe with anger and frustration, while the other evoked love as sincere as his own in return. Now, if only Bruno . . .

Sleep slithered over her again, wiping out the cares of Fern and bringing back the rapture of Catherine, surreptitiously creeping from her cottage at nightfall to keep her tryst with Rafe. "Yon lass is prattling down at the pump again, I've no doubt," Mother had remarked when Phoebe was not back at dusk. Catherine was glad Phoebe was not about, because Phoebe would not have let her sister go without much curious questioning.

The barn near the crossroads was dark and musty, not half so warm and inviting as that up at the Hall. Catherine lifted the latch and entered cautiously, hoping he was already there, his arms held out and a smile on his young dark face to welcome her. She wished she could whisper his name into the gloom.

A rapid scuffle and swishing in the hay alerted her to someone's presence, but no one spoke. A rat, perhaps? She sidled forward into the darkness, tingling with a mixture of hope and apprehension, but no one came to meet her nor spoke a word of welcome. She stopped, frightened. If not Rafe, then who or what had she heard?

As her eyes accustomed to the gloom in the musty depths of the great barn, she looked cautiously about her. Bulky outlines of bales of hay stood silhouetted against the walls, the rungs of a ladder ascending into the invisible loft above, the gleam of a hay fork carelessly cast aside when some farmhand had hastily left for home. She was alone. Catherine turned to go back outside, regretful that once again he was late for their rendezvous.

From behind the door a pair of eyes glowed with menace. Catherine uttered a shriek, and the eyes moved toward her. It was a man, a stranger, and his outstretched hands were no less menacing than the eyes, predatory and intent. She shrank back, terrified, catching her foot against the pitchfork and almost stumbling. He leaped forward with a snarl, and Catherine, terror-stricken, lost track of reason. Unthinkingly she groped for a weapon to fend him off, snatched up the pitchfork, and closed her eyes, holding it before her. She felt his weight against it, felt the heat of his breath brush her cheek, and pushed, desperate to keep the creature away. When no resistance came, she opened her eyes. The eyes still stared, but lifelessly. He was transfixed to the doorjamb, and as she watched in horror, his body slid slowly forward and lurched to the ground athwart the pitchfork.

Catherine stared, petrified and disbelieving. The approach of footsteps jerked her into life, and stepping across the body, she ran out into the night. Rafe came striding jauntily, a smile lighting his handsome face. Catherine, unable to tell him of the horrible nightmarish event in the barn, flung herself into his arms, weeping hysterically.

He cradled her tenderly, trying to calm her sobs. "Come, now, sweetheart, what's amiss? Has your mother been scolding you? Whatever it is, it cannot be so terrible, surely? Come, my sweeting, let me comfort and caress you, and you will soon forget."

She broke away from him, shaking her head violently, till her hair tumbled over her face, clinging in tendrils to the tear-soaked cheeks. She must show him so he could understand the reason for her distress, but she could not face the ugly sight again herself. She gesticulated furiously toward the barn, and as he cocked his dark head questioningly to one side, she began pushing him toward the barn door. He smiled in good humor.

"You are in a hurry, sweetheart—but it should be my place to urge you into the barn. Come, then."

He held out his hand, and Catherine saw his puzzled look when she shook her head and backed away.

"No? Then what? Ah, I have it—you would prefer the copse, is that it? It was always your favorite spot. If ever I lost you, Kate, I should know to find you there. But come quickly, we are wasting time. Tomorrow I must go to London for a few weeks, so let us make the most of precious moments."

His black eyes glowed with affection, and his arm snaked lovingly about her waist. Catherine, sickened at the mental picture of the foul thing within the barn, leaned against his warm strength and let him lead her away. How could she explain, even to Rafe, the corpse there, that the man had been about to attack her? And nothing on earth would induce her to go back there, to lead Rafe in to show him the grisly sight. In her present state of turmoil she could not even think clearly. Gratefully she clung to Rafe's reassuring warmth as they went into the wood.

Rafe was comfort, he was love and loyalty and all that she so desperately needed at this moment. Shivers of terror ran through her body at the memory of the man in the barn, and maybe Rafe was misinterpreting her tremors, her responsiveness, but all she wanted now was forgetfulness, oblivion, ecstasy to wipe out the agony. At no time in her twenty-two years had she felt the need of words as sorely as now. But Rafe more than made up for her inability, his torrent of words expressing love and passion so fiercely that her mind was wiped clear of all else. She sank to the grassy bank beneath him, lost to memory and to suffering.

Time seemed an eternity. When at last she opened her eyes, all emotion spent, she felt now only relaxed and content. All terror and guilt had fled. She rolled over and was startled to find she was alone. Beyond the bed drapes the connecting door yawned wide.

Fern felt dizzy and had to jerk her wits together. She was Fern now, not Catherine, alone in her bed in Brackenroyd Hall. But she slithered the bedclothes back and stared down—she was naked, and the door to Bruno's room stood agape. Surely . . . No, he could not have come in here. She would certainly have awoken.

She lay back, trying hard to reorient her mind to the present, but half of it was still luxuriating in the bliss of moments ago. Catherine in her copse, filled with love, while Fern battled to understand.

Bruno could not have come into her room. He had made it plain he did not want her as his true wife, of one flesh, so what reason could he have for opening the door? But she lay naked, her nightgown lying on the floor alongside the bed. She frowned, puzzled and uneasy.

The drugs in his laboratory. Could he have drugged her and then stripped her? No. She had taken great care to accept no more drinks from his hand. But he was a clever man; he could have found some other means to drug her, in her food, perhaps. Anger burned at the thought of it. No man of integrity would drug his bride in order to ravish her. No, not Bruno. He was a man of strength and determination. He would not stoop to surreptitious methods.

In an unguarded moment Fern almost felt regret that he had not. To be made love to by Bruno would be . . . would be . . . She brushed the daydream aside, irritable with herself for her weakness. Picking up her robe, she draped it about her shoulders and crossed to the door. Bruno lay asleep on the bed in his dressing gown. Silently she withdrew the key from his side of the door, inserted it on her own side, and locked the door.

It was only as she was about to climb back into bed that she saw the gleam of silver under the light of the bedside candle. It was the ring, the one Bruno had used to hypnotize Phoebe, the one Rafe had offered her last night and then forgotten.

She picked it up. A hollow laugh escaped her lips as she read the words on it. *Amor Aeternus.* Love Eternal. So Bruno *had* been into her room while she slept.

But what had he done when he came? Fern felt a mixture of shame and joy at the thought of what he might have done, and was angered with herself. At last, as dawn was breaking, she could bear the indecision no longer. She rose, put on her night robe, and opened the door to his room. He still slept as soundly as a child. She advanced to the bedside firmly.

"Bruno, I want to speak to you."

He stirred and rolled over, a half-smile lifting the corners of his lips. His eyes opened, dark and still bemused with sleep, and he looked up at her with tenderness. Fern bit her lip, undecided how to ask the question that burned within her.

"Did you come to my room in the night?"

The question was sharper, more staccato than she had meant it to sound. He evidently read the hostility in her tone, for the smile fled and his eyes darkened.

"Do you need to ask?"

Embarrassed, blushing with shame, she blundered on. "I am confused. I cannot remember clearly." She could not confess to him that she barely distinguished between Fern and Catherine, that she never quite knew when she changed places, so quickly and easily she seemed to slide from one to the other now. "I found the door open when I awoke, and I seem to remember . . . but I cannot be sure . . ."

He was sitting up now, curiosity in the depths of those eyes, and a sardonic twist to his lips.

"What do you think you remember, Fern? That your husband came to you, as a husband should?"

She hung her head, ashamed at herself, then jerked her head proudly upright. "You made love to me, did you not?"

"And if I did? Your response was most gratifying. But why do you seem so confused, for you were anything but confused at the time."

Fern glared at him. "You knew—you must have known—that I was unaware of what was happening! You took advantage of me!"

"Really?" His thick eyebrows shot up questioningly. "Then your response was remarkably warm in the circumstances."

"You treated me like . . . like a woman of the streets!"

"And you reacted like one."

Fern gasped, stung by the cruel retort. But she was totally unprepared for his next move. He rose leisurely from the bed, crossed to the marble-topped washstand where lay the contents of his trouser pockets. He picked up some coins and returned to her, holding out two golden sovereigns.

"I think perhaps you would consider this adequate payment in the circumstances?" His black eyes bored fiercely into hers. Fern felt fury boiling. She dashed his hand away so that the coins clattered across the parquet floor and rolled under the bed. Then, without thought, she dealt him a fierce blow across his cheek, watching the skin redden over the bone, but he did not move.

She ran from his room, tears burning her eyes. It was clear that as she had lain savoring the caresses of Rafe, she had unwittingly received those of her husband, and she hated him for it. But no more. Never again would he come to her bed; she would see to that. As her rage cooled, Fern dressed for breakfast. When at last she was ready to go downstairs, she heard a sound by the door. Turning, she saw a sheet of paper protruding from under the connecting door.

Curiously she picked it up and read the words in Bruno's firm, upright hand: "Madam, the village will expect an heir to Brackenroyd within a year of our marriage."

She stared at the note, aghast at its coldness and bald statement of fact. No words of atonement or of affection, simply a terse statement as if it were a business letter. "Madam" indeed!

Brackenroyd would wait long for its heir, she resolved. A very, very long time.

Chapter 13

"I'm sorry, madam, the master's gone away."

Mrs. Thorpe's smile was apologetic as she placed the break-fast dishes before Fern, conscious that it was embarrassing for her to know more of the master's movements than the mistress did.

"Gone? Did he say where?"

"Something to do with the dam, he said. Bilberry Reservoir is giving him cause for concern, so he was to go and see the reservoir commissioners. He'd be back in a few days, he said."

"I see. Thank you, Mrs. Thorpe."

Fern was both irritated and disappointed. No doubt after their last encounter Bruno was loath to face her again and so had deemed a message via the housekeeper politic, but it was hurtful to learn of one's husband's movements only through a servant. And she was sorry he was gone. After the terrifying experience of Catherine in the barn, she had need of his company, of his reassuring strength. He was so like Rafe in appearance, and yet so unlike in character.

The Hall too seemed unaccountably desolate without his vibrant presence. Fern wandered disconsolately from room to room, restless and undecided what to do. Last night's events had quite unsettled her, the jumbled dream of Catherine's tragic mishap in the barn aggravated by the strange way Fern had awoken, recalling the comfort of Rafe's arms—or were they Bruno's?

With a pang Fern realized she was aching for the feel of those arms about her again. For all her irritation and anger against Bruno in the past, she needed his reassurance now, and despite herself, she missed him.

Throughout the day Fern's sense of disquiet persisted, and by night she lay restless in her bed, conscious that Bruno no longer lay in the next room. His absence caused an ache which, though she knew it to be irrational and groundless, nevertheless tormented her. However she reasoned with herself that she hated him, distrusted him, feared him even, still she longed for his return.

Sleep brought no peace. She lay crouched in a truckle bed in a corner of the cottage, listening to Phoebe's screams reechoing about the rafters of her little room, wide-eyed and terrified.

"Don't take on so, Phoebe," Mother was murmuring soothingly. "Tha'll make thissen ill, carrying on in that fashion."

"Ben, Ben!" Phoebe sobbed, her face scarlet and contorted with hysterical weeping. "He were to have wed me. What shall I do now? Oh, Ben! Who could a done this to thee!"

She crouched by the hearth, rocking to and fro in her agony and heedless of her mother's attempts to console. Catherine lay numb, stricken with horror. The man in the barn, the man with the menacing eyes and grasping fingers—he had been Phoebe's lover, the swain she had been so proud of. Remorse and guilt flooded Catherine. To have killed a man was sin grievous enough to ensure hell in the hereafter, but her sister's lover!

"Come, now, lass, give over yelling like that—canst see how tha's frightened thy sister?" Mother was urging the grief-stricken Phoebe. But for half the night she sat crooning to the girl while Catherine lay silent, overcome by the enormity of her crime. Useless to confess, to try to explain. Phoebe would never forgive, even if she could understand the reason which had driven Catherine to it.

Even Mother, with all her warmth and kindliness, would be loath to believe the truth, even if Catherine were to express by dumb show that she was the cause of Ben's death, the more so as there was no way Catherine could mime his menacing approach to her. No, best to stay as she had always been, dumb and unobtrusive. Perhaps in time she could find some way to atone to Phoebe.

Gradually Phoebe's wracking sobs and screams gave way to silence. In time she became withdrawn and sullen, and Catherine could see Mother shake her head sadly behind the girl's back.

"It's shock, tha knows. It takes some that way," she murmured to Father. "But she'll get over it, given time. It's a new lad she needs."

"It's a bit more work she needs to occupy her idle hands and give her summat to think about," Father retorted, but not unkindly. Catherine watched her sister fearfully, lest her sharp eyes detect the guilt that Catherine felt certain was stamped all over her face.

Not even in Rafe could she confide the truth, for he was less able to understand her signs than her family. He was content to accept her as she was, wordless and trusting. And now that she had Phoebe's work to attend to as well as her own, there was no opportunity to see Rafe for a time, even after she heard he was back at Brackenroyd Hall.

Phoebe began to go out again, down to the village pump for water in the evenings. And Catherine noticed how the group of girls clustered about the pump ceased their gossiping whenever she approached. But it was not long before the usually garrulous Phoebe had reinstated herself with them, and then it was on Catherine's approach that the sidelong glances were cast her way. Catherine was still riddled with guilt and afraid. Did her guilt show in her expression?

Then rumors began drifting to the Radley cottage.

"Witchcraft? What flummery! Never heard such nonsense

195

in my life!" exploded Mrs. Radley when a neighbor sat whispering by the hearth. "That lad died 'cause he had a pitchfork stuck through him, and there's nowt supernatural in that. Some tramp, happen, or some gypsy who was stealing from the barn, that's who did it, if tha asks me."

Catherine sat silent but apprehensive at the table, her fingers shelling peas while her ears strained to listen.

"But that's what they're saying, Mistress Radley," the neighbor defended herself. "I'm only telling thee what they're saying in t' village."

"Who says? And who in t' village is capable of witchcraft, I'd like to know? These are dangerous times we live in, neighbor, and to accuse anyone of witchcraft is a certain way to send that body to their death."

"Well, there's old Mother Uttley . . ."

"Who's done nowt but good for us all. Why, she cured thee of a toothache not a month gone."

"Aye, but them as can cast good spells can happen cast evil ones too."

"Fiddlesticks. Tha's no cause to speak ill on Mother Uttley, so leave the poor creature alone. Besides, she's learned our Catherine a useful potion or two. Our lass has learned a lot from her."

"Aye, that's what they're saying."

Mistress Radley's eyes grew wide in disbelief. "Tha's not saying, surely . . . Tha can't believe . . ." She glanced quickly across to her daughter. "Catherine, leave t' peas, there's a good lass, and fetch in some milk from t' cowshed. I shall need some for t' baking in a minute."

Catherine rose obediently but lingered outside the cottage window, opened for the sake of a cool breeze on this hot afternoon.

"Who's been saying such cruel things, neighbor?" Mistress Radley was demanding in a fierce whisper. "Who'd dare say owt agen my Catherine?"

"Well, to be honest, mistress, it was your Phoebe."

"Phoebe? Never!"

"I heard her wi' my own ears. She reckons as Ben was

lured to his death by an evil spirit, and there's precious few hereabouts as know how to cast spells. Then she said as Mother Uttley was ill abed that night and so couldn't a harmed him. So that left only . . . only . . . ."

"I'll not have it," Mistress Radley shouted, and Catherine trembled at the rage in her mother's voice. "They'll not say a word agen my poor girl, blighted as she is, but good and pure for all that. They'll not threaten my poor lass!"

"It's Phoebe as says it," the neighbor stammered. "I'd not have repeated it else. But there's some as is anxious to report the matter to the authorities. Tha knows how they hunt witches out."

"I know. I've heard of them witchfinders and what they do. They'll not come pricking and ducking my innocent lass, and I'll thank thee to put the lie to this evil rumor. Good day to thee, neighbor."

Catherine shrank back behind the corner of the cottage as the neighbor emerged, her foot crushing a patch of her beloved mint-scented geranium and sending up the pungent aroma to envelop her. A sweat of fear banded her forehead. So by mischance the villagers had guessed the culprit, Ben's murderer, but for the wrong reasons.

Witchcraft, they said. Catherine shuddered. It was unbelievable. Phoebe must believe her filled with spite or jealousy to want to occasion her lover's death, and by such stealthy means. Oh, it was so cruel! To be justly accused of murder was one matter, but to be wrongfully accused of devil's work for malicious reasons was more than heart or soul could bear. Catherine felt giddy with fear and horror. She stumbled across the green to the sanctuary of the church.

Torment wracked her. Even in the sepulchral gloom of the deserted church she could find no peace. The faces of the saints enshrined in stained glass seemed to frown down on her and it was in vain that she tried to pray for guidance. Guilt weighed heavy on her soul, dragging her down to inevitable hell fire. Catherine moaned in agony.

Two village women came down the aisle bearing clusters of flowers for the altar. On seeing Catherine, they glanced nervously at each other. In the somber silence their whispered words carried clearly to her ears.

"That's her. Never think it to look at her, wouldst tha?"

"Fancy having the nerve to come into church after what she's done. Face of an angel and soul of a devil, that one. Who'd a thowt it?"

They gazed up at the altar as if they half-expected an avenging God to crack a thunderbolt down on the sinful maid, and Catherine could only stare helplessly at them. If these women who had known her all her life could believe such evil about her, what chance would she have of convincing the authorities that Ben's death had been only a tragic mistake? Again the dizziness enfolded her, the vivid colors of the stained glass swimming and merging in the shafts of sunlight.

Rafe! Oh, Rafe, come to me, help me! she cried inwardly. Through the eddying mist that threatened to submerge her, she heard a woman's voice.

"She'll get her deserts. Tha knows what t' good book says: 'Vengeance is mine, saith the Lord.' He'll see to it she pays for what she's done."

"Aye," agreed a vindictive voice. "Soon as t' witchfinder gets here, she'll suffer. I hear as pricking t' devil's mark and t' ducking stool never fails."

"She hasn't t' devil's mark, has she?"

"Oh, aye. Phoebe says it's clear as day, just under her left armpit. And that cat of hers must be her familiar, I reckon."

Oh, no, it was too cruel! A mole interpreted as a condemning mark, and a hairless pet like Tibb as a familiar spirit—how credulous people could be! Catherine felt desperate, alone, and terrified in her mute world. Oh, Rafe! For pity's sake, help me!

She opened her eyes. In her hand a candle glowed, and with the other she was rattling a doorknob. Fern steadied herself, fighting to hold on to a time and a place. She was here, in Brackenroyd Hall, in her bedroom, and struggling to open the door to Bruno's room. And her voice was crying plaintively for help. Footsteps came scurrying in the corridor, and someone knocked peremptorily at the door.

"Are you all right, madam?" It was Mrs. Thorpe's voice. Fern opened the door to her wearily.

"Is anything wrong, Mrs. de Lacy? I heard you calling for the master. He's not home yet, remember." Her welcome face, framed in rag curlers, expressed concern.

"It's all right, Mrs. Thorpe. A bad dream only. I had forgotten the master's absence."

The housekeeper's anxious face softened. "He'll be back in a day or two. Now, can I make you a hot drink to help settle you?"

"No, really, thanks. I'll be all right now."

"Very well, then. Good night, Mrs. de Lacy."

After her slippered feet had scuttered off down the corridor again, Fern blew out the candle and climbed back into bed. She felt disturbed and somehow guilty, as if Catherine's guilt had rubbed off onto her. But then, she *was* Catherine, with only an interval of time separating her former life from her present one. Nevertheless, she felt remorseful. She had deserted Catherine just at her moment of greatest need. She must endeavor to return as soon as she could.

But throughout the rest of the night Fern could not sleep. She tossed restlessly, thinking of the villagers and their hatred of the Radleys. "Tainted blood" they had called it, the only relic of the story of Catherine that had come down to them. Poor Catherine, all these centuries unjustly condemned as a witch, shadowing the lives of all succeeding Radleys like a menacing cloud.

In the morning Mrs. Thorpe searched Fern's face anxiously. "You look very pale, madam. Are you sure you're not sickening for something?"

"I slept badly, that is all. Perhaps fresh air will revive me. The day is warm and sunny, so I think I'll ride out on Whisper. Please ask Malachi to saddle her up for me."

It was a mild and beautiful May morning as Fern rode down to the village, undecided what she would do when she arrived there. As she drew up by the village green, Edgar Amos was standing sunning himself by the lych-gate.

"Good morning, Mrs. de Lacy. I was just thinking of you. Quite a coincidence you should ride by."

"Of me? Why?"

"That old register where we found Catherine Radley's death quite intrigued me. I've just been reading it again. Curious, but there seem to have been quite a number of deaths in strange circumstances just about that time, the summer of 1642. Come, I'll show you, if you're interested."

Dismounting and tying Whisper to a fence rail, Fern followed him into the vestry. Specks of dust rose from the ancient ledger as he opened it, hovering in the sunlight that fell from a high window. Fern read the faint, spidery script with difficulty.

On Julye xii William Brygg was drowned at Park Mylne as he crossed over a narrow bridge. A soden tempest of wind blew him into the water, and the water was unnaturally greate.

Jennett, wyfe of John Marsden, as she comed from ye pasture from milking, ye xxi daye of Julye, was struck by a thunderbolt and died.

Agnes, wyfe of Richard Littlewoode, within xi dayes of she was delivered of a child, rose out of hyr childe bedde and went privily to a little well not halfe a yarde deepe, and there drowned the childe.

All these deeds by instigation of the devil, and more yet we wot not of, perchance.

Fern straightened up from poring over the ledger. Amos was watching her, his fair head cocked to one side speculatively.

"What do you make of that, Mrs. de Lacy?"

She shrugged. "Some poor old parson who was unduly superstitious, no doubt."

"Or a wave of hysteria swept the village. It was a bad year for the village. The crops failed, owing to storms, and the register lists a number of stillbirths. These events would frighten the villagers. It was the era of witch-hunting then, you know, when Matthew Hopkins, the self-appointed witchfinder general, was terrorizing the south."

"What do you make of it, then?"

He frowned. "Taking into account the hatred that has always been felt against the Radleys, the ancient belief in their tainted blood, and the curt way in which Catherine's death is reported simply as 'departed this life,' I think it was she who was suspected of witchcraft."

"And her death? What caused that?"

She would discover, sooner or later, how Catherine died, but the question was of burning importance. She hoped Amos would not notice the eagerness in her voice.

"I don't know." He rubbed his chin thoughtfully, his gaze clouded and far away. "There are more records I've not yet read. Perhaps I shall find the answer there, and then I'll let you know."

He followed her out of the church into the sunlight. At the gate he cupped his hands to help her mount, then shaded his eyes against the sun to watch her ride off. Fern felt choked by the dust in the vestry, the claustrophobic air of the village, the knots that bound about her heart, and longed for air to breathe freely. The moors. That was what she wanted—the vast space and freedom of the moors.

Up and up she urged Whisper, up over the crags on the crest of the hill and away across the vast expanse of moor, where there was only solitude and strange silences, across an endless succession of heather-clad undulations which melted in the purple distance into the sunlit sky. Up here she could breathe again, here where it seemed as though a person could ride for days without seeing a human face or hearing a human voice. The moors held a terrifying power, even on this fine day, for she remembered how in the gloom of winter their dark, frowning presence had dominated the landscape.

Near the lapping waters of the reservoir she dismounted and let Whisper graze on the short, springy turf. Fern stared across the rippling, expressionless waters and felt miserably alone. Here, in the high free air, the burden of guilt seemed to weigh less heavily, but she longed for Bruno to come back, for his nearness to allay the suspicion of fear and impending tragedy that darkened her mind. She needed his strength, his reassuring rationalism, to try to extricate herself from the turmoil of Catherine, who was more in her than Fern. Differentiation between herself then and now was becoming increasingly difficult and less definable. She felt she would go out of her mind unless help came soon.

In the distance a thin wreath of smoke coiled up into the air. Fox Brow. Ellen was at home, alone but for old Hepzibah. Impulsively Fern resolved to go and see the young widow. Perhaps she, in her half-crazed world, could understand and help.

Ellen's door was already ajar when Fern dismounted. Fern hesitated on the step. Ellen was close to Bruno, his friend and confidante—would it be wise to reveal one's doubts and anxieties to her, especially when one's doubts included that close friend?

Ellen's light voice called from within, "Come in, Mrs. de Lacy. I have been expecting you."

She was sitting by the table, her hands composed in her lap. Her eyes searched Fern's face curiously.

"You are troubled, I can see. Sit by me and let me guess at what distresses you."

Fern sat opposite her and felt the gray eyes raking deep, as if searching out her soul. It was a soothing sensation, that someone cared and wanted to help.

"You have the gift, as I told you once. By its means you have discovered the reason for your unhappiness—and that of all the Radleys. Now you come close to the answer, as no Radley has done before."

"What is the answer, Ellen?"

"Love. There are many great and powerful cosmic forces which only the mystics can understand, but the most universal, the most potent of them all, is love."

"Love?" Fern was bewildered.

"It is energy, psychic energy. Love of one's fellow men, the consciousness of becoming one and the same person with another, that is the ultimate power of the universe. Forgive me my philosophical wanderings, but it is the one truth I have learned. You too are learning it now, I believe."

"You mean ... I love Bruno?" Fern's voice was hesitant, reluctant to mouth the words.

"Did you ever doubt it? And your family inheritance, else you would not be at one with your past as you are. But you are still blind. You have yet more to learn."

"What must I learn, Ellen?"

"Patience, understanding. I think you do not yet see how Bruno suffers."

"He suffers?" Amazement rang in Fern's voice.

"Oh, yes, my dear. His is a battle to find himself."

Fern sat perplexed, thinking over Ellen's words. To find oneself. That was the very problem Bruno had once said she had to resolve before she would find peace. And if Ellen was right, he was faced with the same problem himself. It had never occurred to Fern that Bruno, the dark, taciturn man of strength, could have a personal difficulty such as this.

"You forget, my dear, that he is of mixed parentage, and so of mixed heredity. The Yorkshire part of him, wild and unrestrained and imaginative, is at variance with his Teutonic blood. He sees himself as cool and rational, analytical and precise, as a scientist should be, and he cannot easily reconcile himself to the passionate, irrational moods that overtake him from time to time."

"Bruno?" Fern thought Ellen must be speaking of some other man.

"Oh, yes, he suffers as a result. He is a soul in torment, Fern, but through your love he can find himself again, as he was meant to be. You must have patience, for you have found yourself, and he is still to attain that. It will not be long now, though the worst of the suffering is still to come."

Ellen's eyes were misted now, remote and sad. Fern felt she could foresee the tragedy, but something stilled her tongue from questioning.

"It will ... work out right, won't it, Ellen?" Fern's voice was faint with apprehension.

"This time it will; it must." Centuries of hope and sadness lay in Ellen's tone. Slowly Fern rose to go, filled with a new determination.

"Thank you, Ellen. I shall remember what you have said."

Somehow, thought Fern as she rode back toward the Hall, somehow I must resolve the problems of both Catherine and Bruno. And somehow the two problems seemed one, inextricably linked though separated by three hundred years and more. In an inexplicable way she knew that the solution of the one problem would inevitably resolve the other. Tonight she would welcome Catherine's advent and the unfolding of the poor maid's unhappy tale.

But Catherine did not come. By morning Fern felt utterly drained and exhausted from willing her to come, but in vain. She felt afraid, too, afraid that Catherine was slipping away from her, and only by a tenuous thread was the unhappy creature still bound to her. She could not fade away now, to vanish into a limbo of lost souls, forever wandering and wretched. Fern was fretful and sick at heart.

All day she carried the burden of desolation and aimlessness with her, unable to set her mind to anything. By nightfall it seemed too much of an effort to dress for dinner, with Bruno away still.

Mrs. Thorpe tapped at her mistress's door. "The master is home, madam. He's gone down to his laboratory and says he will not take dinner tonight."

Fern's heart leaped into life. Somehow, with Bruno now in Brackenroyd, Catherine seemed a little closer. Despair and lethargy fell from her shoulders. She dressed quickly in a delicate filmy gown and went down to meet Bruno.

The heavy oak door to the old wing swung open as she neared it, and Bruno emerged, bowed and hollow-eyed. On an impulse Fern drew back into the shadows of the corridor until he had closed and locked the door. Then, as he turned to go toward the dining room, she moved forward into the light of the gas lamp on the wall. He stopped suddenly, a light coming sharply into his dark eyes, a look that was at once fierce and compelling.

"Beloved," he murmured.

Instantly she flung herself into his outstretched arms, happiness and warmth suffusing her. His arms enclosed her tightly; then he kissed her. Fern welcomed with delight the feel of his mouth hard on hers and the bittersweet taste of his lips, then drew slowly away.

"I've missed you, Bruno."

The soft words had an effect she could not have anticipated. At once he stiffened and his eyes grew cold. He stood erect and formal, and Fern was bewildered by the sudden change.

"What is it, Bruno? What's wrong?"

He hesitated. "I don't know. I am not myself today. Please forgive me."

It was then that she noticed the gleam in his fingers. It was a frond of hair, a blond tress not unlike her own. He must have been carrying it when she met him.

"What is that, Bruno?"

He looked down at it with an air of surprise, as if he had not seen it before, then raised it to the light of the lamp and examined it, a hint of a smile softening the line of his mouth.

"Where does it come from, Bruno?"

"I don't know. I found it in a little box in the study."

"Then why do you have it?"

He shrugged. "For some reason, I find it interesting. I shall replace it in the box."

In his study she watched him take out a small ebony box from a drawer, opening it to reveal a velvet-lined interior. He laid the curl inside, tied with its faded ribbon, and closed the lid gently. Something in the way he moved his broad, muscular hands over the lid, tenderly and slowly, made Fern ache to recapture the closeness there had been between them in the corridor only moments ago. She moved closer to him.

"There is something nostalgic in a family heirloom, is there not?" she murmured softly. He drew himself up sharply.

"I have no time for sentimentality." His voice was cruelly

sharp, accusing in its denial. For once Fern was not angered by his sudden change; only a pang of pity touched her that always, always he seemed to feel the need to defend himself, to retort and deny. Ellen was right. One needed patience to understand this man. His eyes held a distracted, almost hunted look. Fern took his hand shyly and led him back into the corridor.

"Come, let us go in to dinner, and then we shall go to bed early. You look tired."

He drew his hand away. "I do not wish to eat, nor have I time to sleep. Tomorrow I must go to see the magistrates; the commissioners will not listen to reason about the reservoir."

"You work too hard, Bruno. The problem of water supply is not so pressing that it cannot wait. The mill has functioned quite well up to now."

He sighed and passed a hand across his brow. "You do not understand. I have told you before that you do not understand. I am not concerned with the mill, but our safety. The reservoir dam is in need of repair, and I must get the commissioners to act before it is too late."

"Tomorrow, Bruno. Tonight you must sleep."

He turned on her suddenly, his expression almost savage. Fern involuntarily took a step back. "Tonight I must go to Fox Brow," he hissed softly.

"Fox Brow?" echoed Fern. "To Ellen Stansfield? Why do you go there so often?" He did not answer. "Why, I asked you? Every night almost since our wedding you have gone there, I know."

He was turning away, her question unheeded.

Fern grew angry. She grasped his arm and glared at him. "Why must you see Ellen Stansfield every night, and not your wife? Is she your mistress?"

Fern never saw his arm rise, only the color that flooded his cheeks and the fire in his eyes. But she felt the fierce sting of his fingers on her cheek. Disbelievingly she stared, her hand to her face. Bruno glared at her, anger and hatred staring from his black eyes; then he turned suddenly and strode away, leaving her alone in the empty corridor.

Angrily Fern turned back along the passage. As she neared the studded door to the old wing, she noticed the keys still dangling from the lock. Bruno had evidently forgotten them when she came upon him unexpectedly.

The sting of his hand still hot on her cheek and the bittersweet taste of his mouth still fresh on her lips, Fern turned the key over furiously and opened the door, taking the bunch of keys with her into the darkness beyond.

At the far end of the stone passage a solitary lamp burned, piercing only a part of the intense gloom of the old Hall. Her footsteps echoed hollowly as she crossed toward the laboratory, ringing mournfully in the desolate atmosphere. Tonight the old Hall had the air of an empty tomb, and a frisson of fear went down Fern's spine. Would she ever find Catherine again, to play out the last, tragic scenes of her pitiful life? The fear that she might not gave Fern a terrible, unbearable sense of loss. She picked up the oil lamp, and by its light tried the keys in the lock of the laboratory door.

The second key opened the door. In the circle of light thrown by the lamp Fern could see the bench and shelves, the gleam of bottles and jars. On the bench lay an empty glass. She picked it up and sniffed the dregs cautiously. The smell was familiar. A tentative taste on the tip of her finger confirmed it. It was the bittersweet taste of Bruno's lips. Hemlock, belladonna, laudanum, opium—of all the bottles arranged there, from which ones had he concocted a mixture to drink . . . and why?

Fern relocked the door after her, replacing the keys in the lock of the heavy door to the main house where she had found them, before going down to a solitary dinner. Mrs. Thorpe came in as Cassie was clearing the dishes away.

"Begging your pardon, Mrs. de Lacy, but was supper not to your liking?" she asked anxiously.

"Perfectly, Mrs. Thorpe. I was not hungry, that is all."

The old lady's eyes searched hers. "Are you quite sure you are well, madam? It's not like you to leave your meal hardly touched."

Fern saw her questioning eyes, the speculative stare, and

recognized the unspoken suspicion. Was the mistress of Brackenroyd pregnant already? That was no doubt the gossip belowstairs.

"I am simply tired, that is all. I shall go to bed soon."

"Very well, madam. The master has gone out with Pharaoh, so I have just put away his things in the study. I hope he will not mind."

"I'm sure he won't. What things?"

"Papers, files. Oh, and that little lock of hair." Mrs. Thorpe's eyes misted with nostalgia. "Old Mr. Thomas used to take that blond lock out of its box sometimes and wash it in brandy, to keep it bright he said."

Despite her weariness, Fern was curious. "Did he say whose hair it was, Mrs. Thorpe? An old sweetheart, perhaps?"

"Dear me, no. He said it had been in the family for ages, hundreds of years he said. And he said a funny thing. He said Brackenroyd would never be happy until its owner came back. I never could understand old Mr. Thomas, but he was a very kind and clever man."

Mrs. Thorpe smiled at the memory, and left, leaving a faint scent of lavender water in her wake. Fern rose wearily from the table and had to clutch at the edge for support as a wave of dizziness washed over her. She slumped into a chair by the fireside and felt distinctly nauseated.

She was trembling with apprehension. What on earth was wrong with her? Could the suspicion clearly showing in Mrs. Thorpe's eyes be true after all, that she was carrying Bruno's child? It was unthinkable, to be bearing a child whose conception she could not even remember. Nor could she be certain it had ever taken place. Exhaustion—that was much more likely to be the reason. Or the effect of Bruno's potion she had tasted down in the laboratory. But, no. A tiny fingertip taste could hardly have such drastic effect, when Bruno, having drunk the glassful presumably, had walked out on the moor tonight apparently unaffected.

Or maybe he was affected by the drugs. How was she to know when his behavior was different from usual, when she did not really know the man? But he did change personality often and inexplicably—had this always been due to drugs?

It was odd to remember how she had suspected him of drugging her, while all the time he must have been administering the drugs to himself. But why?

Speculation was cut short by the discreet knock and entrance of Fanny. The maid bobbed a curtsy.

"Begging your pardon, madam, but the Reverend Amos is here and wishes to see you. Mrs. Thorpe says I am to inquire whether you feel well enough to receive him."

"Of course, Fanny. Please show him in here."

Edgar Amos' eyes sparkled as he strode in and crossed to the hearth. "Forgive me, Mrs. de Lacy, for intruding so late in the evening, but I have just discovered among the late Mr. Thomas' notes a story I knew would intrigue you. I had to come and tell you at once."

"Pray be seated, Edgar. Fanny, a glass of wine for the reverend. Madeira, Edgar, or Canary?"

"Madeira, excellent, thank you." He waited until Fanny had handed him the wine, bobbed, and left the room. Then he leaned forward eagerly, putting the wine aside.

"Your Catherine de Lacy was a witch. Or at any rate, the villagers believed she was. Mr. Thomas unearthed accounts— which I can verify, as he states his source in the notes—which told how the villagers suspected her and began to amass evidence against her."

Fern stared at him and felt no emotion. What he told her she knew already. All that concerned her now of Catherine's story was its ending, how she died and how her relationship with Rafe fared. Edgar Amos watched her face curiously.

"Are you not interested, Mrs. de Lacy? I thought you would be."

"You tell me what I already know, Edgar."

His sandy eyebrows shot up. "You knew? Were there other notes of Mr. Thomas' here in the Hall?"

She shook her head wearily. "Tell me, Edgar, does the account say anything of Rafe de Lacy?"

"No, not really, except to mention that he was lord of the

manor at the time and unable to prevent the witch-hunt against one of his villagers, as he was absent from Brackenroyd. Curiously enough, he seems to have returned here on the date given in the parish records as the date that Catherine departed this life."

Fern leaned forward, a gleam of interest revived. "The parish records neglected to state the cause of her death. Does Mr. Thomas' account reveal what happened?"

"He does not state the manner of her death, I'm afraid, but the persecution she suffered leaves one in little doubt. The villagers were unable to try out the usual test for a witch, of getting her to repeat the Lord's Prayer to see if she falters, because it was useless in the case of a dumb girl. Perhaps out of fear or respect for her father they did not duck her in the river either, nor prick the witch's mark she is reputed to have had on her body, but they harassed and tormented her nonetheless."

"So you are in little doubt how she died?"

"What would a poor dumb creature do in such circumstances, unable to run away and fend for herself? I think she probably committed suicide like Annot, for her body does not lie in the churchyard."

Fern felt anger for Catherine flood through her veins, bringing back life and purpose in place of the lassitude of a moment ago. She rose and crossed to the fireplace, to pull the bell rope.

"There you are wrong, Edgar. Catherine did not kill herself. Would you do something for me?"

He rose quickly. "Of course, Mrs. de Lacy."

"Then pray accompany me to Fox Brow."

"Now? It is late, and darkness has fallen. Is it Mr. de Lacy you seek, for I will gladly fetch him for you."

"No, Edgar. It is not Bruno I seek, but Catherine. I must go now, before it is too late."

He was staring at her, openmouthed. "Catherine? Do you mean Ellen, Mrs. de Lacy, Ellen Stansfield?"

Fanny appeared in the doorway. Fern turned to her, forgetting Amos for the moment. "Please fetch my cloak, Fanny, and tell Mrs. Thorpe not to lock up until I return. I am going out with Reverend Amos."

The maid bobbed and withdrew. Fern turned again to Amos. "I meant what I said, Edgar. I need Ellen's help. If Catherine will not or cannot come to me, then I must go in search of her."

Chapter 14

With lamplight gleaming from one uncurtained window as they drew near, Fox Brow had the appearance of a squat, one-eyed monster crouching on the cliff edge. In the moonlight its shape was only indistinctly visible.

"Ellen is still up, at any rate." Amos seemed embarrassed at their late visit, and then Fern remembered that he had probably never visited the house before, since Ellen was reported to receive few callers.

Fern waited while Edgar stepped down from the trap and turned to help her down. As she stood poised on the step, a faint, far-off sound came to her ears.

"What was that?" There was an edge of fear in Fern's voice.

"I heard nothing," Edgar replied after a moment's pause.

"I thought I heard a cry."

"Just the wind over the moors, I expect. Come, Mrs. de Lacy. It is cold out here."

Fern hesitated, transfixed. She could have sworn she heard it—a faint voice calling "Catherine" in a long, drawn-out, despairing cry. She pulled herself together. He was probably right. The wind could sound deceptively human, and especially at night.

It was old Hepzibah who came to the door in answer to Amos' knock. The door opened only inches, restrained by the heavy chain, and Hepzibah's suspicious face, wreathed in rag curlers, peered out at the visitors.

"Mrs. de Lacy wishes to see Miss Stansfield. You recognize me, do you not, Hepzibah?" Amos said gently.

"Aye, Reverend, but we weren't expecting company at this hour," the old woman replied gruffly as she unlatched the chain. "Coom in."

She shuffled ahead of them into the parlor. "H's t' vicar and Mrs. de Lacy."

"Come in and warm yourselves by the fire." Ellen's silvery voice betrayed no surprise as she waved her visitors to the vacant chairs by the fire. It was a cozy scene, lamplight and firelight casting a mellow glow over chintz covers and chenille tablecloth and the frail figure of the woman with a cloud of prematurely gray hair about her gentle face.

"Shall I mend t' fire for thee?" Hepzibah asked.

"No need of more coal tonight. Get yourself to bed, Hepzibah."

The old woman grunted and withdrew. Ellen turned to Fern. "Do you come in search of your husband, my dear, for I fear you have missed him. He was here, but he left half an hour ago."

Fern shook her head. "Do not misunderstand me. I want to see Bruno, yes, but first I must find someone else."

She could see from the corner of her eyes the wondering look on Amos' face as he sat quietly, just beyond Ellen's line of sight. He might think her crazy, but what matter? Finding Catherine—and Bruno—was a problem so urgent that now they seemed a matter of life and death to her.

Ellen's gaze was mistily remote. "He still seeks himself, poor man. But the time is not far off when he will arrive at the truth."

"Bruno?" Fern prompted softly.

"He was like a man crazed with fear—or hate, or some other violent emotion."

"Tonight?"

The soft, misted eyes turned on Fern. "Aye, tonight. He talked of wild things, meaningless jumble. I could make no sense of it. He was like a man possessed, or drunk."

Amos cleared his throat apologetically. "I too have seen him in that condition, I'm afraid, Mrs. de Lacy. I did not wish to alarm you with undue fears, but I do wonder if Dr. de Lacy does not perhaps, um, imbibe more than is good for him."

"Not drink, but drugs," said Fern quietly.

Amos was startled, but Ellen showed no reaction. Fern leaned toward the older woman and took her hands. "Tonight I found the emptied glass in his laboratory. Did you know he took drugs, Ellen?"

Ellen nodded slowly. "I knew he used to, when he first came here, for he told me about it. His work was concerned with the human mind, he said, and the causes of hallucination."

"So he took drugs himself?" Amos queried.

"One could not measure the effect of them on an animal's mind, so it was necessary to use a human subject for experiment, he said."

Fern remembered how she had suspected him of drugging her, how he had interrogated her about her resulting dreams. She stared at Ellen, who shook her head again in mute reply.

"What better subject than himself, he decided, for he could best gauge the results on himself." Ellen's eyes clouded in bewilderment. "But he told me some weeks ago he was discontinuing the experiments. They were having side effects he found unpleasant, he said. I thought he had stopped."

"He has not. I found the evidence tonight."

"Then there must be another reason."

"He could have become addicted, perhaps," Amos interjected, but it was an explanation Fern could not accept. Bruno was too stubborn, too self-willed to allow himself to become dependent on a prop.

Suddenly Ellen withdrew her hands from Fern's, and rising, walked slowly to the table. "Now I think it becomes clear. Dr. de Lacy has been discovering something of the truth about himself—so much I have gathered from his ramblings—and he does not like what he learns. It would seem he tried to discontinue the drugs because it was by their means that he was finding out."

"Then why is he taking them again?" Fern asked hesitantly.

"Because he is strong. Though he dislikes it, he will find out the truth. It gives him pain, of that I am certain, and I think it also brings him fear."

The atmosphere was tense. Amos tried to lighten it with a staccato laugh. "What devilish secrets can the poor man have in his past that he does not like to recall? Some foolish misdeed in his youth, perhaps? But then, what man in Christendom hasn't committed some trifling misdemeanor he would prefer to forget?"

Ellen did not seem to notice the vicar's presence. "But then, it was not primarily about Dr. de Lacy that you came, my dear. Have no fear, his problem will be resolved very soon now. I feel it."

"Are you sure, Ellen?"

She nodded sagely. "As soon as he comes to terms with his Yorkshire blood instead of trying to deny the wild and passionate part of himself. He has been brought up in Germany, taught to think like an objective, reasoning creature, and he believes it wrong to be a slave to one's feelings. But one cannot deny what is in the blood. Heredity will have its way."

She was sitting now at the table, chin resting on cupped hands, a halo of lamplight about her head. Fern went to sit in the spindle-backed chair opposite her.

"It was not about Bruno that I came, but Catherine. I cannot reach her, Ellen. You must help me."

She saw the woman's eyes soften in answer to the pleading in her voice. Amos pulled his chair nearer the table. A coal settled noisily in the hearth, and the firelight grew dimmer. In another room a clock began to chime softly, but whether it struck ten or eleven, Fern did not notice. Her gaze was fixed on Ellen's translucent face. Ellen did not speak, but Fern could feel the atmosphere in the little room thickening, and she knew Ellen was mentally in communion with her, willing Catherine to return. For both of them the intrusive vicar did not exist.

Shadows gathered about the corners of the room. The old clock on the draped mantelshelf ticked relentlessly on, seeming to grow louder in the silence that fed the growing tension. Amos cleared his throat nervously, but the two women were unaware of him.

"It's getting cold," he said in a brittle voice at last. "Are you sure you wouldn't like me to put more coal on the fire, Mrs. Stansfield?"

Ellen's eyes did not waver from Fern's. It was true, the room was becoming very cold, the chill seeming to climb from Fern's feet to her knees. For a moment she began to doubt the wisdom of what they were doing, but the die was cast. Catherine *must* be reached. . . .

She felt the muscles in her back and her neck begin to stiffen with tension, and the shadows in the corners seemed to move nebulously and start to take shape. The nape of her neck prickled, and she heard Amos cough. Fear began to gnaw her, and she started to pant in shallow, panicking breaths. Ellen's hand reached forward to close over hers, and her touch was as cold as death.

"Do not fear." Ellen's voice was faint and musical, like a distant harp.

For the first time Fern saw Amos' face, white and tight with fear, his pale eyes staring. It was as if he saw something terrifying in the shadows. A strange, soft moaning sound pervaded the house, a sound infinitely pathetic and hauntingly tragic. Fern closed her eyes and willed Catherine to come, to take possession of her body. She was near now; Fern could tell by the terror in the air, the terror Catherine had felt before her death, a terror so powerful it had persisted through the centuries and kept the restless spirit wandering in search of exoneration.

You are near, Catherine, I feel it, so near. . . .

Suddenly the door crashed open, and Hepzibah rushed in, her face blanched and her rheumy old eyes popping. Instantly the charged atmosphere reverted to normal, and Amos rose unsteadily. Fern could have wept with frustration.

"What's going on, Mrs. Stansfield?" Hepzibah demanded, her body shaking so violently she had to clutch the back of Amos' vacated chair for support. "Summat's up, and I can't understand it, such fierce cold and funny noises. I don't hold wi' such goings-on, and though I nivver interfere as a rule, Mrs. Stansfield, I'm that shaken I mun speak. Summat wicked's about to befall us. I can feel it!"

"It is gone now, Hepzibah. Go back to bed, my dear. All is well. Nothing will happen to you." Ellen's voice was reassuringly firm, and Hepzibah let herself be cajoled back to bed, muttering emphatically that no sleep would come to her that night after what she had experienced. Many prayers would be necessary to chase away the malign influences. Fern, however, could barely control her vexation, fighting to keep back the tears. Amos was still tense and bewildered.

"I don't know what was happening in this room a few moments ago, Mrs. de Lacy, but I too would like you to know that I do not approve. Table-rapping and suchlike have become fashionable pastimes with the gentry, I believe, but if that is what you and Mrs. Stansfield were up to, a séance of some kind, I should point out that it is a very dangerous practice."

"It was no séance, Reverend. Mrs. de Lacy has a natural affinity with her past," Ellen said quietly.

"Well, whatever it was, it will bring no good," Amos averred emphatically. "I am not one to deny the psychic abilities of some people, but I do not hold with tampering with unknown forces."

"The forces are not unknown to Fern and me," Ellen countered, firmness latent in her mild eyes.

"Nevertheless, one can inadvertently release powers one is unable to control. Admittedly, I have no direct experience of such matters myself, but I have colleagues of the cloth who have been hard put to it to exorcise the evil influences which have been evoked in this way. I think it is time I escorted Mrs. de Lacy back to the Hall."

Fern had never seen him so forceful, but there was no doubt that fear directed his words. He was shaking still, his blue eyes widened till the whites gleamed in the lamplight. His fingers trembled as he helped her put on her cloak.

Ellen accompanied them to the door, standing on the threshold while Amos helped Fern into the trap. The pony whinnied restlessly. A bank of cloud, thrust by a rising wind, scurried across the moor and obliterated its light.

Fern's cloak flapped about her as they drove away. "The wind's getting up," Amos remarked in a voice aimed to sound calm and natural. And indeed it was. Across the moor Fern could hear it rising and howling, then sinking to a mournful moan before gathering fresh breath to howl again. By the time they reached the Hall, heavy raindrops were spattering the wide flight of steps. Amos seemed distinctly relieved when, having seen Fern into the Hall, he was able to stride away down the drive in the direction of the church.

Cassie brought a cup of hot chocolate as Fern prepared for bed. She looked pinched and cold, and her hand trembled, rattling the china cup in the saucer as she placed it on the night table. Fern climbed into bed and sipped the hot liquid gratefully. There was a chill in her bones which had begun in Ellen's little parlor and which it seemed would never be driven from her body again.

"Aren't you going home tonight, Cassie?"

"No, madam. Sometimes I stay t' night if t' weather's bad. Mrs. Thorpe lets me sleep in t' kitchen. It's nice and warm there."

"But it's only just begun raining. Couldn't you have gone home before, at your usual time?"

The girl hesitated before answering, plucking nervously at her starched apron. "Aye, well I could, but I didn't want. It were cold—very cold considering t' time o' t' year—and them dogs were howling, and I were scared."

"What dogs, Cassie?"

"Them hounds, madam, them Gabriel hounds. Surely tha must a heard 'em when tha rode out wi' t' vicar."

Fern cast her mind back to when they arrived at Fox Brow, when she was dismounting from the trap and thought she heard a voice cry out. It must have been the same pathetic sounds Cassie heard.

"Tha heard 'em once, Mrs. de Lacy, 'cause I remember thee telling me. Didst not hear 'em tonight? They mean death, tha knows."

The girl's face was pallid and her eyes wide. She too could feel the tension in the atmosphere. It pervaded not only Ellen's house but also the Hall and Brackenroyd village, it seemed. And it was unusually cold, as she said, unnaturally cold for a May night.

Fern patted the edge of the bed. "Sit a moment, Cassie, before you go down again."

The girl hesitated, mindful of constant exhortations not to presume familiarity with one's betters, but her need for company and consolation overcame her misgivings. She sat warily on the very edge.

"Have you taken chocolate in to the master, Cassie, or is he already asleep?"

"No, madam, he's not come home."

So Bruno was still out there on the moor, wandering in the rain and the wind. Where could he have gone after leaving Fox Brow? He must be troubled indeed to forgo the warmth and comfort of his bed. No doubt Pharaoh was with him.

"Of course, it must be Pharaoh you heard crying, Cassie."

"Pharaoh?"

"The master's wolfhound. If Dr. de Lacy is still out walking, the dog is probably miserable in all that cold and rain, and howling for his bed of straw by the fire."

The girl looked only half-convinced, but she did manage a weak smile. Fern patted her hand reassuringly.

"Go down and sleep now, Cassie. All is well."

At the doorway the maid turned. "I hope as how tha'rt right and all's well, but I fear it's not. I can feel evil in t' air, thick like I could touch it wi' my hand. I'll not sleep till that wind and cold has gone."

"Say your prayers, Cassie, and no harm can come to you. Blow out the lamp and go now, and sleep."

Fern was anxious to be rid of the girl, for she sensed it too. Excitement quivered in her. The air was pregnant with shadows, with emotions she knew could only mean that Catherine was close. It was as if the wraith hovered patiently outside the latticed window, mutely entreating Fern to let her in. Whatever magic Ellen and she had worked between them in their silent communion in Fox Brow, it had evidently succeeded in bringing Catherine close again. Fern tingled with expectation.

Shivering, she rolled over in the bed, and her knees encountered an averted back. Instantly the other occupant of the bed sprang upright.

"Don't touch me, hellcat. I fear thy touch worse nor thy silence." It was Phoebe, her eyes flashing fury in the light of the moon that glimmered in through the low window. She lay down again, curled suspiciously on the far edge of the truckle bed.

For a moment there was silence in the little room; then Phoebe began muttering in the shadows. "It's all thy fault, tha knows it is. None i' this village comes owt for thee now, for all are afeard of thy powers."

Useless to deny, impossible to repudiate, Catherine was forced to lie helplessly listening to her sister's vicious words.

"It were thee as killed my Ben. I know it. I saw thee coming from t' barn that night. I saw thee in Rafe de Lacy's arms. Tha were jealous I had a lover too, so tha killed him. But tha'll not escape, Catherine Radley. I'll see to it tha's punished for thy sins.

"Tha'll not have thy lover, I swear it. Tha's robbed me, and I'll rob thee likewise."

A sob of fear caught in Catherine's throat. There was such vindictive determination in Phoebe's voice that Catherine knew she would do no less than she had sworn. It might well be that she had poisoned Rafe's mind against her already, for

Catherine had had no glimpse of him since that terrible night, even after he had come home. Somehow she must see him again, to try to convince him that her action had been only in self-defense. But how? For the thousandth time Catherine cursed her blighted tongue, which would not curl itself about the words she needed.

Phoebe was still murmuring, plotting aloud the scheme she knew Catherine could not divulge. "They all begin to believe me that tha'rt a witch, and before long I'll convince 'em. Thy Rafe'll not come near thee then."

It would not be hard to do, thought Catherine. The crops had failed this summer after unexpected fierce hailstorms, Mistress Arnley's third had been stillborn only last week, and poor Jennett Marsden had been killed by a thunderbolt as she came home from milking. Unnatural events indeed, to be explained away only by the presence of an evil spirit in the village, and the local folk would be only too glad of a scapegoat. Already, as Phoebe said, they were half-convinced Catherine was the culprit. No longer did any of them come asking for Catherine's help for a toothache or a wart. It was evident they all feared and distrusted her.

The first glimmer of dawn light was filtering through the little window when the footsteps came tramping toward the cottage, heavy steps ringing when they reached the cobbled yard. Catherine heard voices and her father's angry demand.

"What the devil brings thee here so early in t' morning, Arnley?" he was bawling through the open window.

"Thy lass, Catherine. We've had enough of her mischief. We've talked it over and decided to make certain."

"Certain? Certain of what, tha meddlesome creature? My lass is as good and virtuous as they come, and I'll not have thee say otherwise."

By this time Father had evidently put on his breeches, for Catherine heard him open the cottage door to argue with Arnley. Phoebe was sitting up now, listening intently, her dark eyes agleam.

Mother was in the little flagstone parlor too, her voice angry and plaintive.

221

"Just because the lass is different, tha's no cause to say she's wicked. What hast got against our Kate?"

There was a shuffling of clogs on stone and a few muttered prompts from Arnley's companions. "Well, there's all t' strange happenings of late. Jennett Marsden for one, crops ruined for another, and now my missus is heartbroken over our son."

"It's no fault of our Kate's if tha has only two wenches and t' first lad were stillborn. That's God's will, and tha were best to accept it. Tha'll happen have another lad soon."

"But it's not chance that thy Catherine looked at my missus only t' day afore and scared her half to death. It were t' evil look, thee just ask my missus."

"Flummery!" Mistress Radley was furious. "And Jennett Marsden—did our Kate look at her too? And at t' crops in t' fields? Is that all tha can say against t' girl?"

Another man's voice cut in. "What of soldier Ben's murder, Mistress Radley? A pitchfork doesn't rise up in t' air and pierce a man lest it's by witchcraft. We all know Kate were jealous of Phoebe having a swain, she so quiet and mouselike that no lad followed her."

Phoebe leaped from the bed, pulled a shawl over her nightgown, and went out. Catherine followed, fearful of what her sister would say to augment the accusations mounting against her.

Phoebe stood in the doorway of the little parlor, the group of men near the outer door having moved just inside the room. They stared at the girl, and seeing Catherine just behind her, shrank back farther toward the corner.

"Tha'rt right," Phoebe was saying eagerly, "my sister is a witch. She killed Ben Pickering."

Mother moved forward to clutch Phoebe's arm. "What art saying, lass? Thy own sister." Her eyes stared helplessly from a blanched face.

"Aye, Mother, and I can prove it."

From under her shawl Phoebe withdrew an object which she held forward for all to see. Over her shoulder Catherine could see a piece of wax, crudely shaped into the figure of a man. And transfixing its body was a bodkin, such as all the village women used to fasten up their hair.

"Where didst find it?" Father's voice was barely a whisper.

"Under her bed."

The figures in the shadows drew back yet farther. Fearful eyes turned from the wax effigy toward Catherine, and she saw their terror, their accusing hatred. Even Mother turned to stare incredulously at her.

"It were thee as made t' tallow candles last week, Kate," she murmured reluctantly. Catherine longed to cry out, to deny, to explain that Phoebe had taken the leftover tallow when the task was done. But most of all she felt bewildered, unable to believe that Phoebe had taken the tallow willfully, to incriminate her. She stared helplessly at her sister, who returned the stare with a mocking, defiant smile.

Catherine's confidence waned. Phoebe would win now. Rafe would never dare to consort with an acknowledged witch, and even if in the eyes of the law Catherine was not proven to be a witch, the village would forever believe it. For a moment she felt a new, unknown emotion, a hate so powerful against Phoebe that she inwardly cursed her for her lying, vindictive tongue. Would that the girl were cursed with dumbness as she was, so that she could never lie again!

In the tense air of the little room, the faint mew of a cat broke the silence. From under the settle where she had been sleeping, Tibb came out, stretching her paws and arching her back daintily. The villagers watched in silence as the cat, staring around haughtily for a moment at the intruders, sought out her mistress. Catching sight of Catherine by the door, she crossed leisurely to her mistress and began rubbing herself luxuriously against Catherine's skirts, purring with pleasure. A murmur rippled through the onlookers.

"Her familiar," Catherine heard someone whisper.

"Aye, it seeks to be fed," another replied.

"The witch's mark—she'll give it food from the witch's nipple."

Mistress Radley, confounded by all the terrible evidence against her child, found her tongue at last. "Get thee all

223

hence, home to thy families. There's no cause to come here making mischief. I'll not have all this wicked gossip, dost hear, Arnley? I'll thank thee all to be gone and let us about our work. T' sun's up already, and there's no water fetched from t' well yet. Get thee away home, neighbors, and let's have done wi' all this nonsense."

Arnley shuffled uncomfortably. "Much as we'd like, it's not so easy done, Mistress Radley. That there wax figure has proved all for us. Now we mun put thy lass to t' test."

"Test? What test?" Catherine heard the hollow tremble in her mother's voice. "Tha's surely not thinking of ducking our Catherine, art tha?"

"Nay, mistress. We've talked to t' vicar, and he'll not have us duck her nor prick t' witch's mark neither. He reckons that's only for t' proper authorities to do."

"Thank God t' reverend has a bit of sense at least," muttered Mistress Radley. "What then?"

"He'll let us weigh her."

Father, silent up to now, took a step forward. "Dost mean to weigh her against t' parish Bible?"

"Aye."

"But tha can see how slight she is, nobbut a slender little thing. Your hefty Bible is bound to outweigh her. That's no true test."

"It's fair notwithstanding. It's known as witches can never outweigh t' Bible. T' vicar says we can do it after t' evening service. So tha'd best see thy lass is at t' church, Mr. Radley. Tha surely can't object to a fair test."

Radley stood dumb, aware that a refusal would only incriminate his daughter more. Arnley, his ultimatum delivered, signaled to his companions, and they all shuffled out. As if in a trance, Catherine heard their footsteps fade away across the yard and down the lane until silence settled over the cottage once more.

Little was said of the occurrence, but all day the threat of the evening's trial hung heavy in the air. Mother and Father seemed incredulous, unable to believe that anyone should question their daughter's virtue, she who had freely given so much of her skills to help others. And Phoebe too was silent, but whether because she felt she had already said too much or because she was content with her victory, Catherine did not know.

The July sun was still high over the western horizon when the time for evening service came, and the little church was sultry. Catherine sat with her parents and Phoebe, her heart tilting for a second when she saw Rafe enter and sit alone in the De Lacy pew. He did not look her way, not then or throughout the service.

The vicar hastened away into the vestry once the service was over, as though reluctant to be part of what he knew was to follow. Catherine sat, head bowed, while men clattered the great iron scales to the lectern where the great Bible lay. From the corner of her eye she could see Rafe still sitting as though in silent prayer.

"Now, then, Mistress Radley." It was Arnley who stood before them, holding his hand out for Catherine. Quietly she rose and followed him. Every eye in the church was fixed upon her as hands helped her to seat herself in the great iron pan of the scales. It dipped to the stone floor beneath her weight.

"Now for t' Bible." Reverent hands grasped its bulk carefully, struggling to transfer it from the lectern to the other pan. As they did so, Catherine felt herself rising slowly till her feet were clear of the floor. The Bible's massive weight had proved her guilt.

"Didn't I tell thee?" she heard the excited whispers. She looked up, not to see her parents' or Phoebe's reaction, but to the De Lacy pew. Rafe was leaning against the pew in front, eyes lowered and his face as pale as a sheet. For God's sake, speak now, defend me, or I am lost, she prayed fervently.

"There's no doubt now," Arnley was saying. "Catherine Radley is a witch. God's Holy Book does not lie." Catherine stared beseechingly at Rafe, who rose, stumbling, and made for the door.

Don't desert me, oh, for pity's sake, come back and help me in my need! She screamed silently, but his great shape only lumbered out through the door and was gone. She could barely believe it. Even he, who had sworn undying love for her, had turned his back on her.

Fury gathered within her. Nowhere on this earth was there truth and honesty; no love was pure and strong; no man was to be trusted. If he had no faith in her, then no man alive would ever believe her. Silently she cursed Rafe de Lacy for his treachery. May he wander forever, tortured and suffering as she was now, never to find peace if he did not come to her.

"Art satisfied?" Father was saying gruffly to the group of villagers who clustered about Arnley. "Can we take t' lass home now?"

Arnley eyed the other before nodding. "We mun decide what's to be done. In t' meantime go home."

Catherine felt her mother's urgent hands pushing her toward the door and out into the evening sunlight. Phoebe followed with her father, murmuring as they left the porch, "See, she does not weep, as one might expect. They say witches cannot weep."

"Hush, Phoebe. Tha's said enough," Catherine heard her father retort. To the door of the Radley cottage was but a few yards, and she was relieved to enter the little parlor, out of reach of the villagers' malevolent, distrustful eyes.

"There's mischief afoot; I can sense it," Mistress Radley muttered to her husband. "There's no trusting them when they're in this mood. Lock and bar t' door, Father."

"They'll do no more, saving happen to report to t' authorities. They done do no more themselves."

"Bar t' door notwithstanding." Mother's lips were set in a tight, determined line. "Dost know what night it is? It's Lammas eve, or witch's feast, and a night them out there might well have a mind to do mischief."

Father locked the door without further protest. Phoebe followed Catherine into the little room where they slept, mocking her while they undressed. "They're locked out, and tha'rt locked in, sister. No moonlight meetings for thee in t' woods tonight, neither wi' a coven nor a lover."

Footsteps clattered up the staircase. Mother and Father were going to bed with the sun so as to be ready to rise with the sun for the day's work. Silence soon settled over the

Radley cottage, but Catherine could find no sleep. Inwardly she boiled in a ferment of vexation, anger, and hatred. They all feared and scorned her, the villagers, her own family, and Rafe, whom she had loved and trusted above all.

Gradually anger dwindled to despair. What was there left to live for now? Deep regular breathing from Phoebe's thin curled frame indicated that she was sleeping. A sudden thought struck Catherine. The wax figure, Rafe's stumbling steps and pallid face—had Phoebe in fact shaped the little figure in order to curse Rafe, thus causing his apparent sickness?

Catherine reproached herself. What a wicked thought. Rafe, sick or not, had deserted her, and she could not blame Phoebe for that. Rafe's was the crime, and may he suffer long and miserably for his perfidy.

Such unnatural hate in her heart made Catherine restless. At last she could lie still no longer, and rising stealthily so as not to disturb Phoebe, she put a shawl about her shoulders and looked out of the little window. Under the moon's pale light, which robbed everything of color, she could see the sleeping village street, the gaunt outline of the church tower. Not a soul stirred nor a light showed. Cautiously she unlatched the door and pulled it silently closed behind her.

Up, up toward the moor, where the air was free and she could breathe, anything to lessen the dead weight that threatened to choke her. Catherine's thin mules made no sound on the cobbles as she turned off from the main street and struck uphill.

Brackenroyd Hall's great windows lay blank and expressionless too, she could see as she reached higher ground. The rambling old building had an air of death and emptiness. Somewhere within its thick stone walls lay that faithless Rafe de Lacy, and again she cursed him. If only he would appear now, tall and broad in the moonlight, striding out toward the copse to meet her as he had done so often before. But long as she stared, no figure came.

The copse, that was where she would go, and ease the ache in her temples with the cool waters of the stream on whose bank they had lain and loved. She could see the outline of leafy branches silhouetted against the craggy skyline beyond.

Voices and footsteps below in the valley came to Catherine's ears. She turned and listened. Clogged feet were running on the cobblestones, and men's voices called out.

"Where is she, then? Witches' sabbath, is it? Well, we'll find her."

"There'll be no more spells cast i' Brackenroyd. We've had more nor enough of her cursing."

The footsteps grew in volume, marching down the street in a vengeful, rhythmic stamp. Catherine froze, her palms sweating and nausea trembling in her stomach. They were seeking her, and God knew what they would do when they found her. To flee to the moors was useless, for she would be easily spotted, a running white figure in a nightgown in the pale light of the moon.

The copse. That was the only place where she could find shelter to hide. She crouched amid the undergrowth and prayed, her mouth dry with fear.

The footsteps grew duller as they left the street and crunched over grass. From afar a dog howled, and Catherine felt the sweat prickle on her skin. The Gabriel hounds—that betokened death. She closed her eyes and prayed, but the steps came nearer, crashing up the hill through the bracken, closer and closer, growing in volume until the sound was like thunder in her ears.

"There's evil in her black blood, and we mun put a stop to it," Arnley's voice cried, so close that Catherine felt faint with terror. The footsteps were almost on her now, thundering, roaring.

A hand grasped her shoulder. "For heaven's sake, mistress, wake up! The house is shaking, and it seems like all hell has been let loose!"

She opened her eyes weakly, and the misted figure of Mrs. Thorpe hovered before her. "Go away," she protested, but the housekeeper only shook her again.

"Mrs. de Lacy, please wake up! There's the most terrible storm raging, and Pharaoh has come home without the master. I'm worried for him. Please wake up!"

Chapter 15

For a dizzying few seconds Fern thought the thunder of footsteps still threatened to discover her hiding place. Then slowly she realized that real thunder cracked and reverberated over the Hall, lightning darting in at the windows and cutting across the light of the candle Mrs. Thorpe held in her hand. Another resounding bang and vivid flash brought her to her senses.

Mrs. Thorpe brought her dressing robe from the chair, "None of the servants can sleep in this dreadful storm; I wonder you sleep so peacefully, madam. I'm afraid for the master out in all this."

Rain was pelting wildly against the windows, hurled by a buffeting gale. Mechanically Fern rose and pulled on the robe, mentally screaming to return to Catherine. The girl's terror was bringing her close to death, and it was unthinkable to desert her now.

A bell clanged below. Mrs. Thorpe started. "Whoever can that be at the door in the middle of the night? Surely no one is fool enough to venture out in weather like this?"

She scurried away, and Fern followed. From the gallery she watched the housekeeper open the door to admit a dripping, apologetic Edgar Amos.

"I'm so sorry to trouble you, Mrs. Thorpe, but Dr. de Lacy sent me."

"Is he all right?" Fern heard Mrs. Thorpe ask anxiously.

"He is safe, but he appears somewhat disturbed. He came galloping into the village in all this rain, shouting to everyone to get up and leave. He made me ride Phantom back to warn you to get ready to receive them."

"What is wrong, Edgar?" Amos looked up at the sound of Fern's voice and bowed slightly.

"He seems to fear some catastrophe, Mrs. de Lacy. He was rather agitated and shouting something about it being all his fault. At any rate, he was determined to evacuate the village and send everyone up here. Two farm carts laden with women and children are not far behind me."

"Lord bless us!" exclaimed Mrs. Thorpe. "Then we'd best prepare. Cassie, make up the fire in the servants' hall and get some soup on the stove. They'll be half-drowned in this weather."

Cassie, lurking in the background to listen, rushed off. Mrs. Thorpe took Amos' sodden cloak and hat.

"Mrs. Thorpe, I shall put on a cloak and go down to the village," Fern said. "Keep Phantom ready at the door. There is no time for Malachi to saddle up Whisper."

Amos stared up at her. "You don't mean to go out in this, Mrs. de Lacy? I'm sure I don't know what the doctor fears, but I do think he is being unnecessarily hysterical."

"It is not for you to criticize the master. I am sure he knows what he is about," Fern retorted as she turned to reenter her room. Pulling off her nightgown and donning a woolen dress and riding cloak, she thought quickly. Either there was trouble imminent or Bruno was ill, as Amos hinted. Either way, he needed her help.

Mrs. Thorpe was still in the hall, opening the door again to admit the women and children who tumbled wetly from the carts. Fern snapped orders quickly as she passed her.

"If the servants' hall becomes full when more arrive, open up the old Hall and light a fire. Feed them and give them what dry clothes you can find. I shall return soon."

Malachi stood at the bottom of the steps holding Phantom. Without a word he cupped his hands for Fern to mount. She swung lightly into the saddle and then had to wait, reining in the restless horse, while Malachi shortened the stirrups. Phantom was evidently nervous, the whites of his eyes standing out against his black mane. He too sensed the disquiet in the air.

His great, powerful body reared and plunged forward and galloped off down the gravel drive, the heavy rain beating into Fern's face. The wind still raged, whipping off the hood of her cloak and blowing her hair wildly about her, till the rain soaked it and made it cling damply about her face.

At the foot of the drive two more carts were turning in to the Hall. Fern recognized the sodden figure of Fabia sitting huddled between the others. She reined in sharply.

"What is happening, Fabia?"

Fabia's white face looked up. "Bruno and Luke are rousing the rest of the villagers and trying to find Phoebe. She disappeared while we were gathering the children. I wanted to stay and look for her, but Bruno was adamant I must come up here."

"Did Bruno say what was wrong?"

"He's crazed, Fern. I think he's gone out of his mind. He's raving about the storm being all his fault, an elemental reaction to his past sin. He says the villagers will die for his misdeeds unless we escape to the Hall."

Fern paled. "What sin? Did he say?"

"Not so I could understand. Something about his faithlessness long ago and how he had tried to deny it but now he knew he must atone before it was too late. Fern, I'm afraid. I fear for him—and for Phoebe."

"Don't worry. I'll find them both. Go up to the Hall and wait. Which way did he go?"

"He was heading along the main street, knocking at all the doors, and was going on to the mill."

Fern swung the horse about and rode on down the cobbled

lane that led to the village street. A sodden figure leading a band of bedraggled villagers stumbled toward her. In a fierce crack of lightning she saw it was Fearnley, the mill manager. He waved and gesticulated when he caught sight of Fern.

"Get back, mistress, get back to t' Hall! The master says as t' dam is going to burst!"

She heard his words clearly enough, borne on the whipping wind as she galloped by, but did not stop to argue. If he was right, there was little enough time to find Phoebe.

And what of Bruno? Suddenly she felt no fear for his safety, only a fierce exultation that swept over her. Fabia and Amos might not understand his apparent raving, but to Fern it was clear. Somehow, miraculously, he had come to learn of his treachery to Catherine so long ago, either by means of drugs or by dreams that tortured his sleep so that he was forced to walk abroad at night. No matter how he knew. It was enough that he too was obliged to remember, and to suffer as a result. For a split-second it was Catherine who rode into the village, exulting that her curse on Rafe had had its effect.

Fern reined in on the green before the church. Another vivid flash of lightning ripped through the black sky. The whole main street was deserted, cottage doors left ajar and rain washing in rivulets down the street. There was not a sign of Luke or Bruno or any soul left in Brackenroyd. It seemed that everyone had fled to higher ground, either to the Hall or to Fox Brow or possibly up to Dr. Briggs's house.

A rending crash of thunder split the air, and then immediately another brilliant shaft of lightning, illuminating the rain bouncing on the shining slate roofs and revealing for a moment the eerie stillness of the village, forlorn and abandoned like some shunned ghost town. Fern, soaked to the skin and shivering, sighed and turned Phantom about.

"Phoebe!" she cried out, but her voice was whipped from her by the wind and tossed up among the branches of the churchyard trees, which bent low under the weight of rain. As she urged the horse forward, a faint sound came to her ears, almost lost in the clop of hooves and the wind's roar. She stopped quickly and strained to listen. Was it wishful thinking, or did she hear a child's cry, shrill and terrified, above the roar of the storm?

She slid from the horse and led him by the reins to the schoolhouse gate.

"Phoebe! Are you there, Phoebe?"

No answering cry came from the shuttered cottage, but Fern saw the door of a shed alongside open a crack. Letting go of the reins, she ran to the shed, pushed open the door, and saw a cowering white figure crouched on the floor.

"Phoebe! Thank God you're safe! Come with me, and we'll go to Mother, up at the Hall." Fern's arms were outstretched to the child, but Phoebe only shrank farther, whimpering. "Come, little one, there is nothing to fear," Fern coaxed, but as she approached the child, Phoebe shrieked.

Impatiently Fern grasped her arm and began to drag her outside. Phoebe struggled to break away, and Fern's grasp grew tighter. This was no time to argue.

As if by a miracle, the storm had lessened in intensity. Dull reverberations in the distance now and again indicated that it was moving away, but rain still lashed ruthlessly. Fern tried to cover the child under the folds of her own sodden cloak, but Phoebe still fought to get free.

Phantom—where was he? At the schoolhouse gate Fern looked about for the horse and saw him pawing the ground restlessly under a churchyard elm. A far flash of lightning sparked, and Fern saw his huge eyes widen, the whites staring, and he reared into the air, whinnied in fear, and began to canter away.

"Phantom! Come back!"

It was no use. The last flash had been too much for him. Now all he sought was the shelter of his stable. His hooves clattered wildly along the lane uphill toward the Hall.

Phoebe was still whimpering and scratching. Fern grasped her resolutely and marched her along the lane in Phantom's wake. Holding the drenched child like a half-drowned rat, her dark curls glued about her pointed little face with rain, Fern hurried along the lane, aware of rain trickling down her neck and squelching in her thin shoes. Suddenly another sound came to her ears.

A long, low, ominous rumble made her stiffen. It was not the sound of distant thunder, but lower and more menacing. Involuntarily she found herself grabbing Phoebe up in her arms and running off the side of the cobbled street and up the steep grassy bank.

Phoebe's weight caused her to stumble, gasping for breath, but Fern seemed to sense instinctively that unless she reached higher ground they would never return to the Hall.

She continued to stagger up the slope, her feet slithering and sliding on the soggy grass, till at last, devoid of breath and her heart thudding with effort, she stumbled and sprawled on the slope. Phoebe rolled from her arms.

The distant rumble was growing and becoming louder, a roar now that was becoming a crescendo of sound, cracking and hissing as if all hell were let loose. Fern's heart almost stopped in terror as she recognized its significance. The dam! Bruno had been right after all—Bilberry Reservoir, swollen by the torrents of rain till it could contain no more, had burst the dam! In moments the wall of water would gush down the valley and submerge the village. Fern leaped to her feet and grabbed Phoebe's arm.

"For God's sake, Phoebe, run! The dam has burst, do you hear me? Run!"

Only for a second did the child pause, her head cocked to one side, and then she moved, scrambling up the slope ahead of Fern. Fern followed close behind the diminutive figure in the drenched white frock that clung to her thin little body. They were still far from the top when the waters came.

The little figure ahead turned at the sound of the wrenching, crashing, tearing clamor behind. Fern saw her eyes widen in disbelieving terror and turned, holding the child's trembling shoulders. A massive black wall of water was bearing down the valley, trees torn up by the roots projecting from its inky surface. Thundering, it crashed into Brackenroyd, sweeping down the main street in horrifying fury, tossing the carcasses of cattle and sheep among the cottages and hurling timber in its path. Fern watched aghast. The black monster reached and devoured the long-abandoned Radley cottage like matchwood, and swirled on through the churchyard and the schoolhouse. She shuddered as the shed where Phoebe had hidden broke up and disappeared in the monster's maw.

"Higher, Phoebe, we must get higher!" They scrambled farther up the slope. Fern glanced back at the roaring menace, which, having swept on down the valley, was growing ever deeper over Brackenroyd. Bodies both of animals and of people swirled in the flood; bales of hay bounced along in the torrent alongside dye vats and looms and unrecognizable wreckage of timber. With a sick thudding of her heart Fern realized the mill must have gone. Pray God Bruno and Luke had not been there.

Suddenly Phoebe uttered a scream. Fern looked up in time to see the little figure stumble and totter, lose her footing on the steep slope, and start to roll downhill. Fern lunged forward to grab her, but the child was falling too quickly. Impulsively Fern threw herself after her, terrified lest she should fall into the ever-rising flood.

The little body gathered speed as she fell, and Fern could not keep up with her. She saw the waters coming closer, closer, and still Phoebe's headlong fall continued. Fern cried out as the little white figure splashed as she reached the water. "Phoebe!"

There was a tree still standing at the water's edge, not yet engulfed, and Fern saw with relief that Phoebe's struggling little shape was clinging to an outstretched branch.

"Hold on, Phoebe! I'll help you!"

The water was surging about the child, threatening to tear loose her grasp on the branch. Fern threw off the saturated cloak and waded into the water, feeling it sucking about her skirts. Phoebe's terrified face, encircled in clinging tendrils of black hair, stared at her beseechingly.

"Help me!"

Fern was too distraught to wonder. Reaching the child and grasping her about the waist with one arm and the tree with the other, she struggled to regain a foothold on the slope, but the water tugged mercilessly at her skirts. Inch by inch she pulled herself along the branch, burdened by Phoebe's weight and the sucking current. Mercifully she felt solid ground under her feet and managed to pull herself and the child clear of the flood. Already it had risen several feet, high as they were. Exhausted, Fern scrambled a few feet higher to level ground and sank to her knees.

"You go on, Phoebe, I'll follow."

The child, dripping and shivering, shook her head and crouched by Fern. With a desperate effort Fern struggled to rise and stumble on, holding Phoebe by the hand. The child's teeth were chattering, and the hand was numb with cold. They must regain the Hall and warmth quickly.

At the stream, swollen by rain, Fern paused. It was impossible to cross here, or they would be swept down into the valley again. The copse! By Catsgrave Copse there were stepping-stones, and there they might still be able to cross safely. She struck out for the higher ground. Phoebe struggled on gamely beside her.

Reaching the copse at last, Fern looked back. The waters now were far below and seemed to be growing less deep. No doubt the reservoir, having disgorged all its millions of gallons of water into the valley, now lay empty, and the torrent was flooding on down through all the unsuspecting villages below Brackenroyd. Fern felt pity in her heart. Bruno's vigilance may well have saved Brackenroyd, but what of the poor creatures down the valley?

A despairing nausea clutched Fern as she sought the stepping-stones. Her head ached and she felt giddy with strain. The stones were still there, though the water now gushed over instead of around them.

"Can you manage to cross, Phoebe? Hold your skirts clear and step carefully."

The child nodded and stepped out. With bated breath Fern watched her anxiously, and breathed a sigh of relief when Phoebe at last turned on the farther bank. A wave of faintness swept over Fern again.

"Go on up to the Hall, Phoebe. It's not far. I shall follow you in a moment."

Phoebe hovered hesitantly, reluctant to leave her. Fern waved her on sharply.

"Go on, do as I say. Get out of those soaking cloth_ at once. Your mother will be very anxious about you."

The final words had the effect she sought. Ph ebe ran off into the darkness. Glad of a respite from st .ggle, Fern sank to the soggy ground and leaned her ba k against a tree. The waves of dizziness and nausea wer coming more quickly and severely now. Just for a moment I'll rest, she thought wearily, and then I'll have the strength to go home. If only this sick sensation would go away . . .

Unresistingly she leaned back against the tree; then to her ears came the vague sound of thunder, rumbling on and on and ever louder. Dimly she was aware that it was no longer the storm but the drumming of running feet. Suddenly the bushes parted. Arnley stood there, his coarse linen smock gleaming in the moonlight and his expression one of savage triumph.

"She's here, lads! I've found the witch!"

Hate glittered in his eyes, and she felt too sick and weak to protest. Other feet came running, until a crowd of faces gathered about him, pale and menacing in the moonlight, peering at her, half-fearful and half-malicious.

Before she buried her face in her hands, she could see by their malevolent looks that their fear, bred out of superstitious ignorance, meant ill for her. Well, so be it. She had done wrong in killing, even though in self-defense, and punishment was no more than her due.

For some moments no one moved or spoke. Then suddenly she felt a sharp pain on her shoulder. In surprised disbelief she stared at the tear in her sleeve, and the dull gash that showed blackly beneath. She looked up at her persecutor and saw that it was Arnley who had thrown the stone.

At once the others followed his lead.

"Drive the demon out of her!" another cried as his arm raised in the moonlight and came swiftly down. She felt another piercing pain, this time on her hip, and instantly it was followed by another on her breast. Incredulously she stared, from her tormentors to the wounds and back to their hate-filled faces. More of them were scrabbling for stones in the undergrowth. Arnley bent and straightened again with a large piece of rock in his hands.

"Death to the devil's creature!" he roared, and Catherine sank to the grass, stunned by the violent pain in her forehead. A warm moistness collected on her temple and dripped slowly down her chin. She put her fingers to her head and could not believe the gash, wide, open to the bone beneath. Dimly she heard voices shrieking abuse and hatred and felt the thudding blows to her body, but somehow they brought no more pain.

"She'll do no more of the devil's work!" a voice cried, but it was faint and far away. Then a sudden hush fell, followed by a flurry of footsteps. Catherine lay still, aware only that they had fled and that her life's blood was oozing from her.

Strange she could feel no animosity, no hatred for them, only for Rafe, who had deserted her. She lay sprawled in the grass under the tree that had witnessed their joyful meetings so often, and thought how bizarre it was to see only her own body, spattered and drenched in blood, and feel none of the emotion which used once to flood her veins.

Only disillusionment, and a strangely cold, detached revulsion for the traitor she had once called lover. And then suddenly, as if thought had conjured him up from the night mist, he was there, bending over her.

"Catherine, beloved, I heard the cries down here from up on the brow. What is it, sweetheart? What have they done?"

There was remorse as well as anguish in his dark eyes as he bent closer to examine her. A shudder of distaste shook his broad shoulders.

"Dear heaven, what have they done to you!"

Aye, she thought wearily, turn from me once again, as you did before. What matter now? Too late, too late for accusation and recrimination.

He knelt, burying his face in her shoulder, but not before she saw the brightness—could it be tears? A tinge of compassion penetrated the blank emptiness within her. She raised a feeble hand to his face.

Don't ... weep ... for ... me. The words had to remain unspoken. It was a desperate effort even to think them, for a black mist eddied about her, swallowing her for a second and then receding, though hovering persistently near. She was aware of his face close to hers, his great eyes probing hers and trying to infuse in her the will to live.

"God forgive me, Kate, I never thought it would come to this. I knew they thought ill of you, but not this, never this." His voice caught on a sob. "I should have come to you. Forgive me, beloved. I should have come to you. Forgive me, beloved. I should have come, but at first I thought it best to wait until the gossip died, and then in the church I felt so ill. Oh, God, my Kate, can you ever forgive me?"

Suddenly he leaped up. "I'll take you home to the Hall and send for the physician. You shall not die, Kate, I will not let you!"

But the moment he lifted her from the ground, agony ripped through Catherine's frame, and she moaned. At once he put her gently down again. She knew he had seen the awkward jutting of broken limbs and the bright flow that soaked the grass beneath.

The swirling mist was growing more insistent now, thickening before her, until Rafe's face was only a blur. Death was slow in coming, and the pain was agony. Through the encroaching fog that seeped into her nostrils and clogged her throat till every breath was penance, she could hear Rafe's voice, receding on a constant cry.

"Forgive me, Catherine! I will atone, I swear it! I shall come to you again, beloved, and this time there will be no parting. Come back again, Catherine. Forgive me."

There was a fleeting instant when she was aware of hovering, of pausing on the brink of eternity, and then suddenly she was free. She seemed to be floating somewhere among the branches of the tree where Rafe knelt below, sobbing over a prostrate figure in a tattered, blood-soaked gown of white muslin, and as she felt herself being drawn inexorably away, she found a voice.

"I forgot, dear Lord, I forgot! I laid a curse upon him, to suffer eternal torment! I should have recalled the curse before I died, God forgive me! Let me go back, just for an instant, to erase the curse!"

But no one heard. From afar she saw Rafe rise from his weeping, already smitten with the misery she had wished upon him, and prepare to lift the pathetic little body. Catherine cried out in vain for a second of eternity to return to atone, and her soul knew hell. Forever now she would have to wander in limbo, remorse-ridden and helpless. Her soul would never know peace.

In a vast black void she reviled against the injustice of it all. No one had ever known the truth and come to defend her. No one had cared—or so she had believed until it was too late. Now she knew Rafe loved her, and she knew she would love him until the end of time. Bitterly she sobbed, screaming to get back but sentenced to wander helplessly in time and space that had no ending. Eternity was terrifying.

And then suddenly God relented. A whirling through space and the cool, sweet smell of rain on the moors, and she was home. She opened her eyes slowly, disbelievingly. Interlocked branches of a tree overhead, the springy feel of grass beneath her—it could not be true. Hope rose again in a heart too long accustomed to pain and frustration. Slowly she became aware of a new vitality beginning to throb in her veins. A shadowy face bent over her.

With a surge of joy she recognized his face, hard lines of anxiety and anguish about his eyes. His lips were moving, muttering words of pain. A fierce light suddenly illuminated his black eyes when he saw she was gazing at him.

"You've come back! Oh, beloved, you've come back to me!" There was savage joy and triumph in the words, and she felt new life in knowing she was so loved. But he was not wearing his leather tunic and breeches; instead he tossed aside the tall hat in his hand and pulled off his greatcoat to envelop her tenderly.

Another tall figure came crashing through the undergrowth, a huge hound following at his heels.

"Malachi, go fetch the trap. The mistress is well but weak." The broad-shouldered figure did not move until a few words in German, snapped in a hoarse voice, caused him to nod and lumber away quickly.

She stared up at the beloved face, careworn and fatigued. The mist was clearing from her brain now. Bruno, of course. But it was Rafe's face, full of remorse and contrition, mingled now with joy. He knelt again and cradled his arms about her.

"Catherine, forgive me. I have waited long."

It was unbelievable! Bruno spoke with Rafe's love and concern in his voice. And he had called her Catherine. She stared in bewilderment and tried to struggle upright, but he restrained her.

"Lie still, my love. You have a bad bruise on your temple." His fingers caressed her forehead, smoothing away the sodden hair from the weal. It was as if time had suddenly spun backward. Consciously and deliberately she lifted the curse on him, inwardly and in silence. No more would he suffer the pangs of eternal torment.

The care lifted from his eyes, and the harrowed look vanished. His lips brushed her forehead lightly.

"Soon we shall have you home and safe, beloved, and then I shall never let you from my sight again. So long I have waited. Too long to risk losing you again."

Fern found the strength to speak at last. "How did you find me here?"

"Phoebe told me where you were."

"Phoebe?"

"She came running to the Hall as I was leaving again to look for you. When I asked her where you were, I expected her to reply in the sign language I had taught her. To my surprise, she spoke!"

"What did she say?"

"One word—Catsgrave. It was a miracle, but now her silence is broken, she will learn to speak very quickly."

Fern kept silent. No need to tell him Phoebe's first words

had been spoken to herself, a plea for help when Phoebe feared death. It was enough to know that yet another curse had been lifted.

The rain had stopped, and the clouds rolled away to reveal a crescent moon. By its light she saw Bruno's anxious glances uphill toward the Hall.

"Malachi will be back directly with the trap, and when I have you safely home, I must go and look for Luke."

"For Luke? Wasn't he with you?"

"I sent him on down the valley to warn the villagers in Heatherfield. He hasn't come back."

"Poor Fabia, she must be distraught with worry. Her husband and her child both in danger."

"Phoebe is safe now, and Fabia knows she owes the child's life to you. You have her undying friendship and devotion."

Fern answered coldly. "I owed it to Phoebe. It was no generous gesture, but a debt."

To her surprise, he did not ask why, but simply nodded. "I know, but now it is done. It is I who am still in your debt."

"For what, Bruno?"

Dark eyes regarded her soberly. "You know well, my love. I forsook you in your need."

"Then you remember?" It seemed impossible that Bruno, the clinical, the detached, the disbeliever, could remember that other life. But he did—and he had called her Catherine.

At that moment, Malachi reappeared. Only when Bruno had lifted her carefully into the trap and covered her with rugs and Malachi was whipping up the horse did Fern speak again.

"When did you discover ... about the past, I mean?" she whispered. Bruno's hand tightened on hers.

"I don't really know when it began. When I first met you at Bradford station, I think. I remember feeling a distinct jar of half-recognition when I saw you talking with Amos. And then, when I realized I couldn't possibly have seen you before, I dismissed it from my mind."

"*Déjà vu,* I think you called that feeling once."

The Brackenroyd Inheritance

"Yes. I dismissed your feelings about the Hall as female hysteria, evidence of an unbalanced mind, as I recall."

She smiled wryly. "You did. But when did you have further feelings about the past—and me?"

"Not for some time. And then, when the odd strange dream occurred, of a girl in olden days and her pure and lovable simplicity, a girl with your face and silken hair, I began to think I must be ill. The dreams frightened me, for I always awoke with a feeling of terrible dread and remorse, and I didn't know why."

"So you tried to ignore the dreams?"

"Dreaming had had no part in my earlier, well-ordered life. Everything in Germany was so straightforward, so rational. Dreams, I felt, were a self-indulgence, but there was no indulgence in the dreams that made me wake in a sweat. I could not explain them, and as a man of science I believed there had to be a logical explanation for everything."

"So what did you do?"

"Since you were the focal point of my dreams, I tried to avoid contact with you. I buried myself deeper in my work, or at least I tried to, but I found it difficult to concentrate."

"You took drugs."

"To further my work only. My research was into their effect on the human mind, and I could use only my own brain for experiment."

"You never drugged me. Once I thought you did."

"Because you too were dreaming?"

"They were not dreams. I saw Annot's story and I relived Catherine's. Because I am Catherine."

His hands tightened so hard about hers that Fern winced. His expression by starlight was one of deep pain again, and she felt pity for him.

"I know," he answered hoarsely. "At first I thought the dreams only hallucinations caused by drugs, and tried to ignore them. But the pain they evoked drove me on. In time I came to use the drugs to learn more, and the more I learned of the past, the more I suffered when I realized my guilt. But I could not stop. I had to know the ending."

"And the ending is now, Bruno. Or the beginning."

He looked away from her, down over the fields to the valley below, where only chimneys and the church steeple broke the surface of the waters enveloping the village. His voice was hollow with regret.

"Brackenroyd has suffered tonight. See how it is, broken and humiliated. It is all my fault, Catherine. A De Lacy wronged the valley and is not worthy to be its master."

Fern spoke softly as the trap turned up into the Hall's gravel drive. "And tonight a De Lacy atoned by saving the lives of the villagers. But for your vigilance they would all be lying drowned there now."

He shook his head. "Others will have died down in Heatherfield. Ellen prophesied that death would come."

Fern eyed him curiously. "How did you, always so remote, so aloof, come to befriend Ellen? You went so often by night to visit her."

He was gazing into the distance, up to the moors, as he replied. "It was part of the fantasy that haunted me. For some inexplicable reason, I found that as soon as I came here, even before you arrived, I was drawn to Fox Brow, again and again. It was as if I knew I must be there when the time came. But I did not know the reason. I tried to dismiss the lure of Fox Brow as a silly, irrational notion, but somehow I still found myself wandering up there at night."

"Do you know the reason now?" she asked quietly.

"Yes." He bent close over her, his face almost touching hers. The trap was drawing up by the Hall steps, and figures were crowded in the doorway. "Yes, beloved. It was from the brow that I—that Rafe—heard the cries when Catherine was stoned to death. Only from there could I watch Catsgrave for your return."

Mrs. Thorpe hurried down the steps to meet them. "Thank the Lord you're safe, Mrs. de Lacy! Come on in. I have hot water ready to ladle into the bath for you."

Bruno lifted Fern and carried her in. In the vestibule Edgar Amos was standing surrounded by a group of villagers, still bemused at the suddenness of the night's events. Fabia was clinging to Luke's arm, her eyes, brilliant with joy, betraying her relief on seeing Fern.

"Dear Fern, I am overjoyed," she said softly. "Luke has returned safely, and you saved Phoebe. Tend her well, Bruno, for we have need of people such as the De Lacys in the valley."

Bruno smiled and began carrying Fern up the great staircase. A woman's hand restrained him. It was Mrs. Iredale.

"Mrs. Armitage is right, master. But for thee and Mrs. de Lacy, we'd all be dead. The village'll come to life and prosper again wi' thee and her to care for it, that it will, I'm certain."

Bruno nodded. "We'll do our best. Already the water is falling. Soon we'll rebuild the cottages and the mill, and life will start afresh. We'll talk of it tomorrow. All will be well again in Brackenroyd. I promise."

The murmuring voices of the villagers and the grunts and nods of approval and thanks warmed Fern's cold bones. Mrs. de Lacy, they had called her. She was no longer "the Radley woman," the creature with a dark taint in her blood. Grudgingly, slowly, they were warming to her. In time she would be accepted, one of them, and the true mistress of Brackenroyd.

Kate's spirit was at rest now. No more would Catsgrave Copse be haunted by a tormented soul. And the Radley cottage was swept away, the last evidence of a curse that had blighted the village for three hundred years. Contentment enveloped Fern as she lay, tended by a joyously tearful Cassie, in the big tin bath of hot water before the fire.

Tucked up in bed at last with a stone-hot-water bottle at her feet, Fern inquired about Bruno.

"He's belowstairs, madam, seeing as all the villagers are seen to. Oh, madam, I'm so glad tha'rt alive and well! I thought them Gabriel hounds had sounded thy death cry."

"Not mine, Cassie, but I fear some people down in Heatherfield were not so fortunate."

"Aye, and but for t' master it'd have been all of us an' all. He's a fine man, is Dr. de Lacy."

"Indeed he is. Go down and ask him to come up, Cassie. Then, if Mrs. Thorpe no longer needs you, go to bed."

"Yes, madam." In the doorway the girl paused awkwardly. "And bless thee, madam. There's not so many like thee." Swiftly she was gone, pink with embarrassment.

By candlelight Fern snuggled down under the bedcovers, content as she had never been. It was no surprise when the connecting door to Bruno's room opened and she saw his broad figure in a dressing robe outlined in the doorway. She held out her arms to him. He came forward slowly and stood by the end of the bed.

"How do you feel now, Fern? Does your head ache?"

"No. I am tired only."

He turned back toward the door, and she felt a keen sense of disappointment. But he reappeared in a moment and closed the door behind him. In his hands he held the little box.

"Your lock of hair, Catherine. It has waited long for its owner to return."

She smiled and laid the box aside on the night table; then, opening the drawer, she took out the silver ring and offered it to him. His mouth lifted in a wry smile.

"*Amor Aeternus*. Love Eternal," he murmured as he gazed at its lettering. "Let me now place it on your finger, as I should have done long ago."

Fern gave her hand eagerly. "Will you always call me Catherine?" she teased.

His expression at once became serious. "I think not. We were all at fault, Phoebe and you and I, but the past is best forgotten. I shall call you Fern, for the name suits you."

"You like it? You did not seem to once."

" 'Fern' for 'sincerity.' Your mother chose well, for it suits you admirably. Oh, my love, forgive me. I should have recognized your sincerity long ago. Can you ever forgive me for the way I treated you?"

For a second she paused. Was it Rafe or Bruno speaking, and to Catherine or Fern? No matter. It was all one now, and life held out promise and hope at last.

His dark eyes raked hers, evidently misinterpreting her hesitation. "Fern . . . say you will forgive and forget. I love you. I have waited so long."

There was such humility and pathos in his eyes that Fern held up her arms in compassion and love. She too had waited an eternity for this moment. So much suffering, but it had all been inevitable. She knew it now. History would not be disinherited.

His eyes glowed with such love and joy that she knew the connecting door would remain closed and locked, tonight and always, for he would remain by her side, as he had sworn.

With a fierce surge of exultation Fern welcomed his arms about her. Soon new life would come to Brackenroyd. As Bruno had once wished, the villagers would have their heir to Brackenroyd within the year.

About the Author

ERICA LINDLEY was born in Bedfordshire, England, but brought up and educated in Yorkshire, and considers herself—"but for an accident of birth"—a Yorkshire woman. Married to an education officer, she has four lively children and began writing as an antidote to domestic routine. She now devotes her working time mainly to researching and writing historical novels, but she still manages to take an active interest in community affairs and social welfare.

Have You Read These Bestsellers from SIGNET?

☐ **DECADES by Ruth Harris.** A bold novel of three women bound together by their love for one man. . . . "Terrific!" —Cosmopolitan (#J6705—$1.95)

☐ **THE EBONY TOWER by John Fowles.** Love in all its many guises . . . a superbly romantic work by the author of The French Lieutenant's Woman. Over 5 months on The New York Times Bestseller List and a Literary Guild Alternate Selection. "The most enjoyable fiction of the season!"—The New York Times (#J6733—$1.95)

☐ **THE FRENCH LIEUTENANT'S WOMAN by John Fowles.** By the author of The Collector and The Magus, a haunting love story of the Victorian era. Over one year on the N.Y. Times Bestseller List and an international bestseller. "Filled with enchanting mysteries, charged with erotic possibilities . . ."—Christopher Lehmann-Haupt, N.Y. Times (#E6484—$1.75)

☐ **A GARDEN OF SAND by Earl Thompson.** The big, blistering saga of carnal knowledge in the down-and-out days of the thirties. ". . . brilliant, powerful, sensational."— The New York Times (#J6679—$1.95)

☐ **TATTOO by Earl Thompson.** "A great big brawling book that picks up where A GARDEN OF SAND left off . . . a graphic, hardhitting and violent portrayal of the underside of the American Dream. . . ."—New York Times Book Review. A Book-of-the-Month Club Selection. (#E6671—$2.25)

THE NEW AMERICAN LIBRARY, INC.,
P.O. Box 999, Bergenfield, New Jersey 07621

Please send me the SIGNET BOOKS I have checked above. I am enclosing $_____(check or money order—no currency or C.O.D.'s). Please include the list price plus 25¢ a copy to cover handling and mailing costs. (Prices and numbers are subject to change without notice.)

Name_____

Address_____

City_____State_____Zip Code_____
Allow at least 3 weeks for delivery

More Bestsellers from SIGNET

☐ **MIRIAM AT THIRTY-FOUR by Alan Lelchuk.** She is a sexual adventuress daring to live her erotic fantasies—no matter what the price. . . . A brilliant, savagely intimate novel . . . "Extraordinary . . . a smasher!"—**Boston Globe** (#J6793—$1.95)

☐ **FEAR OF FLYING by Erica Jong.** A dazzling uninhibited novel that exposes a woman's most intimate sexual feelings. . . . "A sexual frankness that belongs to and hilariously extends the tradition of **Catcher in the Rye** and **Portnoy's Complaint** . . . it has class and sass, brightness and bite."—**John Updike, New Yorker**
(#J6139—$1.95)

☐ **THE WOMAN HE LOVED by Ralph G. Martin.** She would gladly have become Edward's mistress, but he wanted her as his wife, his Queen, his Empress. . . . Here, at last, is the full story of the romance that rocked an empire. With an 8-page picture album of rare personal photos, this book was a nationwide bestseller for over 5 months. A Literary Guild Selection. (#J6640—$1.95)

☐ **IF BEALE STREET COULD TALK by James Baldwin.** A masterpiece about the love between a man and a woman. . . . **The New York Times** called this bestseller "One of the best novels of the year!" A Literary Guild Alternate Selection. (#J6502—$1.95)

☐ **ELIZABETH AND CATHERINE by Robert Coughlin.** For the millions enthralled by **Nicholas & Alexandra**, the glittering lives and loves of the two Russian Empresses who scandalized the world and made a nation . . . "Fascinating!"—**The Boston Globe.** A Putnam Award Book and a Literary Featured Alternate.
(#J6455—$1.95)

THE NEW AMERICAN LIBRARY, INC.,
P.O. Box 999, Bergenfield, New Jersey 07621

Please send me the SIGNET BOOKS I have checked above. I am enclosing $＿＿＿＿＿＿＿(check or money order—no currency or C.O.D.'s). Please include the list price plus 25¢ a copy to cover handling and mailing costs. (Prices and numbers are subject to change without notice.)

Name＿＿＿＿＿＿＿＿＿＿＿＿＿＿＿＿＿＿＿＿＿＿＿＿＿＿＿＿＿

Address＿＿＿＿＿＿＿＿＿＿＿＿＿＿＿＿＿＿＿＿＿＿＿＿＿＿＿

City＿＿＿＿＿＿＿＿State＿＿＿＿＿＿＿＿Zip Code＿＿＿＿＿
Allow at least 3 weeks for delivery